Also by Ben Elliott

Gladiator School

First published 2002 by Zipper Books,
part of Millivres Prowler Ltd.
116-134 Bayham Street, London NW1 0BA
www.zipper.co.uk

ISBN 1-873741-68-5

Distributed in the UK and Europe by Airlift Book Company,
8 The Arena, Mollison Avenue, Enfield, Middlesex EN3 7NJ
Telephone: 020 8804 0400
Distributed in North America by Consortium,
1045 Westgate Drive, St Paul, MN 55114-1065
Telephone: 1 800 283 3572
Distributed in Australia by Bulldog Books,
PO Box 300, Beaconsfield, NSW 2014

Printed and bound in Finland by WS Bookwell

THE SLAVE KING

Ben Elliott

Zipper Books

One

A knot of black-cloaked figures fought its way up the steep slope against the cataract of warriors scrambling headlong down it. Heads and stripped torsos were dark with dried blood though double-edged sickles still gleamed; eyes flashed with mingled bloodlust and panic. Within the tight escort of royal bodyguards, which continued to press forward against the tide of retreating men, Aspar was flanked by his parents, King Saphanx and Queen Rosmerta. How could these warriors be fleeing the enemy, wondered the boy? After all, they were Dacians, even though they were not of his tribe.

'The Romans must have breached the walls ahead,' murmured the king half to himself, as if in reply to his son's thoughts. 'These men have fought long and hard; they will go on to the end.' A bubble of defiance swelled in Aspar's chest as he caught the wild battle-cries flung from gaping mouths as they passed. A dragon-headed standard surged above them, its body of brilliant red silk twisting in the orange smoke. Yet the lad knew from the set of his father's handsome face and his mother's unaccustomed silence that the battle now underway would be the last, and that its outcome was beyond doubt.

Above, burning missiles from Roman catapults surrounding the citadel domed the night sky with fire. Like meteors portending disaster, they shrieked just a few spear-lengths overhead. Aspar felt their heat on the back of his neck like the blast from a potter's oven. His mother held her veil over her face against the choking fumes of sulphur and the sparks that descended like swarms of golden insects. The boy felt the sting of them on his arms and legs.

Aspar pitched forward as he slipped on the smooth stone that was treacherous with blood and oil. His father's strong arm circled his waist, bearing him up so that he could regain his footing.

'Steady,' admonished the older man, his mouth close to his son's ear so that the guards should not hear. 'You are king now, remember.'

'Yes, father,' he mumbled in reply, still unsure what the hurried ceremony that had taken place a short while earlier could mean. Yet he could feel the weight of the torque of kingship around his neck, the grip of the serpent armlets on his biceps.

The young man cursed himself for his clumsiness, desperate to justify the confidence his father had placed in him. He glanced in the king's direction but Saphanx stared grimly ahead, sparing his son the embarrassment of his gaze. For a moment, Aspar's knees buckled as the ground underfoot changed from slick stone to a more yielding surface. At first he thought they had hit a patch of thick bracken. Then he felt the vomit rise in his throat as he realised that they were wading through the piled bodies of the fallen. He raged at himself for his weakness. Still his father's expression did not change.

It had been fixed like this since a few hours earlier when, at the height of the battle, a messenger had come from Decebalus, High King of Dacia. Saphanx was summoned to a gathering of the allied kings of the various tribes in Decebalus' citadel. Strangely, Rosmerta and Aspar were also requested to attend. It was then that his father did the thing that Aspar could not understand and which filled him with dread.

He led Aspar outside the royal quarters and, in the sight of his men, placed the jewelled torque around his slender neck and the diadem of kingship on his pale brow. Rosmerta slipped the golden serpents over his upper arms, which, despite his youth, were already thickened by years of drill and combat. With the battle raging all around them, the warriors did homage to the confused boy-king, kneeling before him and touching their lips to the hem of his tunic as though his royal virtue would aid them in their desperate struggle.

The group lurched to a halt. Aspar could see that the chief bodyguard had grabbed one of the retreating men by his leather belt and was questioning him. It was impossible to make out what they were saying over the din of battle. The man darted away like a stone from a slingshot as soon as the soldier released him.

'It's impossible to get through,' the bodyguard bellowed over his shoulder to Saphanx, 'the enemy has surrounded the citadel.'

'We will return to our quarters,' Aspar's father called back.

As the party switched directions, the guards had to summon all their strength to avoid being swept away in the flood of warriors, and pressed back into the crush with powerful shoulders.

Below them, the battlefield stretched to infinity on all sides as though the whole world were convulsed in the conflict: even the heavens were filled with a storm of fire from ballistas and catapults. The iron-clad siege towers that protruded over the walls at intervals like broken teeth disgorged enemy soldiers, who swarmed into the stronghold like flies infesting a dung heap. At several points, they had breached the mighty defences and hordes of troops, formed into tight red squares under the protection of their shields, thrust their way through the defenders. The stones, arrows and spears that the Dacians rained from the battlements did little to stop them. The cauldrons of blazing oil they poured on the legionaries scattered a few screaming, flaming figures as the fiery liquid penetrated beneath their armour to consume flesh with white-hot teeth. But still the troops surged forward.

Yes, this was the end, thought Aspar. Not just a crushing defeat for Decebalus and his allies, including Aspar's father, against the Roman enemy. No, this was something more. Could it be the end of the world, he wondered? Certainly it was the end of his world.

Though he was just sixteen, he had fought in many battles against other tribes alongside his warrior-master Burebista. But he had never seen or even dreamed of a battle like this. Only his mother's tales of wars between the gods came close to matching what he had witnessed in the past weeks of the siege. It was as though the Roman war-god, Mars himself, was hidden in the livid clouds of smoke that hung like a cowl over the battlefield.

But this moment had been inevitable for years, long before Aspar was born, when Decebalus' alliance had first challenged Rome's might. Then again, five years earlier, when Aspar had scarcely emerged from boyhood and his father would not permit him to fight. 'One day, you must succeed me as king,' Saphanx had reminded him. 'To risk your life before you are fully trained as a warrior would be a betrayal of our people: if a leader falls on the battlefield, none of his men may leave it alive.'

That war had ended in a shameful surrender for the Dacians. Their capital of Sarmizegetusa had been occupied and a Roman garrison established within the royal city. The Emperor Trajan had made a show of magnanimity, forging a treaty which authorised the sharing of Roman skills and culture with the vanquished Dacians. Like many other young nobles, Aspar was provided with a tutor who taught him Latin and Greek. He became familiar with the works of the philosophers and playwrights in both languages. Yet Decebalus and his allies had no intention of submitting to the new order. Secretly, they re-armed and prepared for a further uprising.

When Aspar turned fourteen, Saphanx granted the impatient prince permission to train as a warrior. He was apprenticed to Burebista. By day, the older soldier would train Aspar secretly in the arts of war in the forest and, in the fullness of time, as was the custom, by night the boy shared his master's cloak. Although he was a muscular giant of a man, with a pelt of thick blond hair, Burebista was gentle with the boy, who came to enjoy his attentions. Besides, the prince knew that each time his master pierced him with his gnarled weapon, he was planting the divine seed of courage in the young body of his apprentice.

Meanwhile, Decebalus and the allied kings were negotiating treaties with Rome's other powerful enemies in preparation for an invasion of the Roman province of Moesia to the south of Dacia. From the north came the Roxolani and the Iazyges with their cataphracts, cavalry with men and horses encased from head to foot in heavy armour, while from the east came the Parthians with their famed mounted archers which had proved lethal to Roman armies in the past.

One of these was Prince Surena. Now sixteen, Aspar was accompanying his father to joint exercises between Dacian and Parthian troops when the young men first met. Surena was taking a rest from exercises with his fellow horsemen and was standing alone, looking rather lost, pulling his woollen cloak around him for protection against the northern climate, even though it was early spring. When their eyes met, Surena's solemn face broke into the brilliant smile that Aspar would remember often in the years to come. The young prince, who appeared to be around Aspar's age, was clad in fine silver mail, dazzling in the spring sunshine, showing off his lean muscular legs and dark handsome face, with its chiselled chin outlined by a thin dark beard. He bowed slightly towards Aspar whom he recognised by his robes as being of noble birth.

From this moment, the two princes were inseparable, snatching every moment they could together. Aspar no longer shared his nights with Burebista – his apprenticeship now over – but spent them in Surena's arms. Whereas recently he had submitted to Burebista in order to do his duty by the older warrior, he longed for Surena's body whenever they were apart. Their love-making was rapturous and when they would finally settle down to sleep,

Surena begged Aspar to tell him the stories of the heroes and gods that he had learned from Rosmerta. From the lonely, homesick youth he had first encountered, Surena blossomed into a tender companion, full of laughter and play. It was hard to imagine life without the Parthian boy.

Following early victories over the Dacians, Trajan's legions had pursued Decebalus' army to the mighty stronghold of Sarmizegetusa. The Roxolani and Iazyges deserted their Dacian allies: what good would cavalry be in a siege, they argued? The Parthians also withdrew their forces for the same reason, though more graciously. Surena bade Aspar a tearful farewell, begging him to come with him to Parthia and safety until the war in Dacia was settled. Aspar could tell that his parents were by no means opposed to the idea, but he insisted that, as his father's heir, he should stay and fight.

For several weeks after that nothing happened. Aspar had been convinced that the Romans had decided not to give chase. Then, gradually, reports came in from Decebalus' spies of the roads that the Romans were building through the mountains. Everyone was talking about them: each as straight as a die, leading towards the Dacian fortress like the spokes of a wheel. Soon the road builders came in sight. Aspar would watch from the battlements at his father's side as the stone-flagged highways approached by the hour. Then the builders flattened the land at the foot of the stronghold and began to build the camps for the legions that would arrive along the roads. The landscape changed before their eyes as undulating green hills disappeared overnight and the legionaries used the earth to build sloping platforms against the towering cliffs that protected the walled city.

'Are these mere men,' muttered Saphanx watching the slow, deliberate preparations, 'who flatten mountains or raise them at will?' For the first time, Aspar saw his father at a loss and he pitied him. 'What manner of fighting is this?' the king mused more loudly. 'I have been a warrior all my life, but this is an enemy I do not understand. What glory is there in digging and building?' Then he would turn his puzzled gaze to Aspar: 'Perhaps when you are king, my son, you will learn to understand this enemy and how to defeat him.'

Finally the mountains rang with the sounds of marching feet as lines of men poured along the roads in a seemingly endless flood.

The first attack came at night. Out of the silence came the rasping of a distant fanfare. Then another, closer but higher as though from a mountain peak. Others completed the circle, echoing through the valleys. The war-cries of the different legions swept out of the night, enclosing the fortress in a wall of sound. Fires were lit: great braziers of burning missiles illuminated catapults which had been hauled under the cover of darkness onto crags and peaks within range of the stronghold. Ranks of troops were poised to storm the walls with the help of towers which must have been concealed until that moment in adjoining valleys. Then the rain of fire began – it was to continue throughout the weeks of the siege.

Even before the stink of burning human flesh began to permeate the city, the smoke of animal sacrifice hung heavily in the air as the Dacian priests pleaded with their gods for victory. Aspar had always regarded his mother almost as a sister, her manner and looks had always been so youthful. Yet now, for the first time, he noticed shadows under her eyes as she returned from tending the wounded, clutching phials of herbal potions, her robes stiff with blood. Instead of conversing animatedly with Aspar, she spent her hours of rest silently cutting cloth into little strips which she would tie to a bush near a sacred well, each strip a prayer to the gods of her people.

While the battle raged Aspar rarely saw his father, as they were commanding separate companies of men, but when he did return to their quarters, the king looked exhausted and dispirited.

Throughout those weeks, an ominous reminder of passing time, the thunder of the battering rams pounding the great walls could be heard in every part of the city. Even in his parents' dwelling, Aspar could feel the relentless thudding through the soles of his feet. Yet he had never doubted that his father and the other kings would triumph against the Roman enemy. Until the arrival of the messenger from Decebalus that afternoon.

The bodyguards quickened their pace, using their tall shields and spears to lever their way through the throng of panicking troops. It could not be long now before the enemy would break though the last lines of defense and over-run the stronghold, killing, looting, raping. Aspar had heard that the Romans loved to parade their defeated enemies through the streets of their capital before slaughtering them or, worse still, selling them into slavery. This was something his father would never submit to and yet, thus far, the king had given no indication of his intentions.

The small party swung into a group of low buildings. The way was clearer in the narrow alleys flanked by wooden dwellings, most of which were already ablaze. Women and children hurried along in silence, clutching bundles of clothes and treasured belongings snatched at random.

King Saphanx had been assigned one of the few stone structures in the walled city. Once they were inside the throne-room, the guards slammed the great wooden doors, deadening the cacaphony of battle.

Saphanx turned urgently to Aspar, grasping him firmly by the shoulders. 'We had hoped to escape with Decebalus and the other nobles. I feared that it was too late. That is why I crowned you king today. I was right to do this. Now we have few choices. The most important thing for your mother and I is that we should not fall into the hands of the enemy. In a few moments I will rejoin my men and fight with them to the end.'

'I will fight with you, father,' Aspar broke in, flushing.

'No,' said his father, raising his hand in a stern gesture for silence. 'You must do exactly what I say, for the sake of our people and our country.'

Aspar, dreading what was coming next, opened his mouth to speak, but his father silenced him again.

'And for the sake of your mother and I. When I am gone, your mother will do what must be done to ensure that she avoids capture.'

Aspar turned to his mother, fighting back the stinging tears. Her face was pale and serious, her blue eyes fixed on Saphanx's face.

'But you, my son,' said the king firmly, 'must live. Whatever happens, you must live.'

Aspar felt his mother grasp his hand tight.

'We will hide you here as best we can. But even if you are found, you must survive. Whatever they do to you, you must live through it until the day you are able to fight for the freedom of our people once more. You are our hope, my son.'

Aspar struggled to speak, but his father clasped him firmly to his breast then pushed him away. 'There is no time for more words.'

Rosmerta was already crossing the room towards the great carved chest in which she kept her cloth. She threw the carved lid open and Saphanx began to haul out the heavy bales of fine woollen material woven in the complex squared patterns of his wife's people.

'If I know them, the Romans will be looking for gold and not for cloth, which they consider "barbarian",' growled Saphanx, then glanced around the room at the rows of golden helmets, the precious suits of armour, shining quivers and scabbards, Rosmerta's jewel box and the royal diadem itself. 'There is enough treasure here to satisfy their greed without any need to search too hard. So there is a good chance that they will not look under the bales and you will be able to escape later. All the Latin and Greek you have learned may be of help to you in passing yourself off as one of them – a conscripted soldier from a Gallic tribe, perhaps.'

Dumbly, Aspar followed his father's indications. He stepped into the chest and lay in the gap that had been cleared between two large bales deep inside it. As she looked down at him, his mother impulsively took the wooden talisman she had always worn and placed it around her son's neck. Without another word, Saphanx replaced the other bales carefully and Aspar heard the heavy lid fall. He knew that when it opened again, the life he had loved so much would have disappeared for good.

Crushed under the weight of the heavy material, he became agitated, gasping for air. He forced himself to take deep slow breaths. He did not know how long he would have to remain in this hiding place and he could not afford to panic. Above, he heard a muffled knocking as his mother arranged objects casually on the lid. Dimly, he heard the great door slammed shut. Saphanx had gone to face the Roman enemy for the last time.

Now there was silence. Aspar's fingers moved to the wooden talisman at his throat. He could imagine his mother's actions. She would be preparing a mixture of herbs, a skill handed down from her ancestors, as he had seen her do so many times before in order to heal the wounds of fallen warriors or cure his childish ailments. But this time her purpose would be to end life, not to restore it.

He found it hard to believe that never again would he listen to his mother's voice recount the sagas of the gods and heroes of her people as her hands flashed as if by their own volition over her loom or the taut bright surface of a tapestry. From the moment he could talk, he had insisted on reciting these tales back to her, at first in a stumbling, muddled form that made her laugh with delight. Later, however, he began to tell them with the eloquence so admired by her people and even to embellish them with a skill that made her beam with pride.

The chest was hot and stifling and, exhausted by the strain of the past few hours, Aspar drifted into sleep. He was not sure how long he had dozed when he was awoken by muffled shouts and the clash of weapon on weapon. He was suddenly drenched with sweat and despite the heat of the chest felt an icy cold creep about his shoulders. No doubt the bodyguards were defending the royal treasure to the death. But what of his mother? Had her potion performed its deadly work? He had promised his father he would stay alive at all costs. But if she was in danger? For her to take her own life was fitting for a queen, but what indignities might these monstrous Romans submit her to if they found her alive?

A long high scream cut off his thoughts. He knew it was Rosmerta, even though he had never known her utter that strange, high-pitched sound before. It broke off abruptly and there was a momentary pause before men's voices could be heard, rapid and high with excitement. No longer able to hold himself back, Aspar heaved upwards with his shoulders as hard as he could. The heavy bales moved barely a hand's breadth, but the chest lid must have been forced open a little as he heard metal vessels clanking on to flagstones.

The young king glimpsed light as the chest lid flew open and the bales were pulled out from above him. Rough hands tore him from his hiding place and and flung him to the floor. A boot clamped hard against his throat. The cold metal studs dug painfully into the tender skin. A groan escaped his lips as he spotted his mother's body sprawled awkwardly just a few feet away. One hand still clutched the torn clothing to her breast. In the other, a tiny curved dagger glimmered in the torchlight. Blood still gurgled from her throat where it had been opened with a quick, clean stroke. Rosmerta had died a queen. One of the soldiers flung a scarlet cloak over her body, hiding its accusing presence.

'This little coward needs to be taught a lesson,' boomed the soldier who towered over Aspar, shoving the boy's chin back with the toe of his boot for emphasis. A number of other men gathered behind him, eyeing the youth with curiosity. 'Cowering like a girl in a woman's linen chest while his countrymen are slaughtered.' The man stooped, removing his foot from Aspar's neck, only to shove a greaved knee heavily into his chest. Aspar could tell from the elaborate armour, clinking with medals, and from the stiff crest of his helmet, that this was a centurion.

The soldier grabbed a handful of Aspar's blond hair and pulled his head back to examine the boy's face. He gave a slight frown of recognition, glancing towards Rosmerta's body. 'She your sister then, boy?' He hesitated briefly. 'Or your mother?'

'There's only one way to treat little girls, Marcus,' sneered one of the legionaries from behind the centurion, 'especially such pretty little girls.' Aspar had noticed the soldier hurriedly stripping off his armour; he was now tugging on the thick tumescent penis that protruded from beneath his tunic. The boy could see the hunger in the eyes of the stocky dark-haired soldier, who no doubt had been deprived for many months of the satisfactions of the flesh.

'Yes, Livius,' the centurion agreed. He stood up and swiftly drew his sword, placing the tip under Aspar's chin. 'Up, boy, let's have a look at you.' Aspar struggled to his feet, furious that the cramp in his legs made him appear unsteady. The soldiers moved closer, eyes fixed on the young prince, as they slowly removed helmets, let cloaks slide silently to the floor and undid buckles. The soldier Livius, now sliding his fist slowly along his upcurved manhood, drew so close to the boy that Aspar could feel the heat of him and smell his clean fresh sex.

Marcus slid the point of his sword under the silken cord at Aspar's waist, severing it with a jerk. Clutching the neck of the young man's tunic, so skilfully embroidered by Rosmerta, the centurion pulled downwards, ripping it open and exposing the boy's muscular torso, which glowed in the lamplight. Livius tugged lightly at the hem and the garment crumpled to the floor around Aspar's feet, leaving him naked except for a brief muslin pouch suspended from a string at his waist.

To his horror, Aspar felt the flesh of his loins uncoil at the soldiers' scrutiny. The men's eyes slid greedily over the hard contours of his body, pausing at the heaviness of his crotch which clearly revealed a shapely member and weighty orbs nestling in an abundance of dark-blond curls. Their expert gaze also took in the evidence of old wounds, reduced by Rosmerta's healing arts to thin white lines. This was the powerful body of a trained warrior, not that of an effeminate, fearful of battle.

Greaves, skirts of leather thongs, tunics of mail slipped to the floor with a whispering sound as appetites, famished for so long, were stimulated by the promise of so delicious a feast. 'Perhaps it was not because he was afraid to fight that the boy was hiding,' breathed Marcus, in a voice become respectful, 'but because he hoped to survive and continue the struggle. This is one of their nobles. Maybe even a prince.'

'Not a prince,' came the rejoinder from across the room. It was a voice that Aspar had not heard before and one which rang out with authority but also contained a note of silky sensuality. Instantly, the men turned and stood aside. Aspar could see a tall, helmeted figure outlined in the doorway. As the soldier moved into the circle of lamplight with a languid stride, Aspar could tell from his fine armour that this was an officer, a tribune. The face beneath the the gold helmet with its long scarlet plume was dark and strikingly handsome. The proud straight nose and strong chin lent it an aristocratic air.

'Valerius,' muttered the men, nodding their heads respectfully as he passed among them. But the tribune did not acknowledge their greetings. His narrowed eyes with their thick lashes were fixed on Aspar's neck. He stroked the torque softly with his fingertips, almost as if caressing the skin of a beloved.

'A king,' he sighed, slipping his fingers under it to lightly test its weight. 'The torque is the mark of kingship.' He touched the wooden talisman lightly and gave it a quizzical look. 'And these,' he mused, brushing the pads of his fingers over the smooth globes of Aspar's shoulders and tracing the golden serpent coils which circled the young king's clenched biceps, 'are the armlets of majesty.'

Valerius looked up and glanced round the chamber, quickly registering the helmets, suits of armour, drinking vessels and other treasures which crowded it. 'So many lovely things,' he crooned. 'And this –' he ran his fingers through Aspar's tousled blond hair '– the loveliest of all. Mmm?' he questioned, examining Aspar's face for a response. 'The gold and the jewels will enrich the Emperor's coffers as the law requires. But this,' he lowered his voice to a whisper as he trailed his fingers lazily down Aspar's chest, 'this will be mine. Very me, don't you think?' he asked, glancing back at his men.

Aspar pulled away, but two of the soldiers darted behind him, twisting his arms painfully behind his back and thrusting him to the floor at Valerius' feet. 'Take care,' cried Valerius softly, placing a proprietorial hand on the lad's curls. 'I don't want my treasure damaged.'

Aspar tossed Valerius' hand away with a rough twist of his head. 'I am no Roman's treasure,' he growled. 'You were right when you said that I am king. You can call me slave, but I will never submit to you.'

There were murmurs as the men heard Aspar's cultured Latin. 'The barbarian is educated,' exclaimed Valerius, unbuckling his helmet. He drew it from his head with a sigh, slowly turning his head to flex his neck muscles, knotted from days of fighting.

'Is this the dwelling of a barbarian?' demanded Aspar, speaking out firmly now and indicating the richly decorated chamber with a jerk of his head. 'Are these the works of barbarians? Is it barbarian treasure that you covet so desperately?'

'Such a lot to say – and so eloquent,' exclaimed Valerius, untying the sash of bright crimson that circled his waist. Livius, whose rigid appendage still tweaked the hem of his tunic upwards, helped the tribune remove his muscle cuirass.

'Too much to say,' Livius grunted, and his phallus shuddered in a violent spasm. 'I could stop his trap for him.'

'You can have him later,' said Valerius smoothly, dropping a heavy skirt of white leather thongs to the floor. 'When I'm finished with him.' He raised his arms and Livius stood on tiptoe to pull an under-tunic of white linen over his master's head. Valerius' body – slim, hard, sun-darkened – was revealed, his torso a perfect copy of the glossy muscularity of the cuirass he had just shed. He unknotted the white loincloth. His long silken cock was already stiff, curving downwards in an elegant bow shape. The smooth foreskin was drawn back a little, revealing a glossy rounded head. Aspar found himself aroused. But then, painfully, he recalled another hard dark body, one which had invited the submission of a lover, not a slave.

Distracted for a moment, he suddenly found his head pulled back by one of the soldiers and Valerius' rigid brown manhood breached his lips and plunged smoothly down his throat. Valerius gave a long sigh and leant his bent knees against Aspar's muscular shoulders.

Livius' eyes were wide with fascinated lust as Valerius rotated his hips, twisting his tool in the boy's gullet, probing its depths. 'Feed him, Valerius,' he urged, pumping his own weapon. He paused for a second to pull his tunic roughly over his head. His body was broad and heavily muscled, symmetrically patterned with shiny dark hair. 'Let's give him a Roman banquet –' the soldier panted '– fit for a king.'

Valerius grasped Aspar's ears, sliding the young man's head back and forth along the arc of his organ. Opening his powerful thighs, the tribune sank the full length of his appendage into the young man's only-too-willing gullet, probing it with his throbbing glans. 'Let me feel your throat, boy,' he ordered in a low growl as he ground his luxuriant pubic hair against Aspar's nose and cheeks. The boy gagged and the veins stood out on his forehead as he struggled for breath, but Valerius ignored his writhings, leaning his head back with eyes closed, savouring the spasms of the boy's silken throat.

Inflamed by the sight and smell of sex, the other men, who had gradually shed what was left of their uniforms, had begun to seek their own pleasure. Two captured Dacian bodyguards were roughly stripped and lashed to benches with their arms and legs tied securely beneath, mouths and anuses poised for Roman use. A pair of waiting legionaries straddled the benches and forced their raging erections into the defenceless mouths. The moans of half-protest mingled with the victors' grunts of pleasure.

Still pinioned to the stone floor, his arms twisted painfully behind his back, Aspar could make out at his own eye level, between Valerius' thrusts, the muscular arsecheeks of one of the bodyguards stretched apart at the end of a bench. The brown pleated areola of his hole stared vulnerably. Thick-fingered hairy hands began to roughly knead the white cheeks, meaty thumbs stretching, gently at first, the firm muscular ring of the anus. Aspar recognised the big hairy limbs as those of the centurion Marcus.

The young king's eyes widened as he saw the soldier reach for his scabbard which he had discarded on the floor with the rest of his uniform and draw his sword. But, with the blade pointed harmlessly away from the trussed guard, Marcus began to tease the naked hole with the large sphere which decorated the end of the hilt. He exerted a steady pressure, smoothing out the fine folds of the delicate skin which had taken on a rosy hue. Aspar heard a stifled groan which must have come from the bodyguard, though his face was hidden, as it corresponded with Marcus' movements. The centurion paused and reached along the oak table. He held a pot which Aspar knew contained honey and proceeded to generously smear the guard's pursed arse-lips with the amber stickiness.

Now the flesh slowly yielded to the pressure of the hilt's broad knob, twice the size, Aspar reckoned, of any prickhead he had ever seen. The guard continued to utter a long guttural moan, but now it was subtly changed: it had lost its note of protest. Amazingly, the iris of the arsehole expanded, stretched blade-tight, and greedily swallowed the globe in one gulp. Marcus slid the rest of the hilt in after it and began to explore the man's anal cavity with a deft rotation of his wrist. The guard's arse rose slightly from the bench, the muscles clenching and unclenching in response to the centurion's manipulations.

The smooth downstrokes of Valerius' prick, alternated with deep probings powered by the gyration of his pelvis, had relaxed Aspar's throat so that it could accommodate the lengthy endowment with ease. Now the hands that had restrained him raised him from the floor by his wrists and ankles. His throat felt oddly empty as Valerius pulled out swiftly. Too surprised to struggle, he was aware of the strong arms of the soldiers whisking him across the room like a child tossed about in play by a parent. He was heading for his father's ornate wooden throne, set on a dais at one end of the chamber. The sound of booted feet and slightly hysterical chatter told him that the other soldiers were moving alongside him. Shadows on the walls and ceiling, rapidly growing and shrinking showed that one of the men was carrying the lampstand to light whatever debaucheries were to come. Livius, hard sweaty muscles gilded by the glow, scampered ahead of the group.

'The king must be enthroned,' he scoffed with a slight bow and, heaving his powerful shoulders against the back of the great wooden seat, sent it toppling forwards with a clatter so that the tall back fell to the foot of the dais, the legs pointing upwards. The men carrying Aspar flung him full-length against the back of the throne with a force that knocked the air from his lungs. Before he had time to recover, they had lashed his wrists and ankles to the upturned chair so that his arms reached upwards along its legs, and his feet were tethered to the carved back where it lay on the ground.

Valerius' majestic weapon bored between Aspar's lips, still parted as he gasped painfully for breath: the throne had been so positioned that Aspar's mouth could be used by standing on the dais. As Valerius began to thrust frenziedly, Aspar broke out in a sweat as he felt a tickling at his arsehole and realised that his legs had been stretched apart to expose the pale pink lips of his anus, bracketed by two thin lines of delicate blond hair. He shuddered with shame, intensified by the frisson of excitement he was unable to suppress. Something soft and wet was nuzzling the sensitive button of skin, as neat and tight as a second umbilicus. Bolts of excitement shot through his frame as newly discovered sensations were teased into life. Aspar felt his cock leap involuntarily, though it was jammed uncomfortably between his stomach and the back of the throne.

'Come on,' whined Livius, 'let me taste that sweet young mancunt.' Aspar's heart pounded as he realised that the extraordinary sensations that had illuminated his body were caused by Livius' tongue on his hole. He could not hold back a moan of pleasure as he felt the soldier pull his arsecheeks apart and explore the satiny folds with his fat wet tongue. Glancing up, the young man could see the eyes and glistening mouths of the other soldiers, agape with lust. They had drawn so close, he could hear their laboured breathing and even the slithering of foreskins over their juiced-up, swollen prickheads. The air was heavily perfumed with male musk, which acted as a powerful drug on all present, drawing them into a momentary truce.

The boy-king could feel the heat rise in his anus as Livius' busy tongue drove him to new heights of pleasure. 'Loosen that delicious cunt,' ordered Livius and began to circle vigorously over the anal area with the flat of his tongue. Aspar felt an abrupt opening of his rectal passage and heard a long sigh of pleasure from Livius as he sank his tongue deep into the gossamer folds of flesh. By now, Aspar's engorged cock ached, wedged at it was against the throne-back. As though sensing the young king's thoughts, Livius shoved his hand under Aspar's balls and gave an interested grunt of discovery as he felt the rigid member. Aspar let out a yelp of pain as the soldier twisted his cock roughly down between his legs, but the pain was soon submerged in pleasure as Livius caressed the pulsating member with long strokes of his tongue. Aspar could hear the soldier's moans of appreciation as he savoured the long elegant proportions of his pale lance, the abundant white folds of the foreskin now withdrawn to reveal the shapely head of pale mauve. A groan was torn from somewhere deep in Aspar's chest as Livius took the full length of it in his hot throat with one bold lunge.

At this point, Valerius, whose rhythmic stabs had quickened at the sight of Livius' ministrations, tore his sword of flesh from the scabbard of Aspar's throat. Turning and bending forward, he thrust his red manhole against the lad's open mouth. It was hot and slick with musky juices, and though Aspar experienced a moment's revulsion at the thought of performing an act he had never conceived of until now, he found himself intoxicated by the clean and powerful aroma of Valerius' most intimate regions. Suddenly, he found himself lapping hungrily at the little kilt of flesh that bordered the tribune's arse-ring, like a cat starved of milk.

The groans and sighs now loosed from Valerius' lips harmonised with those of Livius and the other soldiers that crowded the dais. Aspar felt himself transported into a trance by the sounds, by the sight of the muscular mounds of Valerius' buttocks, by the feel of the delicate flaps of flesh on his tongue and of Livius' hot mouth tightly encasing his own manroot. A dark face, the face of a strange god – the one the Romans and Greeks called Priapus, perhaps – took form before his eyes, its mouth coinciding with Valerius' hole.

The hole disappeared, but the face remained. The constellation of figures around him reformed into a new pattern of pleasure. Livius withdrew from behind him and Aspar felt his cock pulled through a gap in the back of the throne and the legionary's lips envelop it once more. The group of soldiers before him now drew closer so that the face of the god was crowded by a thicket of raging pricks. He could feel their indignant heat on his cheeks and the reek of their passion. Then, with contrasting coolness, he felt the weight of long muscular limbs against his own. Similarly cool lips nuzzled the long silken hair at his neck.

A voice behind him which he knew to be Valerius' whispered tenderly: 'From now on, let this be your throne, little king,' and, as the tribune spoke, Aspar felt the long bow of the man's dick goring his rear-lips and sliding smoothly into his guts as though it would never end. There was no pain – Livius' preparation had seen to that – only an intense physical pleasure such as Aspar had never experienced before. With its powerful downward curve, Valerius' scimitar pressed upon his intimate parts like a powerful spring. Every time it stirred within him, new sensations were unleashed. Starting with slow, circling motions, Valerius quickened his actions. The thrusts became lightning bolts setting the boy's guts aflame.

The chorus of moans grew louder, higher. Livius' famished mouth sucked powerfully on his painfully swollen manhood. The sacred grove of cocks loomed massively behind the mesmeric face of the god. Aspar's bowels seemed to blaze and melt. For a moment everything was suspended in silence and stillness, and then a tempest of cries and frenzied movement broke out. The floodgates of his loins burst open and he heard Livius' corresponding moans of delight as he imbibed the salty secretions of the lad's ballsac. The mighty spasms of his rectum clutched at Valerius' cock with such force that the man could no longer hold back the burning semen which streamed into Aspar's guts and seemed to flood his veins with its heat. The copse of cocks, now pressed against Aspar's cheeks, appeared to burst into flame as they ejaculated long thin jets and thick gobs of their precious liquid into the lamplight. They fell hotly onto Aspar's hair, into his eyes, his mouth.

Valerius sank against the boy's shoulder with a sigh. 'Oh, what a trophy you will be, little golden king.' He slipped his arms gently round the boy and held him close. 'How the people will admire you. How they will envy me. But you will be mine alone.' Aspar felt the tribune's cock jerk inside him. 'But do not fear, my king. I will be a gentle master.' Aspar could already feel the spring of Valerius' cock growing rigid within him again and, with a deep groan of pleasure, the man's hips began to move once more.

Two

Aspar sat immobile in a long ray of early sunlight that slanted through an arch from the garden. He shifted a thigh which had grown numb after almost an hour pressed to the cold marble seat. The Babylonian artist who had been hired to paint his portrait tutted with exasperation.

'How can I be expected to capture a perfect likeness,' lisped the man with a toss of his long curled wig, 'when you keep moving?' Aspar froze obediently, smiling slightly at the man's heavily accented Greek. To be still yet again felt natural for the young king from Dacia. In the weeks since he had accompanied Valerius to Rome, hardly ever leaving his side, he had felt like a kind of statue, the object of constant admiration from the tribune and his friends, and yet incapable of action. Since the fall of Sarmizegetusa, his mother's suicide and his father's death in the final battle, Aspar had been frozen inside, his will, mind and heart paralysed.

The Roman victory had been followed by mass executions; day after day, thousands of Dacians warriors had meekly lined up to be beheaded. Often, their king or chieftain had already been slain and so, according to custom, it was necessary for them to follow him into death. Occasionally, a centurion would spot an unusually wellbuilt and handsome specimen and have his chains unlocked: the finest warriors were required to adorn the Emperor's Triumph that would take place in Rome. Aspar had watched his race vanish before his eyes, not in the glorious struggle of battle but eliminated with cold Roman efficiency and organisation, according to the inexorable logic of their law. A scribe was always on hand with a wax tablet to keep a careful tally of the numbers despatched. Thousands more would be sent to Rome to be paraded before the people before they were also sent to their deaths or sold into slavery. Already, some 50,000 Dacian men, women and children had been transported to the four corners of the Empire, replenishing the slave markets with much-needed stock.

During the long carriage ride to the port on the Pontus Euxinus, throughout the sea journey and now in the tribune's sumptuous Roman palace, he had allowed himself to be Valerius' plaything, to be dressed and undressed, decked with jewels, crowned with his father's diadem, to have his hair teased into the latest style or the sprinkling of down on his body plucked out the way the older man preferred.

Just as the Roman lust for punishment and revenge seemed limitless, so was their thirst for pleasure. By day and night, Valerius would attempt to slake his desperate longing for the youth, penetrating him in arse and mouth over and over, sometimes with barely a pause for recovery, disgorging his seed into the boy until it ran from the corners of his mouth and bubbled from his swollen arsehole. He discovered the boy's huge manhood, which cantilevered proudly upwards from its mighty base when fully grown – the opposite of Valerius' own down-curved weapon. The tribune gorged on it like a starving man, becoming an expert on its many flavours and perfumes at different stages of arousal, slipping his tongue greedily under the fine loose skirt of skin which hooded the lustrous head. Aspar would not simply passively comply, but found himself responding with almost matching desperation as though to feel something, anything, might remind him that he still lived. He knew that only one person alive could have alleviated his pain. But he was many miles to the east, in Parthia, and lost for ever.

But at the back of the young king's mind, untouchable, was his father's final command; that, at all costs, he must survive. Whatever happened, he was king, heir to Saphanx. Surrounded as he was by a splendour and luxury he had never even dreamed of, he moved in darkness. Yet in the darkness, this one light, like a feeble candle-flame, still guttered. Despite the luxury of his prison, he was a captive and a slave. But he drew comfort from the thought that, till now, he had obeyed his father's command.

Another source of solace had been the friendship he had struck up with Livius who, when not frustrated by weeks of sexual abstinence, turned out to be an affable, considerate young man. He was also a fund of information on every aspect of Roman life. Aspar began to refer to him as 'the oracle', because he was able to answer any question the boy put to him, and with accuracy. Some weeks after their arrival in Rome, Livius reported the capture of Decebalus and the other Dacian leaders who had escaped with him from the fortress. The High King had been betrayed by one of his own men, but had died by his own sword. 150 tons of gold and 300 tons of silver belonging to Decebalus had been captured by the Emperor. Livius, for his part, was entranced by the legends of Aspar's homeland that he would sometimes tentatively try to piece together when they were alone. But the recollections that came with them hurt so keenly that he would end the recitations abruptly, with the excuse of a poor memory.

Although his father's diadem and torque were destined for the Emperor's personal treasure-house, he was allowed to keep his mother's wooden talisman, which he wore always.

'It didn't bring you much luck, did it?' asked Livius one day, respectfully examining the crude figure of the mother goddess.

'That's not why I wear it,' responded Aspar with a blush, his hand instinctively touching the squat little form.

'"Paint the perfect likeness of Bathyllus,"' proclaimed Valerius in

Greek to the Babylonian artist. 'Remember what the poet said,' he warned him, '"Bathyllus must the model for Phoebus be". This must be the portrait of a young god. To set the people of Rome gasping – and cheering. Careful!' yelled Valerius, with a jump.

He lay naked on a couch, draped in white silk while a small army of expert beauticians lavished their meticulous skills on his sleek brown body. Alipilarii plucked hairs from his armpits and torso, unctores applied perfumed oils, jatraliptae buffed his skin to a sheen with mittens of swansdown. Valerius scowled at the picatricus, who was carefully sculpting his pubic bush into a triangle of neatly curled rows.

He aimed a kick at the boy's head, sending him sliding across the marble pavement. 'Be more careful with that hot dropax.' He turned his attention back to the portrait. 'Angle the easel this way: let me see it,' he commanded the artist, sharply.

With an upward glance and a sigh of exasperation, the man moved the easel to face the tribune. 'Though your worship's exquisite taste is reknowned, it is impossible to appreciate at this stage what the final work will be,' he said with exaggerated deference. 'This is a mere sketch.'

'Hmm,' Valerius pondered. The portrait was several feet high and consisted of a head-and-shoulders likeness, many times larger than lifesize: it would allow all the spectators at the Triumph – even those at a distance – to appreciate the full impact of Aspar's beauty. Or it would if only the accursed Babylonian could get it right. 'No, no, no,' said Valerius irritably. 'You haven't captured the set of the eyes – they should be wider and the lips should be fuller, more sensual, pouting. I was told you were the finest man available for this kind of work and I am paying you a handsome fee. I intend to get my money's worth.'

The Babylonian's mouth hardened into a thin line. He stroked his long curled beard and, with a stiff bow, jerked the painting back into position.

Valerius' gaze became tender as he glanced across at Aspar's oval face, at the mouth that looked almost sulky when serious. His eyes travelled down the boy's long, exquisitely muscled body, his torso narrowing to a slender waist and hips, like the statues of the bull-leapers of Knossos in the tribune's own private museum. He liked the boy to be naked when they were in his private chambers, drawing constant pleasure from the sight of him. At this moment, the youth wore an open robe of shimmering gauze which set off the ripe firmness of his maturing body, and to which the southern sun had lent a golden bloom.

The carved bronze doors swung soundlessly open, closing again with a whisper. Livius moved across the gleaming floor with his usual busy swagger. He whispered in his master's ear and Valerius beamed.

'About time!' he exclaimed. He turned onto his stomach so that he faced a broad open space beyond which lay a large swimming pool hung about with golden curtains. The slaves immediately set to work on his underside, the pictatricus carefully plucking the hairs from around his arsehole. 'Let them enter.'

The doors were flung wide to admit a procession of handsome youths dressed in richly coloured robes, accompanied by a Syrian tailor who flapped around his boys in a state of great excitement, posing them carefully before the gilded curtains of the pool, adjusting an arm here, a leg there, worriedly clucking over a hem or a golden clasp. Livius looked on from the sidelines with an amused smile as Valerius summoned the models before him, one by one, and discussed the garments in great detail with the anxious tailor. The legionary winked at Aspar.

Valerius' palace had teemed with activity since the officer's return with Trajan's victorious army. Indeed, all Rome hummed with the preparations for the greatest Triumph in Roman history, marking the largest expansion of the Empire for decades and a haul of booty unmatched in the Imperial annals. The tribune was determined to take advantage of the celebrations to make his mark.

Each morning, Livius would wake him and Aspar at first light. Often they would have slept little and the silken sheets were stiff and rank with repeatedly spilt secretions. After a quick wash, the day would start in a chamber immediately adjacent to Valerius' bedroom. Here he would receive the clients who would come to do him homage in return for some kind of financial, material or even moral support. They would gather outside the doors of the palace from before dawn. Many of these were poor Roman citizens who would leave happily with a few coins and enough provisions to keep their families fed for the next twenty-four hours. They would have money to while away the afternoon and evening in the baths. Thus, like many of their fellow citizens, they could avoid work entirely.

Valerius spent most of his time, however, with freedmen, his former slaves who now bore his name. As it was forbidden for a Roman from one of the old noble families to engage in trade, Valerius had freed a number of his most trusted slaves and set them up in business as merchants and manufacturers. He now enjoyed a handsome profit from these enterprises as well as from the vast tracts of farmland he had bought up not only in Italy but throughout the Empire. On the first morning that Aspar witnessed these proceedings, Valerius had told him, with a smile, that he was about to be introduced to the 'Valerian Empire'. But Aspar knew that this was more than a joke.

Before they had left Sarmizegetusa, he had been present when Valerius had presented the Emperor Trajan with the spoils captured from Saphanx' throne room. Indeed, Aspar had been part of the booty and had been decked out in royal robes and jewels for the occasion. The youth had noticed a spark of interest in the Emperor's eyes when he had asked for Aspar to be brought before the throne that had been set up in Decebalus' captured citadel. A cloud of anguish had passed across Valerius' face for a moment: he too had noticed Trajan's response to the boy-king. But, with a magnanimous wave of his hand, Trajan signalled his acceptance of the treasure and released the lad into Valerius' keeping as his rightful share of the spoils of war. Aspar now knew that Valerius had been anxious to make the best possible impression. Since it was the custom for Emperors to choose their heirs, formally adopting them, the Valerian Empire could indeed become a reality.

Certainly, Valerius behaved like an Emperor: he never seemed to actually do anything, but was happiest when he was issuing orders and had others scurrying frenziedly about him, carrying them out. By mid-morning, after he had finished with his clients, he was ready to start on the matter that most concerned him at the moment – preparations for the Triumph and the banquet that would follow. There would be many feasts that night, all financed by Trajan himself. The Emperor's own festivities would, of course, be unequaled, but Valerius was famous for his elaborate revels and he hoped on this occasion that his party would eclipse every other in Rome, and that news of its splendour would reach Trajan's ear.

The tribune had spent hours poring over plans for costumes and decor, listening to readings from the Greek authors and poets for inspiration, talking with composers – mainly Greek – and auditioning their music. Now, finally, the costumes he would wear to the banquet were ready. There were to be many of them, each a different colour matched to the many settings that were being constructed at one of the officer's villas in the countryside of Latium beyond the city walls – Valerius' palace in the elegant Carinae district, huge as it was, could hardly accommodate his ambitious plans for the event.

That afternoon, Valerius went out into the city on an errand. Unusually, he took Aspar with him. The tribune made frequent trips to the city's lavish emporia but, until now, he had always left Aspar behind. In fact, since his arrival, the boy had only been outside the palace once before. On that occasion, the city had been in inky darkness and since then he had only been able to glimpse its sights from the balconies of the palace, which afforded a fine view over the Forum and the Flavian amphitheatre. Even now he could see little, as they travelled in a curtained litter: Valerius did not want the people of Rome to set eyes on his treasure until the day of the Triumph. The litter was accompanied by a procession of Valerius' pedagogia, his harem of boy-slaves, most of whom had groaned at the sight of Aspar when he had turned up at the tribune's side.

Powerful Nubian slaves bore the two men through the city. The chief led the bearers in a rhythmic chant to which their steps kept time. Into this he wove directions, instructing his team to raise or lower the litter in order to smooth out an incline, to slow down when they reached the densely packed shopping streets and to navigate corners. These were the only clues as to the path they took, besides the cries of street-sellers, cooking smells from open-fronted tabernae and the stench of the gutters.

After a brief journey, the litter was set down gently and Valerius drew a curtain aside to reveal the atrium of a fine town-house. A fountain played in the centre of the courtyard: it took the form of a giant phallus mounted on two vast balls and sent up a powerful jet of water. A heavy perfume, contrasting with the reek of the streets, hung in the air; Aspar guessed that it came from the waters. The walls were decorated with rich frescos, graphic depictions of male rapes – he recognised that of Ganymede by Zeus; another mighty ravisher he knew to be Hercules taking the virginity of one of his many youthful loves.

The decor suggested that this was one of the capital's reknowned male brothels. His hunch was confirmed as, with a jangle of jewellery and a swish of silk, a heavily made-up man swept into the courtyard and swooped dramatically down onto one knee before Valerius as he stepped from the litter. It was difficult to make out his age under the paint which had hardened like plaster in the deeper wrinkles, but Aspar guessed he must be over sixty.

'My Lord,' he intoned. 'Such an honour to welcome you in my house of pleasure.' He spoke a fine cultured Greek.

'Not so humble, Glaucus, I think,' retorted Valerius, taking in the frescoed walls, 'considering what it cost.'

The old man spread his hands with an oily grin. Aspar now recognised him as one of Valerius' clients whom he had seen regularly at the morning audiences, although on those occasions his face had been unpainted. So this was yet another of the tribune's arm's-length enterprises – surely not one that an aristocrat would want to admit to.

'What brings you here, my Lord? Your requirements must be special indeed; I know that you prefer me to deliver the finest samples to the palace, familiar with your tastes as I am...' This last phrase was uttered in a tone of wonder and trailed off into a whisper; Glaucus had spied Aspar who was still seated in the litter, dressed in a wispy confection of a delicate shade of cream trimmed with crimson. His finely worked sandals were dyed a matching wine-red. As Aspar slipped his long muscular legs to the mosaic floor and rose to his full height, the old Greek eyed him greedily, his fleshy lower lip drooping with astonishment.

'Yes, lovely, isn't he,' chuckled Valerius, amused at the brothel-keeper's lecherous expression. 'But he's mine, you old Silenus. You've got plenty of other boys.' Valerius hooked an arm round Aspar's neck and lazily explored the lad's ear with the tip of his tongue.

'Indeed! The finest in Rome, of an unmatched variety, culled from slave markets the length and breadth of the Empire.' In his confusion, Glaucus had slipped into his habitual sales-talk, but, spotting Valerius' look of scepticism, he recollected himself. 'Of course, I do not need to tell you this, my lord: it was, after all, on your own advice that I thought to establish my business on these lines.' With a low bow, Glaucus led the way into a triclinium furnished with luxurious couches. 'Please forgive my lack of hospitality, Lord. Your sudden presence here has caught me unawares.' With a tinkle of bracelets, Glaucus indicated a couch decked out with lavish fabrics from the east. The couches were designed for couples and Aspar lay alongside Valerius as he had become accustomed.

'Can I offer my lord some refreshment? Some vintage Falernian wine?' he asked, summoning a pretty young slave, a Syrian type with dark eyes and curly hair. The boy was stark naked, a state which, Aspar came to realise, was the uniform in Glaucus' establishment. Having dealt with these formalities, the old Greek had recovered his composure, though his eyes continued to slide back to Aspar. 'As I was saying, my lord, what special requirement has brought you here today? A beautiful boy, perhaps one to contrast with this. I think I have the very thing – one as dark as he is fair.'

'Not the pueri,' said Valerius with a wave of his hand. 'For what I have in mind, I need men, strong men, your exoleti – the biggest you've got. And I mean down there, too. What's more, I need a lot of them.'

'I know what you mean,' Glaucus gesticulated, bracelets jingling vigorously, 'I only go for the big ones myself. You can never have enough.'

Valerius raised a sceptical eyebrow, 'But Glaucus, can you afford to be so choosy at your age, and with your looks and figure?' Glaucus drew himself up and fingered his necklaces. 'But then,' Valerius continued, 'you are in the business, I suppose. In fact, this is not for me – well, not just for me: I am planning a banquet at my villa on the night of the Triumph.'

Glaucus' eyes gleamed at the prospect of an important contract. He was also aware of how much business he would attract by displaying his wares at a party which would undoubtedly be patronised by the richest and most powerful men in Rome.

The Syrian slave had returned with the wine. He drew a golden pitcher from a bed of snow in a golden bucket adorned with lewd carvings. The wine was served in matching goblets and sprinkled with rose petals. Meanwhile, Glaucus whispered furiously in the ear of another slave, a long-haired blond, perhaps from Germania, who nodded frequently as the old man spoke. His endowment was impressive: a long white foreskin tapering to a delicate rose-pink.

The German left swiftly and, after a short pause filled with Glaucus' nervous chatter, a curved curtain at the end of the chamber furthest from the couches was drawn aside. A semi-circle of naked men faced them, striking in their variety of colours and builds, from slender blue-black Africans, over six feet in height, to brawny, hairy blonds from the north, a head shorter.

Valerius slid from the couch with a low sigh of approval. He strode slowly across the room to inspect them more closely. Glaucus scurried alongside him. 'Not just beautiful but clean,' he gushed. 'Their bodies fragrant with cinnamon, their breath sweet with mint and honey.'

Aspar remained on the couch and, as he ran his eyes along the line of men, was dazzled: he had never realised before this moment that the world contained so many different kinds of beauty. The Empire, which had drawn such diverse peoples into one, was indeed an awesome thing.

The single feature that the men had in common was the impressive weapon that hung heavily between their legs. Even these, however, showed amazing variety of colour and shape. Aspar's eye was drawn to the mushroom-shaped pricks of some of those from the east and from Africa, who were shorn of their foreskins. But then there were colours ranging from pink to dark purple, and many different shapes – some wedge-shaped, others broadening into the form of a club, or of uniform thickness, like a pillar. Textures ranged from gnarled and veiny like the trunk of an oak tree to the smoothness of marble or milk-white silk.

As he passed down the line, Valerius expertly handled each

man's tool and ballsac to get some idea of their dimensions when aroused. The results were impressive, and in some cases astounding. Seeing what Valerius was after, Glaucus began to perform the same function starting at the other end of the line. Aspar was impressed by the old man's skill. He had heard that such dealers in flesh were versed in tricks that could obtain instant erections in the brothel or the slave market. Now he saw that, as he moved briskly down the line, with a deft pinch or a tweak, Glaucus left each member slowly pulsating, fully engorged as it thrust upwards or outwards, following its natural bent.

Some of the men, perhaps the newest recruits, blushed at this brutal public exposure, others stared stonily ahead. What compromises had they made with their honour, as he had, Aspar wondered, in the hope that one day they might regain their freedom?

His eyes were particularly drawn to one man. He towered above the others. The thick neck and shoulders, the broad thighs in their perfection could have been struck from granite by a Phidias or a Praxiteles. His face, though strong, possessed the classical beauty of a Greek statue in its regular features. Only his manhood, its massive length and girth jutting up and out, had something savage and obscene about it, resembling the appendage of a carved satyr or Priapus himself. But it was not his striking physical appearance that fascinated the young king. It was, rather, something in his attitude and expression, a detachment which gave him almost a regal air, a self-possession which set him apart from his surroundings. In reality, he was as much one of Glaucus' chattels as the golden pitcher or the marble fountain; everything in this mighty Empire, it seemed, was for sale

Aspar was not alone in his admiration of the man with the noble bearing. Valerius had paused before him and was testing the weight of his testicles and the firmness of his erection with delicate fingers that could not encircle its girth. Glaucus noted the tribune's interest. 'This one's new,' he explained eagerly. 'Hermes, they call him, because he is endowed like the god. An Armenian of royal blood. He does not come cheap. Though, of course, to you, my lord –' a low bow '– there will be the usual discount.'

Valerius smiled, partly at the brothel-keeper's greed and partly with the satisfaction at having found what he wanted for the banquet. 'And it certainly won't do any harm to your business to show off your wares to the great and powerful men of Rome who will be attending my feast, will it, Glaucus Valerian?'

The brothel-keeper merely bowed a second time, without replying.

Valerius stood back and glanced along the line. 'I'll take all of these,' he said briskly. 'In fact, I may need a few more – and of every variety.'

'That is our speciality, as my lord well knows,' gushed Glaucus.

'Have them delivered to my villa at Mount Albanus. All except this man.' Valerius swivelled on his heels to face Hermes, who stared impassively ahead. He did not even flinch when the tribune gave his nipples a vicious tweak. Valerius looked directly at Aspar: 'This one we'll take with us.'

His passions aroused by the feast of male beauty on display at Glaucus' house of pleasure, on returning to his palace, Valerius hastily ordered a private supper to be set out in his chambers. He summoned his bath attendants – his 'toilet accessories' as he preferred to call them. Those who were to take part at that evening's impromptu festivities – himself, Aspar, Hermes and Livius – were washed, oiled, perfumed and dressed in fine matching robes of white linen trimmed with an intricate golden border.

In the garden, slaves were setting out a sumptious cold feast of meats and exotic fruits, most of which Aspar did not recognise. Another group was busily lighting lamps that glowed in the purple dusk. In Valerius' chamber, flickering candelabra turned the golden drapes into pale sheets of flame and scattered the mosaic walls with points of fire.

'I think we can dispense with these,' said Valerius as the last of the slaves withdrew, closing the bronze doors behind him. He slipped out of his robe: his oiled body shone in the lamplight. Beneath the neat V of his curled pubic hair, his prick already curved steeply downwards, fully engorged. Hermes meekly stripped off his garment, exposing the muscled symmetry of his abdomen.

Valerius silently moved the men into position. 'Let us worship your name-sake, Hermes: god of the phallus, the fount of life,' he whispered, gently pressing Aspar to his knees before the huge bulk of the Armenian. The veins already bulged, picked out in pale purple and blue on the column which had begun its marvellous ascent from a bush of coarse dark hair. It seemed to defy gravity as it rose and thickened. One hand on Aspar's nape, the other on the godlike endowment, Valerius manoeuvred the fist-sized head into Aspar's mouth and began to exert a steady pressure on his neck. Aspar clutched at Hermes' rock-hard calves as the still-hooded glans pressed at his throat. It seemed against the laws of nature that so large an object should penetrate further, but then he felt the oily head slip from the thick fleshy hood and begin to slide down his throat. Aspar panicked as he realised that the organ, which already felt as though it would choke him, was still growing.

As he tried to pull away, Valerius held his head firmly in place. 'Just relax,' he whispered hypnotically in the boy's ear, 'you can take it.' Hermes let out a groan, a deep echoing sound that made Aspar's heart leap. At the same time, the man's huge but gentle hands gripped his shoulders, dissolving the last of his resistance. Now able to fight the urge to retch, the youth found that he could comfortably breath through his nose while containing Hermes' cudgel in his maw. Still it grew, pushing outwards and upwards. Aspar's own prick danced and shivered, slapping against his hard stomach, stimulated by the Armenian's bulk in his throat.

The musk of Hermes' body, mixed with sweet spices, intoxicated the boy still further. As the unwieldy appurtenance began to slowly slide back and forth, Aspar was intrigued to feel how its temperature varied – hot at the tip and the root, cooler in the shaft. The boy felt his senses dissolving as Hermes' virility invaded his body. The other men were now shadows on the fringes of his vision. Valerius seemed to be sprinkling something on a brazier before a statue of Dionysus. A pungent but not unpleasant smell filled the room, further enhancing Aspar's sense of total abandon to pleasuring Hermes' rod of life, the sceptre of the god whose name he bore.

Another deep groan broke from Hermes' breast and Aspar felt a tremor shake the mighty oaklike legs. A hand clasped his own manroot and he realised that Livius was now crouching behind the Armenian giant and slurping hungrily at his arsehole. Aspar slipped his hands up the solid thighs and onto the spheres of his buttocks, as hard at the balls that men use for exercise in the gymnasium. He pulled the mounds of flesh apart and Livius responded with eager grunts, digging deeper with his tongue, savouring to the full the manly flavour of Hermes' hole.

Strong hands were now pulling at Aspar's hips, lifting them swiftly so that his feet almost left the ground, his full weight hanging for a moment on the Armenian's giant cock so firmly anchored in his throat. As Valerius' hands pulled his arsecheeks apart, the evening breeze cooled his raging hole. A blob of spittle, aimed with practised accuracy, landed tantalisingly on the pink halo of puckered skin, which quivered expectantly.

The tribune exhaled with pleasure as the boy's orifice blossomed in welcome, allowing the full length of his arching member to slide slickly home into the lad's vitals. A strangled cry emerged from Aspar's throat, crammed as it was with man-meat.

All other thoughts vanished from his mind as Hermes and Valerius increased the vigour of their thrusts, timing them so that one pulled back as the other thrust in. The boy was only aware of the single fiery javelin that pierced his body from hole to hole. Even the friction at his loins as Livius pumped his dick dimmed in comparison to his awareness of the pricks inside him: their heat, their hardness, the pleasure they were insistently drawing from his body.

There was an aching emptiness in his bowels as Valerius suddenly withdrew his rigid bow. Bodies rapidly rearranged themselves around him and he felt an intense pressure against his anus.

'I don't want to hurt the boy,' a voice rumbled softly behind him.

A determined whisper came back: 'He can take it.'

Valerius' familiar prick slid down his throat in a single stroke, lubricated by Aspar's own salty arse juices. Large hands gripped his slim waist firmly and, as the force on his slippery hole increased, he felt the aperture slowly expand. The ache began to build as the Armenian giant's glossy purple dickhead pushed inexorably against the boy's frail defences. A shattering bolt of pain caused Aspar's knees to buckle as Hermes' battering-ram breached his sphincter and the huge bulk started to ascend, seemingly without end, into his guts.

Aspar felt his rectum respond with a violence he had never known before. His anal canal constricted convulsively around the vast weapon, almost stopping his breath with the force of the movement. He could not hold back the groans that echoed from the mosaic walls along with Hermes' animal bellowing. The rectal muscles bore down with such force on Hermes' prick that, for a second, Aspar feared he was going to shit. But the other man's deep roars of ecstasy assured him that this was not the case.

'Yes,' thundered Hermes, 'give me that cunt-juice. I can feel it flowing round my prick.' For a moment, the waves of sensation in the lad's entrails subsided. He heard his arsehole squelching noisily as the giant churned his member around inside. Then the boy let out a yell as the sensation returned with even greater intensity.

'Yes,' called the Armenian again, pounding with increased vehemence. 'The juice. Give it to me,' he boomed. Aspar's intestines seemed to turn inside out and he could feel the copious fluids streaming down the back of his thighs. Again and again the spasms racked his bowels, sending shockwaves through his body which glowed to its extremities with profound pleasure. It seemed impossible that the feeling could continue at such a level of intensity, but each time it subsided for a few seconds, Hermes' sturdy manhood would unleash it with renewed force. At last, Aspar's legs began to tremble and threatened to fold under him.

Without withdrawing their phalluses, Valerius and Hermes steered the youth across the chamber so that he could rest his torso across a narrow couch. Time was suspended as the young king gave himself up to the hammer-blows of Hermes' man-pole. At last the Armenian's tortured howls became deafening. He began to fuck Aspar with such abandon that the lad could feel the secretions shoot from his arse as the man slammed into him and, as he pulled out, could hear a sucking noise reminiscent of the sea drawing out of a rocky cleft. Hermes' cock moved so fast that it burned like a sword in the forge and, with a final convulsion of his innards, Aspar felt the hot streams of the Armenian's man-milk gushing into him and mingling loudly with the juices of his hole. Pressed downwards by the edge of the couch, his own prick froze for an instant of aching hardness before forcing out the semen in long excruciating ejaculations.

Aspar felt himself spiralling down into a void until his descent was abruptly checked as, with a searing pang, he felt Hermes pull out of him. He was dimly aware that Valerius had withdrawn from his mouth. Then his hole lit up again as Valerius lunged into him. The tribune began to hammer urgently into his guts, stimulated by the lubrication of Hermes' generous outpourings and the boy's own hot fluids. Despite his exhaustion, to Aspar's amazement, his anus responded yet again with orgasmic contractions, drawing howls of animal pleasure from Valerius such as Aspar had never heard from him before.

Hermes' weapon, no longer fully erect, but still tumescent, appeared before his face, slimy and dripping in the lamplight. The man gently ran his fingers through Aspar's blond hair as the boy licked his own sticky sap from the majestic manhood. Slowly, the mighty column rose again and Hermes fed it gently into the boy's gaping throat. Livius meanwhile had positioned himself under the couch, taking Aspar's semi-erect penis between his lips and breathing new life into it.

Before long, Valerius was unable to fight against the hot sloppiness and muscular grip of the young king's rectum and launched into a roaring climax. This time, all four men, urged on by each other's cries and frantic motions, reached a single massive crescendo, undamming fresh floods of ball-juice.

In the silence that followed, Aspar was aware only of the huge club of flesh, gradually softening now that it had discharged its salty load into his throat, and of the large paw that tenderly caressed his head.

The Dacian king saw little of Valerius as the day of the Triumph approached. The tribune spent most of his time out at the villa, supervising the preparations for the banquet. Every now and then, however, he would check on the progress of Aspar's portrait, gazing at it through narrowed eyes and shaking his head. 'The expression's not right,' he told the indignant Babylonian. 'You haven't captured his spirit.'

Since Livius was in charge of preparations for Valerius' part in the Triumph, he remained behind at the palace, and Aspar spent much of his time in the soldier's company. Valerius had given Livius a further task. Trajan had declared a hundred and twenty three days of games to mark the Dacian victory. The ambitious young tribune had been chosen as editor of the first day's events in the arena; it would be his task to plan the programme, selecting the contestants and animals to take part. From Livius, Aspar learned that eleven thousand animals were to be slaughtered in the games and ten thousand Dacians would compete against trained gladiators. The boy was certain that, for the majority, this would be merely a protracted and bloody execution. When Aspar pressed him on Valerius' plans for his editorship, the legionary was uncharacteristically evasive.

As the schemes for the celebrations unfolded, Aspar became increasingly conscious of the immensity of Valerius' wealth, but even more of his limitless ambition. Livius recounted how the tribune had been orphaned at an early age, coming into his inheritance as a youth. On their demise, his few elderly relatives had added further to his fortune and, with the help of his own commercial skills, he had expanded his 'Empire'. Yet this did not satisfy him; political advancement was his main aim. Livius had heard a rumour that Valerius had introduced his favourite architect, Apollodorus of Damascus, to Trajan and that the tribune would therefore be involved in extravagant new building schemes the Emperor had planned. During this period, Valerius received the news that he had been accepted into the College of Augurers, an honour he had long desired. But the office he coveted most of all was that of Senator, and all his present efforts were focused on this goal. Although he treated Aspar with the tenderness and attention one might show towards a favourite pet, beneath this the boy came to sense a steely ruthlessness.

Three

The white marble monuments of the Campus Martius, the great park to the north of Rome, dazzled in the clear October sunlight. Around them seethed the colourful throng that would accompany the Emperor through Rome in his Triumph: soldiers decked out with scarlet plumes and cloaks and glittering with gold and silver decorations; huge floats depicting the victories of the Dacian campaign; platforms bearing important prisoners to be carried shoulder-high; and cartloads of dazzling gold and silver booty.

Valerius adjusted Aspar's diadem and torque. The lad was dressed in full kingly regalia, as his father's heir. He had even been allowed to wear a sword at his side. Reluctantly, Valerius agreed that he could wear the ugly wooden talisman, as long as he kept it hidden.

'Although you represent one of the defeated in the procession,' whispered Valerius, 'for today at least you will truly be a king. The Romans hate the idea of a king for themselves, but they love to see one: royal visits to Rome have always been most successful. I know you will hold yourself with dignity, little king.'

Valerius called Livius, who led Aspar to his place on a vast wheeled float depicting the fall of Sarmizegetusa. Aspar, who had been there, could not stifle his astonishment at the lifelike tableau fashioned by a team of skilled sculptors, artists and scene-painters. He knew that Valerius had secured the commission from the Emperor's staff to supervise the design and building of this scene, the climax of the Dacian campaign. The tribune had lavished care, taste and, above all, a great deal of money on the task. The battered walls, the siege engines, the swarming troops of both sides armed with swords, falxes, slings, arrows, lances: all were shown in amazing detail. Aspar mounted the wheeled float and took his position at the front on a raised platform, shaped like a turret in the city walls. The massive portrait, finally completed under Valerius' watchful eye, had been fixed against the side of the tower, so that even the furthest member of the crowd would be able to appreciate Aspar's beauty.

The structure was enormous, rising to the height of a three-storey building. From where he stood, the lad could make out the techniques of forced perspective employed by the artists: figures and buildings were reduced in scale the closer they were to the centre of the float, at the furthest point from the spectators, while objects at the sides were lifesize. Indeed, some Dacian prisoners, all men of high rank, crouched in chains along the edges of the tableau with real Roman guards, swords drawn, standing over them. They wore the helmets and armour of noble Dacian warriors. Some of them appeared so frail, that Aspar suspected that they had been seriously wounded or maimed in the war, although any disfigurements had been artfully concealed under their costumes and their pallor skilfully hidden by theatrical paint. He knew, that despite their appetite for blood in the arena, the Romans deplored deformity of any kind in other contexts.

Aspar took his place at the front of the float, standing proudly as he had seen his father do on so many occasions. Beside him, already in place, was the charioteer who would drive the team of sixteen white horses as they dragged the heavy float through the city. The man already had the turquoise reins wrapped around his powerful forearms, ready for the signal that would set the procession on its long course through the capital.

Beyond the horses, Valerius was greeting his fellow tribunes, taking his place at their head as the tribunus laticlavius, chief tribune of his legion. Squinting into the blazing sun, Aspar surveyed the procession stretching arrow-straight, into the distance, along the Via Flaminia towards the silhouetted temples and palaces cresting the hills of Rome. The burnished helmets of the legions in serried ranks were interspersed with the floats and other splendid exhibits now all assembling in their final positions. Wives and children of the troops who had been allowed into the Campus Martius to wave off husbands, sons and fathers, proudly took their places on either side of the column. Glancing over his shoulder, the boy saw the line stretching endlessly behind.

From the direction of the city, a brassy fanfare rang out and, narrowing his eyes against the sun's brilliance, Aspar could make out a tight phalanx of mounted Praetorians crossing the open parkland and occupying a position near the front of the procession. He knew that at the centre of this formation, riding in a golden chariot, his face and hands painted traditional victory red, was the Emperor Trajan himself.

The Imperial trumpets rasped out a second tattoo. From the head of the parade, an arrow arched high into the air, trailing blue streamers. A chant went up from the men at the front of the column and spread along it in a wave, past Aspar and off into the distance: '*Io Triomphe, Io Triomphe*,' – Behold the Triumph! At the same time, bands positioned every few hundred feet, between each cohort, began their regimental marches, each one different, blared and hammered out with gusto on percussion and brass, each competing to drown out the others.

A second arrow cut through the egg-shell blue of the sky and the procession, a long gaudy serpent, began to move. The charioteer at Aspar's side cracked his reins, his powerful upper arms bulging, and, as the horses sprang forward, the float trundled into motion with a fearsome creaking and groaning, like a ship on a heavy swell. Aspar grasped at the plaster form of a ruined building to steady himself. A great cheer went up and the young king glanced to his right: across the shining curve of the Tiber, a crowd had gathered to witness the start of the procession. Already, Aspar could see tiny figures running along the bank towards the city so that they could reach it in time to see the display at close quarters.

When the Triumph entered the first of the two Circuses, the cheers of the gathered thousands hit Aspar with physical force. For the Romans, always avid for entertainment, this was the show to end all shows, a lavish spectacle. The horrors of war forgotten or, perhaps, adding a dark thrill to the proceedings, the event was characterised by a definite bawdy tone. The soldiers sang dirty ditties containing endless verses purporting to describe the Emperor's sexual exploits – with both men and women. The crowd singled out their favourites in the procession and bawled obscene suggestions or else made their desires plain by gestures. Valerius was a particular favourite. 'Suck on these, handsome,' called out a buxom whore from the balcony of a brothel in the Vicus Longus, hauling a large pair of breasts from under her robe. 'Want to plant your spear in my cunt?' cried a boy-prostitute, perched in an arch high up in the outer wall of the Circus Maximus. He turned and saucily brandished his shapely behind, exposed for business under his hitched-up tunic.

The crowd cheered their own men and the conquered enemy indiscriminately, showering them with rose petals. The parade wound tortuously through the city streets, some of them so narrow that the great floats passed by a hair's breadth, testing the skills of the charioteers to the limit. Aspar noticed that, as he passed, the volume of cheers subsided by a degree as the crowd commented excitedly on his appearance. He had the impression of a growing interest as the day wore on, as though word of his arrival were being carried ahead of the parade. As it passed the rich villas of the Carinae district, where Valerius' own palace stood, he noticed matrons with their rich robes and elaborate hair styles lean forward eagerly from their balconies to scrutinise his face.

Though his large portrait had been placed below him, they would only be satisfied with the original. The young king passed so close to some of them that he could see the lust in their eyes as they exchanged excited comments. Some tossed golden bracelets and other trinkets onto the float as marks of favour. Valerius, clearly taking pleasure in the interest his conquest had aroused in the city, shot a triumphant grin over his shoulder at Aspar from time to time.

As they passed the great bulk of the Flavian amphitheatre, whose tiers of arches were famed even in far-off Dacia, the procession drew to a halt. There was a long pause, in which the crowd gradually fell silent. Suddenly, a roar went up from the nearby Forum and was taken up throughout the city. Aspar felt sickened as he realised that the delay had marked the moment when the head of the procession had reached the Capitol: the cheers meant that a representative of the Dacian leadership – for Decebalus himself was already dead – had been executed by strangulation.

Now the Triumph approached its climax as the Emperor ascended to the Temple of Capitoline Jupiter, where white oxen would be sacrificed in thanksgiving. The floats were assembled side by side in the Forum, a living frieze recounting Trajan's most glorious campaign. Imperial attendants, clad in scarlet robes interwoven with gold thread, were unloading the gold of Decebalus and his allies from the carts: a mountain of gold, silver and precious booty was rising before the temple of Vesta, shimmering in the afternoon sun. The populace gazed in awe as the pile grew, almost blocking the temple from view.

Fanfares cut through the roar of the mob, signalling that the omens of the Imperial sacrifice were good. How could they not be, thought Aspar? The gods – whatever gods there were – were surely with Rome. His father had bade him get to know his enemy. The day had been a revelation, a demonstration of Rome's invincible glory and might. How was it possible to oppose such power? the young man pondered, acutely conscious of his frailty and insignificance.

His thoughts were interrupted as Valerius leaped exuberantly onto the float beside him. 'You were a great success,' he whispered, grinning broadly at the boy, 'you are the talk of Rome.' Aspar could only smile wanly at his master.

As soon as the formalities of the Triumph were concluded, Valerius set out with Livius, Aspar and the rest of his party for his villa on Mount Albanus where the banquet was to be held, though many members of the household, such as Valerius' harem of slave boys, had already been sent ahead days in advance in order to help with preparations. Aspar travelled with Valerius in his chariot while the others followed in mule-drawn carts. The tribune soon left his entourage behind, tearing down the Via Appia, before turning off into the hills for the last part of the journey.

Aspar's first sight of the villa was at sunset. It overlooked a volcanic lake, round and smooth as a mirror, cupping flaming streaks of cloud in its depths. Valerius' country home, he informed Aspar, had been designed by Apollodorus of Damascus, who, he confided, was destined to be the Emperor's own architect. The villa scaled the gentle slope of Mount Albanus in curved tiers of slender pillars, each colonnade a different, delicate shade of marble – rose, sea-green, apricot – the hues intensified by the rich evening light. Pergolas, heavy with late blooms, arched over terraces and stairways that meandered artlessly among the tall cypresses.

In groves between the trees, towered the pointed crests of five great silk pavilions – black, azure, scarlet, purple and gold – which had been erected to house the night's festivities. Vast expanses of the fine material rippled in the soft mountain breeze, catching the sunset's fire in its folds, while the gold and silver pennants that festooned the structures trembled like birch leaves.

Valerius' team of 'toilet accessories', who had arrived earlier in the day, were waiting in the villa's splendid baths: a series of arched rooms, encrusted with glittering mosaics, which followed the curve of the mountain and afforded spectacular views across the lake. The team got to work with perfumes, oils and strigils, and soon Valerius and Aspar were sleek and fragrant. Their hair, one blond, one dark, was meticulously coiffed in the shoulder-length style fashionable among Roman dandies. Their brief tunics were of filmy, translucent silk, white interwoven with silver, and their cloaks of an equally light fabric, crimson shot with gold, that billowed at the slightest movement.

'This will be a night of surprises.' Valerius smiled eagerly, slipping his arm round Aspar's waist and hurrying him along one of the villa's curved terraces. A yellow crescent moon hung low over the smoothness of the lake. 'The guests at my banquets expect to be astonished and so I always have to devise greater wonders. But this banquet I have planned especially for you. I think I have surpassed my own reputation for the strange and the marvellous: I have kept the preparations secret because I want to savour your reactions. If today your name was on the tongue of every citizen of Rome, tomorrow, as news of the banquet spreads, it will be the talk of the Senate and the Imperial household.'

They emerged into a paved courtyard in front of the villa. Aspar froze. Hundreds of torches in the shape of giant phalluses were borne aloft by slaves robed as the phallophoroi who marched in fertility festivals such as the Floralia and the Saturnalia. A slave, dressed in the comic mask and costume of an ithyphallos, scampered up to Aspar, brandishing a massive wooden penis attached to his waist; at the end of it flared a lighted wick. Similar figures rushed to and fro providing entertainment, as well as light, for the feast.

By their glow, he saw that a fleet of light chariots was drawn up in rows in the courtyard. In each stood a naked charioteer. To each, however, in place of horses, four muscular nude men had been harnessed. Their identities were concealed by stylised horses' heads. Black bodies had been matched to black heads, brown to brown, while other teams had been painted white or piebald. One team had been painted with black and white stripes like the teams of orynx in the Circus.

Even more extraordinary, however, was the harness that bound them to the chariots: a light yoke linked each group of four, positioned just above their crotches, while the bridle fitted tightly around their pricks and testicles. Many of them were tumescent or even displaying full erections as a result of the stimulation. Aspar guessed immediately that these were the men he had watched Valerius select at the House of Glaucus. Clearly delighted at the effect created by the assembled fleet, Valerius giggled as he indicated that Aspar should mount one of the chariots.

Climbing beside him, Valerius grasped a whip and cracked it lightly across the backs of the team. Muffled grunts of pain could be heard through the horseheads as the men moved forward along a paved driveway that wound down the hill through flowering oleanders. With another lash of the whip, they broke into a trot and the chariot picked up speed. Some of the ithyphalloi, with their cock-lamps swinging wildly from their waists, ran alongside the chariot to light the way. Valerius steered with brisk tugs on the reins. These were magnified into a brutal wrenching on the privates of the team, eliciting sharp cries of pain. Hearing these, Valerius began to laugh with exhilaration, cracking his whip and relishing the many bends which allowed him to haul on the reins first one way then the other, although he discovered that, after a while, their members were so sensitised that by constant slight tweaks on the bridle, he could draw a continuous roaring from the 'horses'.

With a last vicious pull on both reins, the chariot drew up before an arched gateway in the garden walls. Aspar could see the mighty shoulders of their team trembling and streaming with sweat. As he dismounted, he noticed that as a result of the pressure and pain from the harness, their huge pricks bobbed fully erect, a raging red etched with blue veins in the torchlight. One of these Aspar could not help but recognise: although the man's head was hidden by the horse-mask, Aspar knew that the colossal erection belonged to Hermes the Armenian.

The other chariots, driven by the slaves, had followed Valerius' lead and were now lining up outside the gate. The guests – all male, mainly young – had already begun to arrive, and a team of servants tethered their horses or chariots in a clearing outside the walls; the man-drawn fleet would provide transport to the villa. Valerius relished his friends' expressions of surprise and delight as they mounted the vehicles.

'This certainly got a reaction,' he muttered to Aspar, as he smiled and nodded this way and that to the steady flow of new arrivals.

Having greeted several hundred guests, Valerius and Aspar drove back to the villa, the tribune cracking his whip and wielding the reins even more harshly on the more gruelling return journey. The boy noticed, through the semi-transparency of his tunic and pouch, the beat of the other man's arched erection.

'Let me show you the opening entertainments of the evening, before supper is served,' Valerius enthused, jumping down from the chariot and snatching Aspar's hand. Slaves were mingling with the partygoers, offering them pickled flamingo tongues, stuffed cows' udders and other delicacies from silver trays. Drinks were distributed in antique Greek goblets painted with slender red figures of men in the most varied positions of coition. 'It's an aphrodisiac,' muttered Valerius, leaning close to Aspar and offering the boy his own cup. 'Wine fortified with powdered horses' testicles. Tastes good, though,' he added, knocking back a slug of the dark liquid. 'Drink up – you'll need it.'

'Do they need it?' mused Aspar half to himself as he looked

around at the knots of young men on the steps of the villa. Many were scantily clad and had already begun to kiss and slip their hands into each other's clothing.

'There's a long night of revels ahead,' smiled Valerius pushing the cup to Aspar's lips. The boy sipped gingerly at first and then found himself quaffing the sweet liquid in a single draught. He frowned slightly, wondering what he should be feeling, but Valerius snatched the cup from his hands and pulled on his arm. 'Come, let me show you the welcome I have provided for my distinguished guests.'

The tribune led Aspar through the excited throng which now moved up the steps of the villa. Passing through the wine-red porphyry pillars, Aspar found himself not in the atrium he anticipated but in a series of interconnecting grottos, each so convincing that it took him a few moments to realise that they must have been constructed by scene-painters for the occasion. Large plaques inlaid with several shades of marble marked out different areas.

'This is the kissing competition,' explained Valerius, moving past one of them, 'it's inspired by the famous one at Megara in Greece which has been held for hundreds of years. It's traditionally for young lads, so each of the guests may choose one of my slave boys to demonstrate his kissing technique.'

The demonstration did not seemed to be limited to kissing, however. Their passions aroused by the pretty nude youths, the competitors had shed their own clothes and their mouths seemed famished not so much for kisses as for other tender parts such as penises and arseholes.

'This was really to keep my boys happy,' confided Valerius. 'Which they certainly seem to be,' he remarked as he contemplated the sea of bodies so raptly engaged on silk couches. A chorus of sighs and grunts rose on all sides. 'The winning guests get to choose the slave boys of their choice. Which the slaves don't know yet, and may not be so happy about.'

A lad with a head of luxuriant blond curls let out a groan as a corpulent guest shafted him with a impressive purple prick. 'For the moment, I think the boys have already had their reward, however,' commented Valerius drily, taking Aspar by the elbow. At this point, Glaucus, fully clothed and sweating profusely, rushed up to lavish compliments upon his patron.

'Not now, Glaucus,' interrupted Valerius, pushing him aside.

'But, my lord,' the man protested, trinkets tinkling with indignation. Valerius ignored him, and moved on.

Disarmed at the lavishness of the party but also at its spirit of abandon, Aspar meekly followed his master to the next grotto. SLAVE MARKET read the sculpted sign at the mouth of the cave, and Aspar was puzzled to see that that was indeed what it appeared to be. Naked slaves on a platform, chained at neck and ankles, were being led forward one by one, while members of the audience bid for them. Once purchased, they would disappear through a doorway with their new master. 'This suits the tastes of many of my guests,' chuckled Valerius in Aspar's ear.

After a few minutes, it struck the young king that there was something odd about these slaves: none bore the marks of slavery, such as shaved heads, brandings or scars from beatings. On the contrary, they sported fashionable hairstyles and their bodies had been carefully cultivated in the baths and gymnasium. Had they all enjoyed the privileges of favourites with their former masters? But if so, why were they on sale? Then the import of Valerius' words dawned on him as he recognised the regal carriage of the young men on the platform: these were not slaves at all, but the sons of noble Roman families. The masters who were bidding for them, on the other hand, burly men of different nationalities, many with roughly cropped heads, were indeed slaves, and of the lowest sort. Aspar had heard of these men of the ruling classes who craved rough treatment and humiliation: it was said that the

Emperor Nero had prostituted himself in the disreputable Subura district, accepting all comers.

Valerius smiled as Aspar's puzzled frown melted into understanding and steered him through a doorway where the masters were leading their 'slaves'. A dimly lit cavern was divided into many niches and in each, scenes of humiliation and punishment were taking place. Gasps and cries of pain rang out as the masters dealt out the rough treatment their new purchases craved. Calloused palms administered merciless spankings, leaving large red handprints on trembling buttocks. Others writhed, chained to the walls as their nipples were wrenched and chewed. One slave choked on a heavy stream of piss that spurted from the long foreskin of his master's meaty member.

Aspar felt a strong wave of warmth spread out from his chest to his head and loins. Valerius' potion was taking effect. He felt his dick unspooling in its pouch as he watched a dark tangle of arms and legs, a group of several slaves and masters fused by pleasure into a single strange beast – a many-headed hydra, or Cerberus – writhing and moaning in ecstasy. He could hear the rasping breath of the masters as they fucked soft arse-lips with all their rough strength. The slaves were feeding with the desperation of the starving from the holes of other masters who had obligingly spread their hairy haunches and were grinding them with gusto against the privileged cheeks of the rich young men. Tonight, for a few hours, they were the masters and they intended to make full use of the privilege. Aspar could smell the sex-aroma of the masters hard-fucking their slaves and could hear the squelching of arse-juices. Clearly the slaves were enjoying the brutality and subjection because they began to bay with pleasure and, unable to resist the burning sensations in their vitals, sprayed white showers of semen over the floor of the cave.

'Come on, we still have to see the best of the pre-supper tit-bits,' whispered Valerius, seeing that Aspar was falling under the spell of the aphrodisiac and the atmosphere of abandon that was already invading the party.

The third of the caves was the largest: a great marble sign by its mouth read simply, THE STABLES. Whereas the atmosphere in the other caves had been rapt and focused, here was furious activity. Slaves dressed as grooms were leading in teams of panting, sweating 'horses', the groups of men who had pulled the chariots, still yoked together in fours. Having finished their tasks of providing transport for the guests, they were about to dispense another service – equally essential, to judge by the queues of whispering young man that had gathered about the mouth of the cave, eyes hunting among the teams for the most desirable phallus.

Each group of four was led to a wooden framework which provided, side by side, a niche for every member of the team. They were chained in place and a covering of hide drawn down over their bodies with holes strategically positioned to expose their jutting privates. The men had been chosen by Valerius for the generosity of their endowments, but now, after several journeys up and down the mountain, the stimulation had swollen their organs so grotesquely that the skin was stretched to shiny tautness. The men at the mouth of the cave licked their lips greedily, their eyes fixed on the rigid weapons which were now almost horse-sized. As soon as a slave had secured each man, he tugged on a pulley which tilted the framework slightly forward, while still holding the 'horse-men' firmly in place.

Valerius watched Aspar's face with amusement as the purpose of this entertainment became clear to the boy. Once the angle of the framework was adjusted, it resembled four male horses yoked together rearing up in the mating position. The limbs of the slaves had slotted into shapes like those of the beasts' legs, while their bodies were covered in hide which matched the headpieces they still wore.

As the teams were fixed in place, the waiting guests, each of whom had earmarked the animal they desired, fought to reach their chosen mate. Servants at the entrance to the cave had to hold back the press to avert a riot. Already naked, the Roman youths fell on their knees before the weapons which protruded obscenely from the hide. They sucked and slavered hungrily over them before leaping to their feet and, turning, sinking their rumps onto the glistening pricks. Some had to rise on tiptoe so in order to reach the tip of a dick with their hole before plunging down on it and taking it deep in their guts. Once each group of four men was impaled, a servant positioned by each team of beasts manipulated the framework with a lever, rocking it – slowly at first – so that the horse-cocks plunged in and out of the hungry Roman holes.

'I thought this up with you in mind.' Valerius grinned. 'Let's try it,' he urged, pushing Aspar towards one of the waiting teams.

Swept away by the communal lust and feeling the aphrodisiac raging in his veins, Aspar stumbled to his knees before the inflated member of one of a team of horses: the broad shaft was pale, though the exposed glans and tightly trussed balls were a shocked scarlet. The boy half tore off the flimsy cloak and tunic, exposing his long brown limbs and cock that already soared nobly from its thick base. His mouth closed over the powerful rod and, in his arousal, he let it slide all the way down his throat. He pulled his head back, tickling at the hard bright glans with his tongue. From within the horse-mask, he heard a long exhalation. Pressing down hard again, the boy felt the bone-like curve of flesh inch its way along the constriction of his gullet. The man uttered a deep groan of relief after his torment before the chariot. Aspar felt a tug at his elbow. Valerius was pulling him to his feet and urging him to take his seat on the horse-dick.

At first the young king experienced a sharp pain as he pushed back on the shiny hardness and it began to penetrate his innards. But soon he could feel the man's heavy gonads knocking against his own and he experienced a delicious fullness. Glancing along the line, he could see that Valerius and two other men were also firmly anchored to their horse's prick. The framework began to rock, slowly at first. As Aspar's natural lubrication started to flow, the horse-cock moved smoothly in and out of his arse, massaging his throbbing prostate and sending waves of heat through his body and along his limbs.

Because the thrusts were synchronised for all eight men, the mounters and mounted, Aspar found that his growing moans chimed in with theirs. The loud cries of other teams, some closer to climax, also in chorus, added further stimulation. The slave operating the framework began to quicken the pace and vigour of the strokes until Aspar found that, at the height of each stroke, his feet were swung off the ground and there he hung for a brief moment, skewered on the powerful horse-meat. He felt his anal canal bear down hard with the intense sensation. The floodgates of feeling opened deep within him and the waters of pleasure burst, rushing towards the bestial club sheathed in his rectum and streaming down his legs. His ears rang with unison roars of the studs and those on which they were breeding; to his surprise, his own cries were part of the chorus. Linked by some mysterious circuit of lust, the note of hysteria in their bellowing signalled that for all eight, a dizzying climax was approaching. And then it broke over them like a tidal wave. Aspar felt the horse-flesh stiffening full-length into his guts and inseminating him with gush after gush of its fertile fluid. Stimulated by its own copious outpourings, the horse's prick juddered and immediately launched a second generous libation into the boy's hot entrails. His own vertical column was stimulated into a frenzied dance and, after an agonising moment of utter rigidity, sent long white streamers of jism upwards across his chin and along his chest. At the same time, he could see Valerius' head thrust forward, his eyes narrowed and his mouth distorted in screams of frightening intensity.

After a dip in the tepidarium of the baths, where there was a continuous stream of men sluicing and primping themselves, Aspar and Valerius donned fresh tunics and headed for the banquet.

'This is another surprise,' Valerius confided as servants drew aside tapestry curtains depicting phallic gods, and he and Aspar led the guests into the feast. It had been laid out along a broad terrace that overlooked the moonlit lake. As his friends streamed past them, Valerius stood back to drink in their gasps of amazement. He was famed for using only the most exquisitely fashioned utensils at his parties. This time, he had gone one better. Together with a team drawn from Rome's leading cooks, he had created a banquet in which exotic delicacies were served on living utensils of equally delectable young men, their skin colours careful chosen to complement the dishes.

For a moment, the guests wandered along the terraces admiring the masterpieces of the culinary arts that had been set before them. Six Nubians knelt in a tight circle facing one another, their laps forming a great ebony bowl for exotic fruits – Aspar identified pomegranates, dates and figs as well as strawberries, quinces and raisins, mixed in with strange forms he did not recognise. The slaves wore jewelled turbans to match the flesh of the fruits. On the paler skin of a group of Syrian youths, a splendid display of poultry had been set out – swans, pheasants, peacocks, flamingos, all cooked and sewn into their original plumage. The boys forming the receptacle sported headdresses of brightly coloured feathers.

At various points on the table, young men had been posed in the guise of gods: here was a Cupid with his arrow about to fly, there a young Hercules strangling snakes (stuffed and ready to eat). Aspar guessed that there were a hundred or more of these statues that could be glimpsed along the winding course of the terrace. Each had been coated with a thick layer of coloured foodstuffs: sometimes several shades had been used on a single statue: Cupid appeared to have been painted with some kind of honey glaze that shone like gold in the lamplight, Hercules was covered with garum, the much-prized fish sauce. One statue was smeared with green-dyed eel roe, another with a red fruit sauce.

Their curiosity satisfied, the guests fell on the feast. And hunger was not the only stimulus; they soon realised that rather than using bread to scrape garum from a statue, more pleasure was to be had by licking it off directly. From an immaculate still-life, the scene was rapidly transformed into one of mayhem, with guests rolling in sauces and lapping greedily at the platters which began to sprout new knobs and handles. Before long, the young Romans were washing down the feast with the milk that springs from men's loins.

'Now for the climax of the feast,' said Valerius, surveying the scene with satisfaction. He served Aspar with a wine-coloured liquid from a ornately sculpted golden bowl. One of the handles of the bowl, a gold-painted slave, smiled lazily up at him. Aspar emptied the cup in a few gulps, recognising the potent brew he had imbibed earlier that evening.

The guests looked up from their activities at the sound of loud music and singing. A column of ithyphalloi, swinging their cock-torches, was clearing a way through the crowd. They were followed by an actor in the guise of Dionysus, followed by a train of lusty satyrs and a band of flute and harp players. 'Come with us to the kingdoms of love,' they sang and danced off down the terrace until they disappeared round the side of the mountain. A team of slaves with towels and bowls of rose water followed, and the guests rapidly washed away the remains of the most recent revels before hurrying off in pursuit of Dionysus' procession.

Following the others, Valerius and Aspar came to a large circular balcony. A marble plaque several feet high had been set up with the legend THE KINGDOMS OF LOVE carved on it in large letters. Below, inlaid with different colours of marble, was a map showing the five pavilions that had been set up in the garden. Each of five stairways that led down from the balcony was carpeted in the appropriate colour. Servants were waiting for Valerius by a bronze cabinet. They stripped both the tribune and the young king of their garments and dressed them in open-fronted robes of silver silk.

'I had these made – one for each of the kingdoms,' Valerius explained as he guided the boy down the stairs which led to the Kingdom of Ganymede. 'We must put in an appearance at all of them but I have planned that we shall linger a little longer in one, designed especially for us.'

The azure pavilion was decorated to resemble the home of the gods on Mount Olympus. The silk walls were artfully painted with cloud mountains and temples in the Greek style that gave a convincing illusion of limitless vistas. The floor of the chamber, however, appeared to be an immense cloud on which a number of guests were lounging. As he stumbled on to it, Aspar realised that it was made up of white air-filled cushions upon which bleached raw wool had been piled to give a light, fleecy effect. What was most extraordinary about this setting was that the sky seemed to be filled with great winged eagles carrying off youths, just as Zeus had abducted Ganymede. Round they flew, swooping low and rising towards the azure empyrean of the pavilion roof: Aspar could feel a rush of air and swish of wings as they passed. The piercing cries that he heard, however, were not those of birds but the lust-calls of ravisher and ravished. It was not until he had studied the scene for a few moments that Aspar began to understand the ingenious devices that had been constructed by Valerius' team of experts, who were all accustomed to creating impressive effects for Rome's theatres.

Young slaves – as they dipped and glided overhead, he recognised many of them as members of Valerius' harem – had been secured by harnesses so that they each appeared to be in the clutches of a giant wide-winged eagle. Within each eagle, one of the party-goers was concealed; the rapturous expressions on the faces of the youths and their shrieks revealed that, beneath the artifice, the ravishment was real.

Aspar watched a guest being strapped into an eagle costume and saw how, as he took his place, he inserted his engorged tool into the expectant hole of his Ganymede. Once the two were securely locked into this position of coition, a system of pulleys on the end of a long flexible pole raised them up and, as one slave rotated the pole, another manipulated the ropes, raising and lowering the god and his helpless prey. The rise and fall in the shouts of pleasure suggested that the sensation of flight added a peculiar intensity to the simple act of penetration. Certainly the wildly flailing limbs of the youths and their frantically jiggling erections suggested as much. Frequently, these would stiffen into regular contractions, scattering showers of silvery man-seed on to the clouds below.

Sporting matching robes for each of the pavilions, Valerius and Aspar continued their tour. The purple Kingdom of Dionysus commemorated the love of the god of wine and revelry for the mortal Polymnus and how, having lost his beloved in death, the god had wandered the hills of Greece with a wooden replica of his lover's manhood as his only consolation. This pavilion provided phalluses not only of wood but also of glass, gold, bronze and many other precious materials, of the most extraordinary forms and dimensions, for the guests to choose from. Some preferred to be the receptors of these tools while others took delight in administering them: willing slaves performed both services.

The scarlet tent of the Kingdom of Hyacinth was one of the most beautiful, Aspar thought. An Arcadian setting of blossoms of many varieties framed a lake filled with wine. Beyond the fragrance of the flowers, Aspar detected a faint sweetness which reminded him of the aphrodisiac he had drunk earlier; doubtless the wine was liberally spiked with that efficacious brew. A lifelike polychrome statue of the youth Hyacinth, beloved of Apollo, stood upon a small island in the lake. A bronze discus was embedded in his brow, commemorating his tragic accidental death at the hands of his lover. Red wine spurted from the wound, replenishing the lake.

On the shores, among the flowers, naked erotic dancers, cinaedi, gyrated lasciviously while watching guests cavorted in the red liquid, taking frequent deep draughts, their privates expertly attended to by trained spatalocinaedi. These eunuchs had been carefully selected and castrated at the moment of adolescence when their rods and balls had reached perfect ripeness. Aspar could already feel the aphrodisiac he had drunk at the feast performing its fortifying work, but Valerius scooped a cupful of the red waters of the lake and bade him drink deep: 'For the pleasures ahead,' he urged. As they left the Pavilion, Glaucus hurried towards them, jewellery rattling in agitation, but Valerius silenced him with a vigorous sweep of his hand, leaving the old pimp frozen, his mouth agape.

The golden tent of Narcissus was even more splendid. Its central feature was also a shallow lake, but it was clear, touched with just a hint of blue. Recalling the fate of Narcissus who fell in love with his own reflection, great bronze mirrors had been set up all around the pool and even its bed was a massive mirror. Lamps in amber globes suffused the scene with warm light. The lake and surrounding landscape heaved with rutting groups and couples, focusing with quiet intensity on their own reflections which receded into infinity all round as though in an unlimited multiplication of pleasurable sensation.

'This is the Kingdom I devised for us,' murmured the tribune in Aspar's ear as, with a rustle of black silk, he drew back the curtain that masked the entrance to the Kingdom of Orpheus. Aspar followed him inside and was immediately enfolded in thick blackness. He felt Valerius' hands slip his robe from his shoulders, leaving him naked and feeling strangely vulnerable in the impenetrable darkness. Valerius hooked his arm firmly around the boy's slender waist and pushed him forward. 'This Kingdom is inspired by my experience of the divine mysteries at Eleusis, in Greece,' he confided in the lightest of whispers. Aspar was struck by the fact that the darkness of the pavilion was matched by an apparent total silence. But then he gradually became aware of the laboured breathing of many men and an undulating sea of sighs that spread all about him.

'It is forbidden on the pain of a terrible curse to divulge the Eleusian mysteries,' continued Valerius, carefully manoeuvring the lad down a steep slope, 'but what I saw there inspired me to create a similar divine experience – a passage through the underworld, a total surrender of body and reason to the god of life and nature.'

As well as the subdued sounds of rapture from a hundred throats, Aspar was becoming aware of other sensations: a heady aroma of male sex on a vast scale, the heat of many bodies and feathery touches of exploring fingers on every part of his anatomy – legs, loins, torso, face. The warmth intensified and he felt hot flesh pressing in on all sides. A hot mouth clamped hard on his upright cock, hands opened his crack and a slippery tongue began to worry at his throbbing hole, while another entered his mouth, vigorously fencing with his own tongue. Other hands moved purposefully over his back, his chest, kneading his leg muscles. 'Surrender,' whispered a voice from the darkness which he dimly recognised as that of Valerius. 'Give yourself up to the god. I am here with you.' Involuntarily, Aspar's knees buckled, yet he felt himself borne up on an undertow of flesh. Another mouth, cooler this time, sucked hard on his prick, exerting a steady friction on the slick head. The lips on his lovehole sucked hard at the pucker till it became hot and engorged. He felt the suction increase so that the entire ring of flesh was taken into the man's mouth, clamped between his lips like a ripe plum. Now the tip of his tongue darted in and out of the smooth aperture.

Firm hands pressed on Aspar's shoulders, forcing him down until his nose caught the intoxicating whiff of arousal and his lips were prised open by a tautly hooded prick arching eagerly upwards. It jammed with satisfying firmness into Aspar's throat. Other hands tugged at his ankles, pulling them from the ground and depriving him of his last shred of control over his own body. His legs were swung apart and a powerful smell of fresh male sweat struck his nostrils as hard burly hips pushed between his parted thighs and something heavy and blunt pressed urgently against his already lubricated arse-lips.

The probing in his throat, the hard pounding in his gizzard, the sucking at his crotch blended into a single powerful sensation of ascension; he was rising upwards towards some mysterious peak of intense revelation. He was acutely conscious of fingers and tongues running over every pore of his skin like rivulets of water. The sighs and breathing all around him swelled like the gurgling of a stream. Up, up, he soared, like the organ that hammered away in his guts. Far below, he heard cries and a convulsive movement told him that thick spurts of cock-juice were coursing through his intestines. As one man's pillar withdrew, in plunged another, hot and gnarled with a thick foreskin that he could feel clicking against his sphincter with each stroke. He was aware of great gobs of semen flowing into the mouth that sucked greedily on his own member. Yet he felt no diminution in his ardour. On the contrary, his manhood remained stiff, and still he felt himself float further skywards. Cock after cock emptied its precious nectar in his throat and he felt a warmth swelling within him as though they were filling his soul with the divine spark of their loins.

The life-giving fluid streamed from his mouth and anus. As a spent prick pulled out of his gullet, another mouth met his, lapping the dripping seed from his lips, while a third noisily sucked the salty ambrosia from his open cunt. Still, he felt himself soaring up, up towards some obscure revelation. A burning pang shot through his loins as another manroot thrust into the raging crater of his sensitised rectum which now overflowed with the hot lava from innumerable ballsacs.

In his trancelike state, Aspar was still able to recognise the down-curved manhood of his master. Sloshing his hard appendage back and forth in the come-bath of the boy's hole, Valerius leant forward and moaned in his ear, 'All those others were just to prepare for this, my little king. I am the priest of Dionysus: this is the phallus of the god inside you.' He hammered at the boy's anus until his whole body shook. 'Let me impregnate you with my divine seed.' Violent shudders racked the tribune's body as his arched weapon flung jets of sperm into the boy's anal canal. Hot streams were released from Aspar's bobbing pole, as many famished mouths and tongues jostled for a morsel of his flying jism. At that moment, his ascent reached its peak and he began to fall in a rapid earthward spin. But Valerius' strong arms clasped him firmly and he knew that they would keep him unscathed.

The familiar raucous blare of captured Dacian dragon trumpets rang out in the packed amphitheatre as the Emperor, accompanied by the Senators, entered the royal box for the inauguration of the victory games. A discreet gap of a few days had been decreed to allow for recovery after the night of the Triumph. Banquets had been held all over Rome – including a lavish event at the Emperor's palace on the Palatine Hill. It was Valerius' party, however, which had set all the tongues of Rome wagging and, as he stepped into the editor's box in the amphitheatre, Aspar at his side, whispered comments rippled around the tiers of spectators. The tribune noted with satisfaction that the Emperor Trajan, just a few feet away, was craning his neck to examine his companion: clearly, he was aware of the gossip that had swept the city.

Valerius had made sure that his young protégé would live up to expectations. Certainly he looked very different from the bedraggled youth that had been presented to the Emperor in Dacia. Both men wore togas of the finest white wool, embroidered with broad purple borders in silken thread. The warm brown of Aspar's long muscular arms stood out against the brilliance of the fine garment. The young king's hair hung to his shoulders in ringlets of spun gold so that he resembled a youthful Alexander or an Apollo. Although Aspar's own crown and torque had been returned to the Emperor's private treasury, Valerius had decked him out with a diadem, necklace and jewels which had been looted from one of Rome's enemies centuries earlier, and had eventually found their way on to the open market.

Oblivious to the scrutiny of the mob, Aspar awaited the start of the event anxiously. Thousands of Dacian warriors would fight over the weeks of the celebratory games and most of them would stand no chance of survival. The splendour of the amphitheatre was overwhelming; all the power of Rome focused in this circle of marble. Cooling fountains, dyed red, green, blue and yellow, rose high in the air round the edge of the ring, filling the stadium with exotic eastern perfumes.

The youthful king had not forgotten his father's words; his task now was to survive and bide his time until the opportunity arose to regain his freedom. Besides, he knew that there was nothing he could do to help either the men of his own tribe – now his own subjects – or those of the allied tribes who would fight to the death today. His only concern must be to control the bitterness and rage of seeing yet more of his countrymen slaughtered by Rome.

Another trumpet blast rasped out and doors swung open at the far end of the arena. Aspar's heart skipped a beat as the long procession of men circled the arena, massing in orderly rows before the Imperial box. He was taken aback to notice that, far from wearing armour, as he had expected, the men were quite naked but for helmets which completely covered their heads, reducing them to faceless fighting machines. He blushed, sharing the humiliation they must be feeling.

Valerius smiled, his emotions for the boy aroused at the sight of his burning cheeks: 'It's customary for gladiators to walk naked in the opening parade,' he explained in a low voice, 'many are proud of their bodies and this is a way to attract the attention and support of powerful citizens.' Indeed, the amphitheatre echoed with the buzz of whispered comments on the men's physical endowments.

More disturbing, however, was the fact that many of them wore golden helmets marked by the familiar high Dacian crest. Some resembled those worn by his own tribesmen; they had been fitted with protective visors covering the face, as was the custom in the ring. At least this meant that Aspar was spared the torment of watching the death of a man he recognised. He searched the rows anxiously to see if he could spot the burly form of his warrior-master Burebista, but, to his relief he could not.

As he held the office of editor for the day's events, it was Valerius' task to give the signal for the each contest to begin. Over the course of the afternoon, the shadow of the circular awning moved around the ring. From time to time, at the start of a bout, the tribune would whisper the names of the combatants to Aspar. Each contest pitted one or more Dacians against a corresponding number of professional gladiators. In every case, the fight concluded either with the slaughter of the Dacian, unused to the tricks of the arena, or with him disarmed and at his opponent's mercy. In these cases the final decision rested with the Emperor but, in every case, the crowd, still intoxicated with vicarious victory, bellowed for blood. Trajan, ever anxious to please his people, bowed to their wishes.

Towards evening, with a flourish of trumpets, the last Dacian warrior strode out into the arena. Clad only in his helmet, he was a commanding figure, tall and long-limbed. He bore the long oval shield and deadly curved falx of a Dacian soldier. The setting sun picked out the fleece of fine golden hair that covered his legs and torso. Across the ring, a dark stocky figure emerged from the gates. The crowd rose to its feet with a great shout, and blossoms and rose petals were tossed into the arena from every direction. He was a retiarius, armed with a net and trident – clearly a great champion and a favourite of the Roman mob. This was a fight anticipated by all, the climax of the first day of the games. Valerius sat upright in his marble seat, motionless, one hand laid idly across his pro-gramme, a half smile playing on his lips.

Aspar felt sadness well up inside him for this fine-looking anonymous warrior. He knew that he stood little chance against an expert gladiator; and this made him feel his own powerlessness more keenly. The arena fell silent – even those in the free places at the topmost tier ceased their chatter. The gladiator began to en-scribe slow circles on the sand, gradually closing in on his oppo-nent. The Dacian inched round, crouching like a mountain lion, sizing up the other man. The gladiator moved in closer and lunged with his trident. At this, the warrior flung his shield aside and began to wield his falx with two hands in lethal arcs. The gladia-tor leapt back, astonished at the other contestant's speed and strength. Indeed, unbroken by the rough journey from Dacia and months in captivity, the man's spirit drew gasps from the crowd. They watched with bated breath as the warrior whirled the giant sickle around his head with such swift movements that at times it was invisible. So deep was the concentration of the populace that it was possible to hear the whistling of the weapon as it sliced through the air.

For a moment, faced with a tactic he had not yet encountered, the gladiator was taken aback. But he had tricks of his own to call on. He simply turned tail and fled across the arena. As the Dacian followed, still spinning his weapon, the gladiator wheeled round and hurled the net, taking the other man unawares. Caught up in the mesh, the warrior desperately tried to free his weapon, but before he could do so, the gladiator had circled behind him and with one tug on the net brought him heavily to the ground. The Dacian attempted to lash out with the falx, but the gladiator stamped hard on his wrist. Throwing the net back from the Dacian's body, he thrust the trident towards the man's muscled chest, grazing it with the points.

The victorious gladiator used the tip of his sandal to push back the visor of the defeated Dacian. The man raised his bowed head. Aspar gasped, clutching at the marble parapet. The fallen warrior was King Saphanx, his father.

The boy wheeled round to face Valerius. 'You knew,' he hissed at him. 'You planned this,' he accused, indicating the programme on the tribune's lap.

The other man shrugged, without meeting Aspar's gaze. 'I don't run the Empire. Is he not our enemy? At least he had the chance to fight. He put up a good show.'

'You could have prepared me,' said the boy, his voice cracking. 'He's been here all these weeks. I could have spoken with him again. Why did I have to find out this way?'

'He was the Emperor's prisoner, not mine.'

'That's all that interests you, isn't it? Making an impression on the Emperor. I'm just a bauble to you, aren't I,' murmured Aspar, 'without feelings.'

Valerius stared into the arena, impassive.

Aspar shot to his feet and the movement drew Saphanx' attention. He started as he recognised his son. He reached out an arm towards him in a gesture of appeal, and his cry rang through the amphitheatre: 'Aspar, remember my words. Live on – win back our freedom.' Though he spoke in his native tongue, the crowd sensed the defiance in his tone. Pandemonium was unleashed. How dare this wretched enemy of Rome publicly challenge his conquerors?

The stands became a sea of shaking thumbs. Aspar struggled for breath and the ellipse of the arena began to tilt dangerously. Valerius grasped the boy by the waist to steady him, but Aspar knocked his arm aside.

The Emperor stood up from his couch, holding a white silk handkerchief of judgement. A deafening chant was taken up on all sides: 'Death to the barbarian!' Aspar's gaze shot to the fluttering scrap of silk upon which his father's life depended. He glanced back at Saphanx whose eyes were fixed on him, filled with confidence and strength. From the corner of his eye, he saw the handkerchief released and float gently towards the bloodstained sand of the arena. Saphanx stared boldly at his opponent as the trident plunged towards his throat. A powerful arc of bright blood spurted upwards, streaming over the gladiator, who received it without flinching, like an initiate of the Magna Mater bathing in bull's blood. Saphanx's head slumped back on the sand and a loosening of his limbs marked the departure of his spirit. Aspar felt the arena lurch. Was it an earthquake? Abruptly, it tilted on its side although the people seemed glued in place, and the young Dacian, now undisputed king, toppled into blackness.

Four

Night had fallen when Aspar awoke. He was back at Valerius' palace in the bed they had shared for so many weeks. He dimly recollected being carried into a private chamber under the stands at the arena where Livius had given him wine to drink. There must have been something in the cup along with the wine, for now his head felt heavy and dull.

The events of the afternoon came jostling back into his consciousness and the feelings he had tried to stifle since his arrival in Rome seethed within him: grief, anger – especially anger. Anger at Valerius for keeping from him the news that his father still lived; but anger, above all, with himself. He had allowed himself to be lulled into a delusion that the young aristocrat saw him as anything more than a plaything, less than human. He had tried to follow his father's command, to stay alive at all costs, but now he felt that somehow he had betrayed the trust Saphanx had placed in him. Looking into his father's eyes that afternoon had made that clear.

The light of a single lamp cast a flickering orange light on the coffered ceiling. Aspar could make out a still figure silhouetted against the lampstand. As he tried to sit up to see better, the silk covers rustled and the figure turned towards him. It was Valerius.

'Are you awake?' came his voice, gentle with concern. The tribune climbed onto the bed and approached Aspar on hands and knees. He pushed back the damp hair from the boy's forehead. 'You scared me, little king. I could not bear to lose you.' He covered the young Dacian with his body and placed his lips on his brow. Aspar could smell the familiar natural scent of his body, mixed with cinnamon and oriental spices. Suddenly, he felt as though his chest would burst. Clutching at Valerius' neck, he pulled his face towards him and sank his teeth into the tribune's cheek with all his strength. The young Roman's shrieks of pain and shock combined with Aspar's bestial roar as he held the other man down with a strength he never knew he possessed. Blood, thick and metallic, trickled over his tongue; its taste enraged him further and made him want to hurt this man who had betrayed him, who had used him. He opened his jaws and clamped his teeth hard into the smooth flesh a second time.

He heard voices and felt strong hands tug at his limbs. Rough fingers were inserted in his mouth and pulled his teeth apart. The young Dacian was carried struggling and howling with fury from the room. The chill night air struck his naked body as he was man-handled out of the palace. He was tossed on to the cold earth floor of an outhouse. A heavy wooden door slammed shut and he heard a clanking of chains and the turning of rusty locks. The young king tasted the blood congealing on his lips, and the rage blazed on in his chest and head. He howled like a chained dog, until his throat was gripped with a painful choking sensation and his breast heaved with sobs: for his father, his mother, for himself.

Aspar was not sure how long he spent in the stone shed, a storehouse for empty amphorae. The ground was freezing. He curled shivering in a corner, one hand clutching at the wooden talisman. Exhausted with weeping, he slept fitfully. When awake, he stared blankly into the gloom: the only marker of time passing was a sliver of daylight under the door, alternating with the solid darkness of night. Although he was given nothing to eat or drink, he felt neither hunger or thirst and longed only for oblivion. One thought tormented him: why could he not have been condemned to the arena like the others? It was too much to ask that he should go on living without hope, condemned to serve the very men who had butchered his people and his future.

Once in the formless blackness of night, he heard soft movements and the warmth of a body. 'Not a sound,' came the voice of Livius from the void. The soldier fed him hot thick soup from a spoon and covered him with a sheepskin blanket. He held him close, rocking the lad and murmuring words of comfort until he fell into a deep sleep. When Aspar awoke the soldier had gone – but food and several hours of rest had slightly dulled the rawness of his pain.

A band of light under the door told him that it was day again, and perhaps not much more than an hour passed before the grating of rusty metal announced the arrival of several slaves. They kicked the Dacian youth to his feet and covered his nakedness with a rough brown slave's tunic. His legs were stiff after what must have been days crouched in the same position, and he stumbled as the servants hustled him through the palace. Several of the slave boys, who had resented his usurpation of their position as favourites, smirked in doorways as he passed. One even stepped out and spat in his face. Aspar did not bother to wipe away the blob of saliva that slid down his cheek.

His escort thrust him roughly through an archway into Valerius' private chambers, leaving him standing unsteadily before the tribune's ornate bronze desk. Valerius was silhouetted against a curtain of golden gauze, staring out across the balcony towards the Forum. Dark clouds clotted the sky, signalling the approach of winter. The tribune, dressed in full military regalia, slowly turned. Half of his handsome patrician face was hidden by a bloodstained bandage. For a moment he contemplated the changes in the boy's appearance: eyes brown-ringed, golden hair matted with sweat and grime, face and body smeared with the filth and stench of the outhouse. Valerius' lip curled with distaste. Sensing the boy's broken spirit, however, he motioned to the servants to leave.

'So,' he said, once they were alone: 'Phoebus is eclipsed.' Aspar saw that he spoke with difficulty, his voice strangely distorted. Valerius approached to within a few inches of the hunched young man. 'I would have given you so much, Aspar. I cared for you as I had never cared for another man. And you repaid my love with this.' He ripped off the bandage and revealed an ugly fissure, black with congealed blood, that ran from his left eye to the corner of his mouth. It had been crudely pulled together with stitches of black thread. 'You know what this has cost me?' demanded the tribune icily. 'My life. My future. There is no place in the governance of the Empire for a man with so obvious a disfigurement. Men in high places require a noble aspect to inspire awe in those they command; like this, I can only evoke disgust. I have renounced my ambitions in Rome and taken a commission in the east.'

He turned away abruptly and strode to the window, where he paused. It had begun to rain and the crowded shopping streets were rapidly emptying. 'You, too, will be leaving Rome soon. Tomorrow, in fact. But you will be heading west – to the gold mines of Hispania Tarraconensis.' He looked back to savour the boy's reaction, but Aspar remained expressionless. 'Your kingdom from now on will be the most wretched the Empire can provide. You will be a Slave King, whose power is no more and who cannot boast a single subject – not even his own fate is his to command. My one consolation, as I spend the rest of my life exiled from my beloved Rome, will be the thought of the living death that you will endure moment by moment.'

The following day, Aspar was chained by his neck and ankles to a couple of dozen other unfortunates who had been condemned to the mines of Hispania – most of them petty criminals or escaped slaves. They were loaded onto a barge bound for Rome's port of Ostia, from whence they were herded onto a ship bound and ready for Tarraco, capital of the province of Hispania Tarraconensis. The sailors were already at the oars, the sail furled until they were clear of the harbour. The sailing season was almost over and the captain was anxious to make haste – however much he might be paid by the wealthy owner of the mines, it was not worth shipwreck on the stormy winter seas.

The condemned slaves were chained to iron rings on deck. The dealers and guards who accompanied them had constructed makeshift shelters to protect themselves from the elements, while wealthier passengers had elaborate pavilions erected for them to keep out the worst of the cold and the wet. Constantly drenched with rain and spray in the days of the crossing, the slaves huddled miserably together in an attempt to gain some warmth and protection from each other's bodies.

Aspar exchanged few words with his fellow prisoners – either onboard or during the gruelling journey overland to the north of the province which, though it meant little to him, was one of the largest and richest in the Empire. They travelled mainly on foot, as the mountain routes were unpaved and too rough for carts. The slave-dealers who accompanied them made liberal use of the lash to keep their charges moving, hoping to make the return journey to Rome before winter set in.

Aquamarine dusk had fallen when the slaves stumbled into a narrow gorge between soaring cliffs, exhausted from the march through the desolate shadows of ridge beyond ridge of barren mountains. Emerging from the pass, they were faced with an unexpected sight: in the midst of such desolation, there was a miniature city. A broad vista of jagged peaks glimmered with a constellation of scattered lights: fires in the mouths of caves; torches illuminating a criss-crossed web of makeshift wooden footbridges; lamps marking out precarious snaking paths cut into rock faces. They had arrived at the mine that was to be their life from now on.

The slave merchants showed their documents to the brutish mercenaries who guarded the great wooden gateway, which, as

Aspar would later learn, was the only entrance to the complex. Escape was virtually impossible. In order to reach the mines themselves, it was necessary to pass across a narrow rope-bridge spanning a ravine. As the line of prisoners inched nervously along the fragile construction, Aspar could hear the roaring of waters from the pitch blackness below.

The prisoners hugged the walls as the guards prodded them along zig-zagging paths which scaled the sheer cliffs. They eyed each other fearfully: chained together as they were, if one were to slip into the abyss, he could take the others with him. Finally, a guard held a thick curtain aside and pushed them blinking into light. Aspar gazed round him with some bewilderment at what seemed to be the richly furnished chamber of a palace. Finely worked tapestries adorned the walls; hundreds of flickering lights hung from many-branched lampstands; there were statues of marble and bronze-decorated tables and chests. A Greek waterclock kept up its steady drip-drip in a corner. Looking up, however, Aspar saw the rough roof of a cave, carved either by nature or man. Who would require this level of splendour in the midst of such desolation?

A couple of pretty youths, sprawled on a couch, languidly eyed the party of prisoners. Their hair was carefully curled and they wore brightly coloured tunics in the short military style. One stumbled lazily to his feet and crossed to the back of the room where he whispered something through a curtain slung across a low opening in the cave wall.

The curtain was pushed to one side and a large shaved head and broad shoulders emerged through the rock doorway. As the man squeezed through the narrow aperture and drew himself to his full height, he presented a commanding figure, a short brown tunic showing off the taut muscles of his long sun-browned limbs.

'I am Diocles, owner of the mines,' he growled in Latin. His poor grammar and heavy accent suggested that he was a freedman; to judge by his figure, a former gladiator or maybe a boxer. He prowled noiselessly along the ragged row of slaves, whose features to a man were almost hidden by the caked dust and sweat of the long journey from Tarraco. He examined each of them with the narrow eyes of a lynx, running the metal-tipped thongs of a lash absently through his fingers as he did so. 'You are all here because you have committed some offence against your owners. Don't fool yourselves: lazy or disobedient slaves won't survive long here. We won't mollycoddle you like your former masters. Any misbehaviour, no matter how minor, will be severely punished.'

He pointed earthwards with his whip. 'In the galleries and shafts beneath our feet there is neither day or night. So to produce the gold the Empire needs, we labour without ceasing. From now on, this is the only life you can expect.' He drew level with Aspar and stopped. Exhausted though he was, the young man's eyelids barely flickered as he met the other man's steely gaze. Diocles moved on. 'If any of you has tried to escape before, let me warn you now not to try the same trick here. There is only one way out of the mines, and that is heavily patrolled. My guards are under orders to kill any slave attempting to escape.

'When you entered these gates, you left behind the world you knew forever. If you accept your fate, you will be treated well and survive. If you try to fight the will of the gods, then your existence here will be wretched and short.'

He indicated with a wave of the whip that the audience was over, but, as the bedraggled line began to shuffle towards the exit with a jingle of chains, he halted it. 'Unlock him,' he grunted, brushing Aspar's shoulder with the lash's leather thongs. 'This one I would like to see alone.'

The guards scrambled to release the youth. As they hurriedly drove the other slaves from the room with brutal jabs from the blunt end of their spears, Aspar stood, swaying slightly with fatigue.

'So,' drawled Diocles, circling him slowly, 'you must be the one: the lad they call the Slave King.'

Holding the handle of his whip at arm's length, Diocles lifted the hem of Aspar's tunic. He raised his eyebrows at the sight of the boy's heavy hooded phallus. As the hopelessness of his situation beginning to dawn, Aspar felt tears starting into his eyes. Now, finally, he realised how rash and foolish he had been. By defying Valerius, he had brought upon himself a fate a thousand times worse than that of a favourite in a Roman palace. How was he to fulfil his father's wishes now?

Diocles moved behind him: the young king's shapely buttocks drew a drawn-out growl of approval. 'He should clean up nicely,' mused the burly mine-owner. Turning to his slaves, he ordered, 'Summon an escort. Take him to my villa and give him a good scrub.'

'What about the lice?' shuddered one of the effete youths. 'Should we shave him?'

Diocles frowned, as though again trying to imagine how the boy might look cleaned up. 'His body and face, yes, but not his head. Give his hair a good soaking in vinegar, though.'

As the man turned away, Aspar noticed one of the slaves shoot a grimace of distaste towards the other.

Aspar took in little on the way to the villa. Night had fallen and beyond the domain of the mines, the countryside was hidden under thick darkness. Besides, he had spent so many days trudging across the harsh Hispanic landscape that he slipped unthinkingly back into an automatic march rhythm: unseeing, unfeeling, so that he could even continue to walk while hovering on the brink of sleep. It was not long, however, before he drifted back into consciousness to find himself passing through a guarded, well-lit gateway and into the drive of a large handsome villa. It was odd to find a development on this scale in the midst of a barren wilderness. Once more Aspar noted the powerful reach of Rome; that even here on the outermost rim of the Empire it could create an outpost of such sophistication.

The house was surrounded by well-groomed gardens. Beyond them, neat rows of fruit trees, orchards maybe, were outlined against the darker sky; perhaps the estate sustained the other farming activities that one would expect to find around a villa in Italia. The interior was no less impressive, with arches giving onto splendid chambers paved with mosaics, their walls bright with frescoes, ceilings domed or coffered. Clearly, the vast wealth produced by the mines made up for any lack of taste in its rough owner, though Aspar did not doubt that behind him stood a prominent Roman sponsor.

The corridors bustled with servants about their evening chores, trimming and lighting lamps, carrying dishes of a kind that would not shame the top tables of the capital. Indeed, here one could easily imagine that Rome was just a short chariot-ride away.

Aspar let out a long involuntary sigh as he slipped into the warm waters of the tepidarium. Before they had allowed him into the water, the slaves had oiled him and roughly scraped away the encrusted dirt with bronze strigils. They had also shaved his body and had made him lean over a bucket as they poured strong vinegar over his hair. He winced when it stung his scalp. Now, as he sank into the soothing bath, he threw his head back to rinse away the burning liquid so that only his face floated on the surface. Points of light from candelabra suspended over the pool danced on its ripples and Aspar had to fight against an overwhelming wave of drowsiness as the heat dulled the ache of his muscles.

The blurred inverted outline of a dark figure snapped him back to his senses. He stared up to find Diocles gazing down at him. Aspar, with only his face surrounded by floating golden hair visible above the water, was once more the flawless young king, the

Phoebus that Valerius had imagined him. The older and the younger man gazed at one another mutely for a moment and then Diocles turned away, muttering terse orders to the servants.

After being dried with enormous towels, Aspar was dressed in a fine tunic of silk and his hair was curled. He was given a thick stew to eat and wine to drink, before being shown to a small bedchamber containing a narrow couch. To Aspar it looked as welcoming as the great featherbed he had enjoyed in the house of his parents. The minute he felt the coolness of its silk covers along his naked body, he plunged into a profound slumber.

He was not sure how long he had been asleep when the servants shook him awake. He felt rested, and it was dark outside the room's one small window, so it must have been at least a night and the following day. Without a word of explanation, the slaves bathed and perfumed him and, leaving him naked, led him into a large triclinium where Diocles and several guests reclined on the couches for their dinner.

Even before they entered the room, gruff male voices raised in some kind of an argument could be heard. The conversation was liberally larded with foul language and blasphemous appeals to the gods. But, as Aspar and his escort of servants emerged from the shadows, the din of voices trailed off. All eyes were on the naked, golden-haired stranger. One man on his hands and knees, brandishing a leg of meat menacingly at another, sank back weakly to a reclining position, the cause of his annoyance forgotten.

'This is our new guest,' purred the owner of the mines, eyes half-closed in a smile of satisfaction as he took in the dazed expressions of the others. Diocles pushed himself up from the couch and padded silently in bare feet across the marble floor to Aspar, who stood mutely blushing at the searching stares of the men. 'The Slave King we have heard so much about has come to pay us a call.' He grinned back at his colleagues. 'A long call, I reckon. So, your highness,' he went on with a mock-bow to Aspar, 'Here's your welcoming committee. Only the nobs, of course, for such an illustrious personage as yourself. Lichas, chief overseer of the mines and his lieutenant, Agatho.' The two men grinned stupidly: they were freedmen, their heads shaved and the brands of their former masters still visible on their shiny foreheads. Their stocky muscle-bound physiques testified that they had spent their lives in heavy manual labour.

'Lycurgus, captain of the guards.' The thin-faced man who had been brandishing the roast joint so fiercely nodded towards Aspar, his tongue lolling lasciviously between his lips. It was a patrician face, thought Aspar, despite the cruel twist of the mouth. What could a man of this sort be doing in this remote corner of the Empire? The son of a noble Roman family, perhaps, who had been disappointed or disgraced in a legitimate military career? 'And finally, a real nob – Menander of Samos, one of the Empire's greatest architects. Without him, our work here in the mines would be impossible. Oh, and his assistant Habinnas.'

Menander smiled and bowed: it was impossible to gauge whether this was done with irony or sincerity. Nevertheless, his manner and dress marked him out from his colleagues as a man of breeding. He was still young, dark-haired and clean-shaven, with the long straight nose and perfection of features that is found occasionally among the Greeks. A youth at his side – presumably Habinnas – glared at Aspar sulkily from under his curled tresses.

Aspar recognised the architect's name – perhaps Valerius had mentioned him in connection with one of his many building projects. 'We are honoured to have Menander here,' continued Diocles, his mouth curling slightly as though at a private joke. 'His techniques have made this mine one of the richest sources of gold in the Empire. But he has improved our lives in other ways, hasn't he, boys?' The men obligingly guffawed along with their chief.

Diocles moved away into an unlit area of the chamber. Jerking his head, he indicated that Aspar should follow. With a light touch on the boy's arms, the servants manoeuvred him in Diocles' direction.

'There's not much to do out here and we get bored,' Diocles explained as he walked, 'especially those of us who are used to the pleasures of Rome. So someone – or something – new is always welcome.' Diocles had stopped before a bulky rectangular object concealed under a silk sheet; it towered over him. He placed a large hairy hand against one of its upright sides. Servants silently lit standing lamps positioned around the mysterious monolith and Diocles' guests – who had followed them – were gathering in the warm glow. 'He's always thinking up ways to keep us entertained, is Menander. By a piece of luck, he's come up with this new gadget in time for your arrival. How about that, Menander? A king to unveil the latest product of your genius?' After another chorus of coarse laughter, Diocles stepped aside, indicating that the architect should commence his demonstration.

With a twist of his wrist, the Greek swept the light covering from his invention. Aspar saw smiles of understanding suffuse the faces of Diocles and his men. The young king, however, stared in complete mystification.

'I have dubbed this the Spinning H,' explained Menander with quiet satisfaction.

The construction Aspar saw before him did indeed resemble a large wooden letter H, set in a larger framework of axles and pulleys.

'If your highness would like to step this way, I will demonstrate,' he suggested with scrupulous politeness. The slaves pushed Aspar forward and, before he could react, they had stretched his arms upwards and apart, fixing them to leather straps at the topmost points of the H, while his legs were splayed and his ankles lashed with similar leather fastenings to the bottom ends of the uprights. He found himself suspended by his extremities, stretched across the frame in a taut X-shape. His middle was pressed against the crossbar of the H and here was fixed a wide leather belt which the men secured around his waist. One of them pushed gently against one of the uprights and Aspar experienced slight dizziness as his entire body rocked back and forth.

His limbs were drawn so tightly that only his head was free to move but, glancing downwards, he saw that the cross-bar of the H slotted into a larger cradle: thus the whole letter was pivoted in the centre and could be swung through three hundred and sixty degrees. Menander turned a handle and Aspar felt his stomach turn over as the H tilted forward and he was facing downwards, his body held horizontally. Menander adjusted some pulleys to lock the H into position. Looking up, Aspar saw Diocles and his guests stripping off tunics and togas, their eyes fixed on him, glinting with the many possibilities offered by the Spinning H. Menander was checking the workings of his machine and busily jotting notes on a wax tablet.

Aspar recognised the powerful legs that moved into position just below his head as those of Diocles. The thick tool that was inserted into his mouth, however, came as a surprise. It was sweet and salty at the same time, and somehow at once hard and soft. A metal ring glinted in the thick curled hair at the base of the man's cock and Aspar could feel thick knotted veins bumping over his lips as Diocles began to slowly rock his hips. The head was hooded by a heavy, loose foreskin, and this meant that the entire rigid length was swathed in a velvety softness that slipped back and forth across the engorged blood vessels. In spite of the initial distaste he felt at finding himself so humiliated and vulnerable, Aspar began salivating in reaction to Diocles' delectable manhood. When the man began to thrust hard, Aspar found his throat opening willingly to accommodate the full length of his virility.

Meanwhile, the others had wasted no time exploring the other accesses to the boy's body offered by the Spinning H. A crouching figure beneath him, which he recognised from his thick head of hair as Habinnas, squeezed and pulled his nipples, digging into them sharply with his nails and looking up at the young king with a spiteful smile on his cherubic lips. Aspar's legs, pulled wide apart, stuck out horizontally behind him and he could feel hips brushing down the inside of his thighs. A luxuriant, coarse pubic growth tickled his gaping anus and a bolt of pain shot through his loins as sperm-heavy testicles thudded against his own. But that was nothing to the delicious torment that was to come.

Without the least preparation of the boy's dry, tight pucker, a broad hard weapon of flesh gored his bowels up to the hilt with a single remorseless blow. His whole body sagged with the agony that was at the same time pleasure, but his scream ended in a choking retch as Diocles stopped his throat with a vicious thrust. The cock pulled endlessly back in his rectum until the rim of the glans grazed his sphincter; then it hammered in again with excruciating friction as Lycurgus, the captain of the guard, took his pleasure.

Soft lips closed over Aspar's cock – which, in spite of his pain, was already rampant – and began to glide up and down it with a practised smoothness. It had to be Menander, his oral technique as precise as the lines of his inventions. Swallowing the full-length of Aspar's upstanding member in his slick throat, the architect began to massage the half-hooded head by rotating the root of his tongue. Aspar heard the man's muffled exclamations of delight as the boy's salty love-juice oozed in pearly droplets from the lips of his slit.

Habinnas plucked at his nipples with cruel suddenness and Aspar felt the pain like lightning bolts shooting into his groin, exacerbating the mounting ache. The fire that seared his vitals was subsiding to a warm glow as his fuckhole began to loosen. The strength of the feeling provoked a steady stream of arsejuice and the captain's pounding made a sound like footsteps on wet sand.

Aspar's brain, confused by so many impressions, still told him that something was missing. With a loud crack, a calloused palm exploded against his smooth butt-cheek. Another man – one of the overseers – had joined the party. There was a scuffling beneath him. Menander and his assistant withdrew from their crouching positions, signalling, without the need for a word to be spoken, a transition. The now-raging manrods pulled out of either end of him. The room appeared to flip over as Menander span the H, and Aspar was on his back. Faces furious with sexual concentration grouped round him in the lamplight. The men fell on his body like preying animals. His head was pulled back and a dick, slick with his own savoury arse-juice, lunged into his craw: it belonged to Lycurgus, the butt-fucking captain, who now mouth-fucked him just as ruthlessly. His lips levered open to their fullest extent by the jabbing monster, Aspar could only let out a strangled cry as Diocles' pillar skewered him, the hard walnut of its glans hammering at his intestines. The boy could feel an orgasm rushing to overwhelm him. Habinnas gobbled at his blazing erection, inflaming it with the friction of the roof of his mouth and the rough flat of his tongue, while elegant Menander worked skilfully on his nipples, alternating tender stimulation with stabs of torment. Aspar could feel the leather thongs of Lichas' lash testing the soft skin of his torso with gentle strokes. Agatho stood by him, leering as he pumped his own swollen prick, eyes greedily drinking in the activities of the others.

All thought blocked out by the multiple sensations in his throat, nipples, dick and hole, Aspar's body began to shake as the tidal wave of an orgasm flooded over him, starting deep in his rectum and radiating outwards to the tips of fingers, toes, phallus. As the two poles battered him in both directions, he was shaken by another arse-orgasm, and a third. Juice splashed from his hole as Diocles filled it with his hard smooth tool. Groans of pain and pleasure shook the young king as one internal convulsion followed another, until his slender muscular limbs trembled and he was pushed to the point of exhaustion.

Once more, without a word, Menander ceased his activity, as did the others. The architect swung the H into vertical position so that Aspar stood upright once more. He signalled that Diocles should resume his post, and, as the man stepped onto the frame and reinserted his blue-veined cock into Aspar's hole which now hung open and slavering, a gasping mouth, Menander gently attached his employer's spreadeagled arms and legs to the uprights of the H, so that they matched those of the boy. A loose belt was looped around Diocles' waist so that he could continue to probe the young man's anus, whilst being held comfortably in place. Aspar started to moan again as a further spasm was triggered in his sensitised rear.

The architect rotated the frame until the two men were upside down and turned enquiringly towards the others. Habinnas stepped eagerly forward onto the frame on the opposite side from Diocles; Aspar's raging gristle was just at mouth height for him and Habinnas downed it with a gulp. The architect fixed his young assistant's ankles so that they lay alongside Aspar's wrists and his arms against the boy's legs. By the time he was firmly lashed into position, the young king was straining against his bonds, so acute were the feelings in his rock-hard column and his aching prostate under constant assault from Diocles' fuck-weapon.

Menander took up his wax tablet and, carefully inspecting the position of the pulleys, jotted down more notes. Setting down the tablet and stylus, he began to manipulate a handle at the side of the machine. Slowly, the great wooden H with its three interlocked passengers began to spin through three hundred and sixty degrees. At first, it moved slowly and the moans of Aspar and the other men rose and fell in chorus. Then, as a system of gears clicked into place, the speed increased and their shouts melded into a drawn-out roar.

Aspar felt the orgasms of his bowels increase in speed and penetrate his entire body. The faces of the watching men became long orange streaks and the world tumbled around him. His hole and cock felt like gaping wounds, streaming with the most intimate juices of his body.

The machine now span at such a velocity that the spectators could only see a blur of heads and bodies. For Aspar, several things seemed to happen at once: his cock stiffened and the heat rushed to its tip like a flaming arrow; in his hole, Diocles' manhood strained with bone-like stiffness; the H suddenly seemed to fly off its axis and then whirl wildly, unfettered, through space. He came in Habinnas' mouth as Diocles ejaculated hot streams of spunk into his hole. But this was different from anything he had experienced before. It was as though he was spurting not just from his cock and arse but as though his whole body had been ripped open from top to toe and was ejaculating its juices in every direction: he was caught up in the power of a sex god and was fertilising the world in one great cosmic orgasm.

He was not even aware of the H coming to rest and two of the other men taking the places of Habinnas and Diocles. Gripped by the intense, wholly novel experience, the men wanted to try the Spinning H again and again. So dizzying was the sensation for Aspar that, when Lichas, driven into a frenzy by his own ride on the contraption, began to strike the boy's spinning body with the lash, he was unaware of the welts that it left on his skin.

The dark outlines of the mine's jagged peaks were already visible when Diocles' guards half dragged the boy into a cave where other slaves were huddled around the dying embers of a fire and dumped him on the bare rock floor. Aspar was too exhausted by repeated penetration and his own racking orgasms to take much notice of his surroundings.

*

Two unblinking eyes stared out of an encircling curtain of darkness. The silence and stillness were so deep that, for a moment, Aspar wondered if he had fled his former life altogther and entered the underworld. As he tried to move his limbs, however, the aches left by the rigours of Menander's machine and the marks of Lichas' lash felt real enough. So did the prickly bed of straw beneath him. Aspar realised that he must be in one of the caves of the mines.

He raised his head to see better: the eyes blinked and tilted to one side. Then they approached till they were a hand's breadth from his face. He felt warm, sweet breath on his cheek and the glow of a body next to his and gradually, by a scrap of blue moonlight that filtered into the cavern, he made out a face. It was that of an Ethiopian, his skin smooth and dark as a ripe plum. It was strikingly handsome face with a calming stillness in the small, regular features.

He pulled back a cover which had been laid over Aspar's bruised, torn body. Examining the boy carefully, he took a bowl from the floor by Aspar's side and gently bathed his wounds with a cloth. The liquid in the bowl smelt of wild herbs and stung slightly, though the feeling quickly subsided to a pleasant tingle. There was a grace, almost a nobility in the young man's movements that made Aspar wonder if he had been a king among his people.

For a moment, it passed through the young king's mind that if this Ethiopian was familiar with the healing power of herbs, maybe he also knew those that could grant death.

As though sensing Aspar's thoughts, the man began to murmur in a rumbling musical voice that the young Dacian found almost hypnotic. 'Your spirits are strong,' he told him, gently tending the wounds. 'I have sat here and watched over you for many hours. My spirits communed with yours. They told me that you have endured much and that now you feel weak, but they are strong and you will be strong again, they say.'

The man sat back on his heels and smiled down at the boy. The smooth muscles of his dark body in repose conveyed a feeling of peace and strength, like a crouching idol hewn from a cube of granite. He placed a cool dry palm on Aspar's forehead and the boy felt the other man's inner calm and power coursing through his own body. Frowning, the man leaned in and stared at the wooden talisman at Aspar's throat. He lifted it gently, turning it over and examining it with care, then looked up into Aspar's eyes.

'I know that you are Aspar, a king from the cold lands of the north. I, too, am the son of great men of my people, men of wisdom, men familiar with the spirits. I am Zosimus of Ethiopia. I was captured by Arab slavers with my whole family when I was still a child. They sold us all to separate masters. I cannot even remember the face of my mother and father. Me, they sold to Diocles, because they need children to work the narrow seams here in the mines.

'I vowed then that I would survive here with the help of the spirits, and I have. I am strong in body, but without my spirits, I would have despaired long ago. Because they whisper to me that all is not lost: hope still lives. For the moment, you are weak in body, but it is in the chaos of the outer world that we find inner strength. I have brought you to a secret place deep in the caves so that you might recover your strength. Now, you cannot see a way ahead, but you are born of great leaders and your destiny too is great.' Aspar could already feel the strength of his body returning as the young Ethiopian smoothed his brow. 'Now rest, my king, rest.'

Five

'Where have you been lurking?' demanded Habinnas, furrowing his pretty forehead as Aspar, his physical strength rapidly restored by Zosimus' ministrations, returned supported by the Ethiopian to the cave in which he had been slung some twenty four hours previously. 'The guards said they'd left you here and I've been hunting for you since yesterday.'

Zosimus sprang to the boy's defence. 'He wasn't ready for work yesterday.'

Habinnas opened his mouth to give a smart retort but, seeing Zosimus' lowered brow, thought better of it. 'Well, you're lucky Menander didn't report you missing,' he continued to Aspar. 'Lichas would have been only too delighted to dish out a few more strokes of the lash – but for real this time.' He scowled, 'For some reason, Menander wanted to give you a chance. He's too kind, that master of mine. I'd have had them on your tail in no time at all, by Bacchus.'

Zosimus silently handed Aspar some water in a crude clay cup and a hard wedge of dark bread.

'Anyway, get a move on. You're late already this morning.' Habinnas moved towards the mouth of the cave. 'Oh yes,' he snorted, turning back, 'another stroke of luck – you've been assigned to Menander's team. That means special privileges and no heavy work down the mines – for as long as you behave yourself, that is. Otherwise you'll die of exhaustion on a treadmill or end up at the bottom of a pitch-black shaft.'

Aspar chewed dutifully on the tasteless hunk of bread as he and Zosimus followed Habinnas along the narrow paths cut into the cliff face. The Ethiopian insisted that he would be glad of the nourishment during the long gap before they were given their one proper meal in the early evening. Aspar stepped gingerly along the track which fell away on his right into the deep shadows of a ravine. Zosimus, however, leapt from boulder to boulder like a mountain goat, sometimes performing a sideways run up the almost sheer cliff wall on their left and bouncing back down on to the path.

He too worked with Menander, he explained as they went. He was in charge of the architect's precious instruments. Slaves chosen for their intelligence had the task of assisting the architect with a quick and highly efficient method he had devised for extracting gold from the rock. The Empire's need for gold was insatiable and the faster it could be mined the better. The blood-red rock of the mines was honey-combed with galleries and shafts after years of mining silver, copper and tin.

Menander's idea had been to divert the waters of a nearby river, flooding these cavities with enormous pressure so that entire sections of the mine were carried off in the stream. The resulting debris was then sifted for the precious deposits. It was the job of Menander's assistants to help him survey the terrain through which new channels were to be cut and decide which sections of the mine should be collapsed. Finally, they supervised the delicate demolition operations.

The architect was standing on a flat raised area, squinting through a copper instrument mounted on a long pole when Habinnas announced Aspar's reappearance. He turned his cool, intelligent gaze on the boy. 'I knew you would resurface sooner or later. Where did you get to?' he asked with rhetorical vagueness, his gaze drifting on to Zosimus, whose impassive face gave nothing away. The Greek turned back to his work. 'Leave us alone,' he instructed Zosimus and Habinnas. His assistant flounced off with an indignant snort, but the Ethiopian turned away slowly and not before shooting Aspar a smile of complicity.

'Habinnas has probably told you that the slaves on my team enjoy a much better life than the other miners,' explained Menander in his elegant Greek, delicately adjusting a tiny screw on the copper apparatus. 'I am pleased to have you on my team.' He turned to Aspar: 'I see a spark of intelligence in your eyes. Can you read?'

'Yes,' returned Aspar promptly. 'I was educated by a Greek tutor from Thrace. He taught me to read and write in Greek and Latin. I am familiar with the philosophers and poets of both languages.'

'Good,' said Menander softly, peering through the eyepiece of the instrument again. 'As you probably gathered the other night at Diocles' villa, there is little entertaining conversation to be had out here and, while one tries to dream up other amusements, it is more than a trifle dull. I need stimulating company and you may well be able to furnish it.' He stood up and looked Aspar full in the eye. 'I also need a new assistant. One who is really capable of understanding the requirements of the work. I am tired of Habinnas' constant whinging. Think about it,' he said softly, turning back to his task. 'I have been a slave, too, though now I am free. No one knows better than I how many of us who serve are made of greater stuff than our masters. We might have much to give one another. You understand what I am offering, don't you.'

Aspar nodded slowly.

Menander continued: 'More than a job. Oh, and by the way, I would like you to describe to me the sensations you experienced the other night on my new invention. I always like to make careful notes on my little experiments.'

Menander kept Aspar by his side over the next few days and found that his interest was rewarded by the speed with which the youth picked up the skills needed to survey the rough mountain terrain.

As they worked, the architect explained that the project they were working on was his grandest yet. One of the highest peaks of the mine – and one of the areas richest in gold – would be brought down by creating a powerful confluence of waterways which had already been formed in the destruction of other parts of the mine. This force would be channelled through the lower shafts and tunnels of the peak and – if Menander's calculations were correct, and so far they always had been – would bring the entire mass of rock crashing down into the flood.

In order to calculate the levels of the various streams and maximise their impact, up to twenty members of Menander's team were to be employed at once, often separated by deep ravines and canals, out of earshot and even out of sight of one another. Aspar soon learned the signals that the assistants would use to communicate their readings so that Menander could co-ordinate all the necessary data for his calculations. Constantly on the move from one team-member to another, Aspar was often exhausted by the end of a long day, but the work was interesting and he was flattered by Menander's praise. It made a change to be valued for his mind rather than his body, after all he had experienced since he had been a captive of Rome.

The best part of each day, however, was when he was reunited with Zosimus in the cave, where the team made their rough lodgings. After carefully cleaning the instruments and packing them away in boxes, Zosimus, who always appeared to have plentiful supplies of all kinds of materials, would make a little wood fire in a corner some distance from the others and they would talk about the times when they were free.

'Tell me something about the spirits of your fathers,' asked Zosimus one evening, his handsome face gilded by the fire's glow.

'I know more about the gods of my mother's people,' Aspar admitted. 'This is one of them,' he added, lifting the talisman at his throat. 'In the long winter nights in our land, she would tell me the sagas that had been handed down since time out of mind by the wise men of her race.'

Zosimus face lit up: 'Do you remember any of those tales?'

'I think I do,' said Aspar hesitantly. The events of the past few months had dug a deep and unbridgeable chasm between him and his former life. On the few occasions when he had tried to comfort himself with memories of his home and his parents, they had unravelled in his mind with the speed that his mother used to unpick a knitted garment. 'I have heard them so often – and told them too. But that seems so long ago now.'

'Try to remember,' urged Zosimus, settling down close to the fire, hugging his knees and fixing his liquid eyes on the blond youth.

Aspar began, falteringly at first; in the past he had always heard and recounted the sagas in his native tongue, and it seemed odd to translate the forceful sayings of his native gods into the precision of Latin. But then he began to forget about the words as, in his imagination, he conjured up the pictures that had lent such colour to his childhood: the horned war-god Cernunnos, the three mother goddesses, and the loveliest goddess of all, Rosmerta, after whom his mother had been named. And while the loves and wars of these beings were far more wonderful and terrible than those of mere mortals, there was something comfortingly familiar about them. Their armour was richer and more splendid than he had ever seen worn by his countrymen, and yet they bore the same oval shields and wore the same crested helmets. The dwelling places of the gods, too, were grander than anything he had ever beheld with his own eyes and yet they resembled in some way the desolate mountain strongholds of his people.

As these images came to life in his mind's eye, the words flowed freely, and Aspar recalled not only the famous deeds of the gods but found himself elaborating more detailed descriptions and even evoking other events in the gods' lives which seemed to come from nowhere. A flush crept into his cheeks and his voice lost the listless monotone it had acquired since the day of his father's death in the arena. He used different voices for each of the gods – a deep booming note for the warlike Cernunnos, and a sweet, high tone for Rosmerta. When he described mighty battles between the gods, he spoke vigorously and illustrated his words with gestures – a sword thrusting, a shield raised – and then his voice would drop to a mysterious whisper to tell of their magical deeds.

While he recited the old stories, his own words acted upon him like a spell. The walls of the cave faded and in their place, mountains were raised, rivers were cut, cloud fortresses reared up – his native land evoked in a living frieze. And at the same time, behind these images were further visions of himself at his mother's feet, listening to the tales she span along with the endless skeins of fine wool, while his father sat by the fireside, oiling his weapons and pretending not to listen.

Throughout the telling, Aspar was aware of Zosimus' still, calm gaze drinking in his words. When he ceased, however, he experienced a moment of disorientation as the pictures in his imagination faded to be replaced by the drab walls of the cave, and it was with a sense of shock that he realised that he was still in the mines of Hispania, still a slave. He was also surprised to see that he was surrounded by staring faces. During the stories, all the other slaves had drawn around them in a rapt circle.

Over the next few weeks, with Zosimus' gentle encouragement, and in response to the pleas of the other slaves, Aspar recounted all the tales of the gods he had learned from his mother. Still they clamoured for more, and so he began to piece together what he knew of his father's gods, though he found that he was forced to to spin these out with invented details and descriptions of his own.

Afterwards, he and the Ethiopian would share the same blanket for warmth; before they fell asleep, they would swap reminiscences of when they were free. Aspar found that, under the stimulus of his story-telling, the memories he thought gone forever came flooding back: the chasm to his past was bridged. Sometimes the pain of remembrance was acute and, as he rested his head against Zosimus' smooth back, he would weep silently. 'Remember,' Zosimus gently reassured, feeling the tears run down his nape, 'your people and their culture will never die as long as they live on in you.'

Aspar genuinely began to dread the evenings when the guards would appear in the cave and escort him to Diocles' villa. Here he would be used as a plaything by the owner and his guests – sometimes up to ten of them – before being dumped, exhausted and demoralised by his illicit lust, in the cave. Here, silently, Zosimus would treat any harm done to him before enfolding him gently in his strong arms. One night, when Aspar entered Diocles' triclinium, he found the guests and host all dressed formally in togas. A small band of musicians played Greek melodies on harps and flutes.

'I have heard there are other skills you have been hiding from us,' called Diocles, summoning Aspar to the table with a wave of his arm. 'Tonight, my king, you will entertain us with your stories – finally you will have an audience worthy of your talents,' he added, grinning around him at the other men. Aspar seated himself on the stool by the musicians that Diocles had indicated. He began haltingly at first, feeling awkward in the company of men who in the past had only been interested in using his body for their pleasure. But soon he was lost in his own narrative and, as it came alive for him, it had the same effect on his listeners. When he concluded his tale with a thrilling account of a battle between despotic gods and defiant mortals, his audience, usually so raucous, remained quite still. Aspar noticed that Menander's eyes shone and his lips were parted in a look of hunger he had not seen before.

Diocles dismissed his guests and the musicians, but beckoned Aspar to remain behind.

'How do you find working for Menander?' he growled, pouring a goblet of wine and offering it to the young king.

Aspar shook his head in refusal. 'It's interesting work,' he replied, 'and something I was already familiar with. My people are skilled builders and I had often watched our architects at work planning the foundations of a fortress.'

'Menander tells me you learn quickly. In fact, he seems very taken with you. He has even mentioned that you might be a suitable replacement for his assistant.' Diocles' scrutinised the boy's face for a reaction, but was rewarded with none. 'Working on Menander's team is a privilege, but your life could be better still. What if you were to come and live here in my villa? No more work in the mines, no need to offer your charms for the use of the men. You would spend your life here with me and be mine alone.'

Aspar could not disguise a look of dismay.

Diocles continued: 'I know this must be a surprise to you, but I have come to care for you over these weeks. I don't just want you to submit to me as a slave, though. I want you to come willingly. Don't answer now,' he added hastily. 'Think carefully about my offer and all that you would be gaining. After all, you were born a king. Look around you, boy – here, you would live like one.'

'A palace does not make a king,' Aspar murmured, almost without thinking: it was a favourite saying of his father's. He noticed the other man flinch and almost felt pity as he read the hurt in his eyes.

'Consider my offer carefully,' Diocles urged after a pause. 'Perhaps if our arrangement worked out, one day you might even earn your freedom, become a citizen.' Aspar's look softened slightly. 'Think about it. I am prepared to wait. I want you to come to me of your own free will. Only that way will you truly be mine.'

*

The north wind was beginning to howl down the crevasses and gorges of the mine. At night, the cave where Menander's team were billeted would echo with eerie whistles and moans. The men would stir uneasily in their sleep, the spectres and phantoms of Aspar's tales sneaking into their dreams, and they would draw together for comfort. Many of them were from warmer southern or eastern regions and they were not used to the rigours of a northern climate. Aspar, however, felt comforted by the sounds which were so familiar to him and would fall asleep contentedly in Zosimus' embrace.

Up at the villa, Diocles' servants were preparing for the Saturnalia, the traditional revels that marked the year's end now just a few weeks' off. Menander's divided his time between working on the entertainments he was devising for the celebrations and completing his great project at the mines. A low grey ceiling had been drawn across the limpid autumn skies and, even though they were given rough woollen cloaks, Menander's slaves shivered in the bitter weather.

Sometimes the temperature would rise a fraction and the air would be filled with large meandering snowflakes. This would prove a distraction to those of the slaves who had never seen snow and Menander would lose his customary calm, urging them to concentrate on his work: it was imperative that the project was finished before the temperatures dropped so low that the smaller waterways froze over. On some days, the snow showers were so heavy that they cut visibility down to zero and it was impossible for the architect and his workers to continue. Besides, the days were getting shorter and the project had to be completed in daylight hours.

Almost all the slaves of the mines were assigned to the numerous complex works involved in the scheme: digging the various channels and rigging the wooden sluices that would hold back the waters until the final moment. Other teams were preparing the galleries and shafts, removing wooden supports to ensure that they would collapse when the full force of the waters hit them. This was dangerous and delicate work as, if the galleries were to cave in before then, the project could be ruined. Zosimus super- vised the workers; no one knew the tunnels, galleries and vertical shafts of the mine like he did. It had been his home since child- hood and he was familiar with every hidden nook, just as other youngsters know the alleys of their city.

Menander's plan hinged on the destruction of one great gallery at the base of the rocky outcrop. The waters would strike this at peak velocity, filling the passages that led off it and rapidly rising to engulf the many layers of workings that had hollowed out the peak.

On most days, Diocles could be seen, anxiously following the work from a high crag. He had given orders to drive the slaves as hard as was necessary to complete the works and, while Aspar tried to concentrate on his tasks, he was constantly distracted by the crack of the overseers' whips.

Finally, the preparations were complete and the day of the de- molition arrived. All those playing a key role in the scheme were in their assigned positions by first light. Menander himself would co-ordinate the opening of the sluices, the timing of which was crucial to provide the necessary impetus that would bring the tar- geted section crashing down. His team had the vital task of con- veying his orders, by means of a system of signals, to the many teams of slaves who were invisible to one another in the mine's maze of interlocking gullies and gorges. The architect had there- fore selected a vantage point on a crag overlooking the chosen peak. From here, he could see both the junction where the various streams would converge and, just by moving a few yards around the rock, the broad channel through which the waters would enter the mountain, collapsing the great mass of rock into the raging flood.

As his closest collaborator, Aspar was positioned at the confluence of the channels from where he could see the architect. At this spot, he would convey his signal along several winding gorges, by means of a relay of slaves, positioned at each bend. Thus, the order to open the sluices should reach the various teams at approximately the same moment.

The chill wind that funnelled down the narrow gullies snatched away the white plumes of the young king's breath. He looked up to the peak where the still figure of Menander waited, stamped his feet to bring back some feeling and pulled his thick red cloak around him. It had been a gift from the architect and was of fine wool from Britannia. He had been hesitant about accepting it, but Zosimus had urged practicality. He could see his Ethiopian friend now: he was positioned at the first bend in the deepest of the channels that forked away from the spot where he was standing. Zosimus' eyes were fixed upon him and Aspar took comfort, knowing that this look signified more than the desire to accomplish the day's task.

He glanced along the other gullies: in each, the first slave in the chain was poised for his signal. Up on the crag, another figure took his place by Menander. He recognised the towering frame of Diocles, anxiously striking his leg with the coiled lash. Aspar sensed that much rode on the outcome of today's operation for the owner of the mines; it was not just a question of wealth, but also recognition at the gold-hungry heart of the Empire. The two men leant towards one another in intense last-minute consultations.

Then Diocles stood back. Aspar stiffened as he saw the architect raise a flag high in the air to herald the start of the operation. Slowly and deliberately, the young king lifted his own flag and checked that each of the other team members had done the same.

He counted slowly to sixty as Menander had coached him: this would ensure that each man in the various chains had time to raise their flags. As he finished counting, he knew that, according to the carefully rehearsed plan, each of his colleagues assigned to the sluices would be ready to give the signal to the teams of slaves who would demolish the gates and send the waters thundering into the channels.

His eyes were trained on Menander. The cold wind had unfurled the flag that he held aloft. Aspar shot a last glance towards Zosimus and the others. All waited, flags raised, motionless. Then the architect's flag curved earthwards. With a lightning reaction, Aspar's flag came down too and, almost simultaneously, those of the other men. There was a pause; a deep and expectant silence. This was the part of the scheme that it had been impossible to rehearse: the moment when Aspar would see the waters come tumbling along the channels towards him. Although these had been cut to accommodate the expected flow of water, Menander had warned the members of his team positioned along the gullies, and especially Aspar at the fork where they joined, that they should scramble up the cliffs as soon as the signal had been given, in case the first powerful wave overflowed the beds dug by the slaves. The agile Zosimus had already shinned some way up the steep cliff face and was crouched on a boulder, facing in the direction from which the water would appear.

Aspar waited anxiously for the first sign that the plan was working. He felt a tremor in his feet. Then there was a deep rumbling that rapidly grew. It became a deafening roar and he could already see streaks of boiling foam shooting along three of the channels. But the fourth – the largest of the channels and the one the boy knew to be vital to the scheme – remained dry. He cried out to the slave positioned along the gully, but his voice was swept away in the echoing roar of the flood. Foam already splashed against his legs as the waters met and seethed along the broad canal that led into the heart of the mountain. He glanced up towards Menander and could see the architect and the mine-owner had moved to the very edge of the cliff and were leaning forward anxiously. Menander was shouting and waving his arms with unusual vigour.

Aspar looked back down the empty channel. There was still no sign of the water. He tried to signal to the slave at the first bend, but he had retreated some way up the slope and was turned away so that it was impossible to attract his attention. The seething waters were lapping around Aspar's knees and dragging at his cloak, but he knew he would have no chance of sending a signal down the empty gully if he withdrew now: the success of the scheme was at stake. Zosimus, standing upright on the boulder, also appeared to be signing to him energetically and shouting, although his words too were drowned out by the tumult of the waters. Diocles was now also frantically gesturing to him. The fourth channel remained dry and he made another attempt to attract the attention of the slave whom he could see in silhouette, standing some way up the cliff and facing in the direction from which the flood should be coming. Suddenly, the man whipped round, waving frenziedly. What could this mean?

In an instant, the empty gully was blocked by a towering wall of water, heading towards Aspar with lightning speed. Becoming aware of the tug of the stream around his thighs, he lunged towards the cliff, but his feet slid on a fine covering of earth and he slipped backwards. Out of the corner of his eye, he could see Zosimus bounding towards him along the bank of the raging waters. The agile youth appeared to be running at right-angles to the cliff face. Already the strength of the approaching flood could be felt in the strong current as Aspar scrambled vainly with hands and feet to haul himself beyond their reach. But the mud and rock crumbled at his touch. Faced with this elemental force of destruction, a single thought gripped him: he wanted to live. And then the torrent broke over his head.

Instinctively, he snatched a breath before going under. It seemed like an age that he was submerged, rolling and somersaulting helplessly until he no longer had any idea in which direction the surface lay, even if he had had the strength to break free of the current. Then, he found himself tossed out of the flood, thrown clear as far as his waist, sucking air into his bursting lungs, before falling back in up to his neck, carried along at such speed that the passing cliffs were a blur. He heard a familiar voice calling his name insistently and saw Zosimus hurtling towards him, leaning over the flood at an alarming angle. He was holding out the pole he had used to give his signal, urging Aspar to seize it as he passed. The boy flung himself against the angry waters with all his strength and felt the pole strike his fingers a stinging blow, but then he had passed it and could see Zosimus rapidly disappearing behind him, though the man was already streaking along the bank in a furious attempt to overtake his friend.

Aspar looked around him desperately for an outcrop of rock, anything that he could grab on to – yet he knew that this section of the channel ran as straight as a spear so that the waters would hit the galleries at top speed. If he was carried into a tunnel, there was no hope. The channel had been constructed so that the waters would fill all the old diggings, pushing up the vertical shafts at maximum pressure. Once or twice, he was swept close to the bank but each time he tried to grab it, his hand ricocheted back violently.

Gradually, he became aware of a subtle alteration in the roar of the waters. The thunder of the flood was drowned out by a sucking sound, as of a vast drain filling up or a bathing pool emptying. Blinking the water out of his eyes, he saw up ahead a blank cliff face, peppered here and there with cave-mouths, each an entrance to a gallery still above the waterline. As planned, the stream had risen to such a height that one level of workings had already been flooded. If he continued on this course, Aspar would be smashed into the sheer mountainside.

There was only one chance. Under the water lay the broad gallery that had been the main target of the channel and which was the backbone of the system to be demolished. If he was able to dive down and allow the strong current to carry him along that gallery, at least he would escape being dashed to pieces. Filling his lungs with air, he plunged down head-first, his body rapidly becoming caught up in the dizzy spin of the speeding flow that entered the tunnel. In his mind, he battled despair. He now stood no chance of fighting his way back to the surface: the lower level of tunnels was flooded and it would be impossible to break free of the current in order to pull himself upwards and escape through a shaft. There was the further risk of being crushed against the rock wall at a bend, or that the pressure of the water would rapidly reach the critical point at which it would bring the whole mass crashing down.

In the pitch dark, he felt himself corkscrew along the gallery at an alarming rate, till a protruding tongue of rock grazed his skull. A flash of white sundered his being: his body streaked away into the freezing black waters while his mind pitched downwards through the rock to a place of warmth and calm. Yet he was aware of something, someone, tugging him back to his helpless, tumbling form.

A winding blow like a rod of iron across his chest brought mind and body jarringly together. He was still submerged but appeared to be suspended in the water which coursed around him. In the utter blackness, it was hard to tell what was happening, but he had the distinct impression that he was moving upwards. Then, he was out of the water and frenziedly gasping for air.

He looked directly into the face of Zosimus and realised that his friend was shouting at him at the top of his voice. 'Aspar, we must get out of here before it goes.' Zosimus was freeing himself of a chain that circled his waist. They were in one of the upper galleries and as they clambered to their feet, Aspar realised that his friend must have lowered himself on the chain down a shaft into the lower gallery: the blow he had felt was his friend's arm hooked around his chest. A vertical column of water shot upwards from the shaft through which they had made their escape and this tunnel too was rapidly filling up.

Supporting his friend with one arm, Zosimus made for a glimmer of blue light which marked the mouth of the tunnel. He explained how he had caught the young king a hand's breadth away from a sharp bend, knowing that he would be close to the wall at that point. If he had been a second later, Aspar's skull would have smashed against the rock like a quail's egg. As they reached the entrance, they saw the water had risen so rapidly that it was already gushing over the threshold of the tunnel. Dragging Aspar behind him, Zosimus picked his way up a steep slope, clear of the foaming stream.

Menander and Diocles were scrambling down towards them. They reached out and hauled the two slaves to the top of the cliff, where they collapsed, exhausted. At that moment, the earth shook and all four turned to see the jagged peak above the torrent quake and tilt. Great clouds of dust rose and jets of water shot into the air as the mine imploded and the man-made flood – now broad as a lake – became a rushing soup of mud and rubble.

Six

Zosimus' lips moved silently as he ground a mixture of herbs in a clay cup with a rough wooden pestle: was he simply recalling the ingredients, Aspar wondered, or murmuring an invocation to his spirits? Adding boiling water from a pot over the roaring fire that he had skilfully kindled in the rough-hewn hearth, he began to apply a hot poultice to the angry raised bruise on the young Dacian's forehead.

'That's quite a medal you've got there – commemorating a very narrow escape,' remarked Zosimus thoughtfully, moulding the paste over the purple swelling. 'Luckily, it won't be permanent.' He had carefully palpated the spot with his long sensitive fingers and knew that no serious damage had been done. 'And look,' he added with surprise, touching the cord at the boy's neck: 'your mother's talisman is still with you. It must have been this that saved you.'

Aspar nestled comfortably among the pile of soft skins on the rough wooden bed. The ever-resourceful Ethiopian had brought him to a cave in a disused area of the mines. At one time it must have served as the living quarters of an overseer: there was a fire-place with a real chimney, so that it did not fill up with smoke, and a proper wooden bed in an alcove apparently carved for the purpose.

His miraculous escape had filled him with a keen appreciation of the simplest sensations: the warmth of the chamber, his friend's care. He found himself sighing deeply again and again.

'What is that sound you keep making?' chuckled Zosimus,

softly patting the poultice with the pads of his fingers and tilting his head on one side to study the results.

'Because, I'm so relieved to be alive,' whispered Aspar clutching his friend's hand. 'I felt the pull of the underworld down there in the water and yet, more than ever before, I knew I wanted to live. You were right – my gods have not abandoned me. Surely this was a sign of their protection: maybe they have planned a some kind of destiny for me. But it is through you they have spoken,' he added. 'You healed my soul when it was sick and now you have saved my life. I owe you everything, Zosimus. Here,' he removed the talisman from his neck and slipped it over his friend's head, 'take it. You are the only charm I need now.'

As he watched his friend tending the other minor cuts and bruises on his body with deep concentration, he felt a warmth growing in his chest. And when, finally, Zosimus had cleaned away the poultice from his brow and, with the lightest of touches, was assessing the decrease in the swelling, the young king could no longer resist his impulses. Sliding his arms around the Ethiopian's strong neck, Aspar pulled the dark sombre face towards him, his whole frame suffused with a powerful wave of tenderness. As Zosimus' lips met his, Aspar felt him release a deep sigh, as though he too had long awaited this moment. Intoxicated, Aspar drank in the sweet breath. Their tongues duelled frantically as their naked bodies twisted against each other until they could not distinguish limb from limb.

Although they had shared a bed with the intimacy of brothers, now each man perceived the other's body as a newly discovered continent, every inch of whose landscape cried out to be explored and charted. Eagerly, they began to gorge on one another, longing to sample the other man's flavours and inhale his aromas.

The chamber was filled with the warmth of the blazing fire and by its light their two interlocked bodies, one fair and the other dark, moved on the softness of the fur blankets like one being, with fierce concentration. Pulling his tongue from Zosimus' mouth, Aspar squirmed under the other man, grasping his hard thighs and levering his head up between them so that he faced the smoothness of his buttocks. Easing the cheeks apart, he lovingly contemplated the dark circle of gathered skin that lay between them. His eyes fixed on the man's lovehole, Aspar drew close and brushed it with the softness of his lips. At the same time, he felt Zosimus lifting Aspar's own hips from the bed, gently parting his arsecheeks. He sighed as the Ethiopian's breath riffled the circlet of golden hair that fringed his own pink love-button.

A groan escaped from both men's throats as their tongues simultaneously tasted each other's delicate arse-lips. Aspar's heart leaped as he breathed in Zosimus' rich musk, and he lapped furiously at the blossom of the other man's hole which shyly began to yield up its moist interior. Aspar pressed his mouth around the silken, engorged flesh of his friend's anus, clamping his lips around it and sucking hard as if on a ripe fruit, teasing out its nectar with the tip of his tongue. Zosimus moaned, grinding his hips with arousal, pressing his hole against Aspar's mouth. He too guzzled on Aspar's arse, probing the red satin folds of its inner sanctum with his muscular tongue.

Pricked by the deliciousness of Zosimus' intimacy, the saliva spurted under Aspar's tongue. Pursing his lips, the boy shot a long jet of it across the loosened arsehole. He watched it ooze between the tender folds, then smeared it across them with slow circles of his flattened tongue. Tracing a downwards path between Zosimus' bulging thighs, Aspar began to nuzzle his weighty testicles, already tight with arousal, taking one in his mouth and thrusting it in and out between his lips with his tongue. Straining his jaw to its fullest extent, Aspar took the other date-shaped ball into his mouth and closed his lips over them, tugging gently and rolling them together. Zosimus moaned and rocked his arse back and forth in response to the deep pleasureable ache that gathered in his scrotum.

Aspar released the balls and, with a quick slide of his shoulders, was under the other man, arching his head back so that he could take the full length of his heavy erection in his throat. At the same time, Zosimus' willing gullet enfolded Aspar's upstanding seed-chute. The two men sank into a deep well of pleasure, penetrating and being penetrated at the same time. Aspar relished the feel of his lover's shiny pink glans churning in his throat and, spurred on by the heat at the root of his prick, pushed hard until he felt his own dickhead skidding along Zosimus' slippery gullet.

Zosimus pulled himself away from Aspar's lips and twisted himself round to face the boy. Their eyes and tongues locked, as they savoured their mingled flavours.

'Fuck me,' the Ethiopian insisted. 'I want to you to fill me with your manseed!' Fired by his passion for the other man, Aspar grasped him roughly by the ankles, parting and levering back his sturdy legs. The young king contemplated the loose-lipped man-cunt for a second before sinking his rigid white pillar into its softness. Aspar sighed as he felt his rod glide smoothly down the satin-lined passage. He grimaced as he frantically pumped Zosimus' hole, his own delicate foreskin slipping back and forth in his partner's copious arse-juice. Zosimus arched his head up from the bed, veins protruding from his forehead as he met the onslaught of Aspar's fuckpole with the involuntary spasms of his anal canal. Feeling this vice-like pressure milking his cock like a hungry mouth, Aspar's prostate contracted to stone-hardness and the jism mounted from his balls in a hot, irreversible jet.

As the foaming torrent splattered his innards, Zosimus' prick reared up rigidly from his stomach and, after a long silent dance of agony, began to shoot thick curdled skeins of white semen across the sculpted muscles of his dark torso.

His lover still helplessly impaled on his column, Aspar kissed him feverishly. 'Implant me with your seed, too,' he begged Zosimus, 'to seal our love.' Without breaking their gaze, the

Ethiopian, still in a state of full arousal, snatched at the gobs of fluid on his chest, using them to anoint Aspar's hot, expectant anus. Aspar felt the man's long foreskin ripple against the smooth muscle of his swollen arse-ring as Zosimus' manhood tore into his guts with an urgent pounding. Aspar felt simultaneous stimulation as his anal canal clamped round his lover's member in a paroxysm of pleasure and at the same time a bolt of pain shot through his already contracted prostate as it threatened to launch a second load of semen.

With a ferocity born of pent-up longing, Zosimus slammed into his lover's contracting rectum and a deep groan burst from him, rapidly rising to become a roaring shout. Eyes wide with astonishment, Zosimus cried out, 'I'm coming. Take my spunk in your beautiful hole.' And he lunged forward again and again, gasping loudly at each painful squirt. Aspar's face contorted with a ferocity of pleasure – and emotion – that enveloped his body and mind. Tears ran down his cheeks as jets of seminal spume soared from his wood-hard seed-shooter.

In the days immediately following Aspar's brush with death, Diocles and Menander were too preoccupied with the extraction of the gold from the debris of the collapsed workings to give much thought to the young Dacian. Nevertheless, the day after the accident, one of Diocles' Egyptian cooks arrived under escort, bearing a dish of lamb marinaded in spices and a dessert of snow flavoured with strawberries and rose petals. Zosimus brought these delicacies, obviously designed to speed the lad's recovery, to Aspar in their cave retreat. They shared the feast, washed down with sweet water from an icy spring that Zosimus had discovered deep in the heart of the mountain.

As he had been excused from work, Aspar spent his days alone in the communal cave of Menander's team; Habinnas informed him of the special privilege with his usual resentful sneer. One afternoon, the young king was filling his time by recalling quotes from the philosophers and writing them on the wall with an ember from the fire when Menander entered. The architect squatted awkwardly on a blanket beside Aspar and presented him with a small wooden box, inlaid with silver figures.

'A healing ointment from the east.'

Aspar smiled his thanks and completed the sentence he was working on. The architect twisted his neck to read it: 'The Phaedrus of Plato,' he murmured in astonishment. 'So, you are familiar with the philosophers. Diocles did say you were educated, but I did not imagine such things were known among the northern peoples.'

'Barbarians, you mean?' said Aspar, raising a quizzical eyebrow. 'I wonder what Socrates and Plato would have had to say on the subject of what constitutes barbarism? Phaedrus was a slave and a captured enemy – and of noble blood, as it happens – yet Plato chose him as the protagonist of this sublime work, to share a dialogue with Socrates on the subject of love.'

'Indeed – it is a favourite of mine, too,' said the Greek, encouraged to reach out and place his hand on Aspar's, which hovered over the lines he had been writing. 'I think we have a great deal in common, young Dacian. And recent events have shown that you are not only intelligent but a conscientious and devoted worker. We could give each other much.'

Aspar gently withdrew his hand and carefully laid the ember in a niche in the rock. 'But for how long?' he asked. 'Remember that, like Phaedrus, I am a slave. Though Socrates enjoyed conversing with the beautiful Phaedrus, he could not grant him his freedom – the boy belonged to his master, the brothel-keeper. The philosopher could admire his looks and his wit, but nothing more. You have had success here; your fame will travel and soon you will leave to work on a greater project. I, however, belong to Diocles and I must stay. What is the point in starting what soon must end?'

Aspar's gentle demurral, however, served only to further stimulate the architect's interest and over the next few days a series of small but exquisitely tasteful gifts were delivered by Habinnas, who tossed them unceremoniously onto Aspar's bed of straw.

As they lay together on the night of Menander's visit, Aspar told Zosimus about his conversation with the architect. The two slaves had created an oasis of life for one another in the midst of an existence that most men would regard as a living death: their greatest fear was that this happiness should be snatched away. Sooner or later, Aspar reassured his lover, Menander would leave Hispania. It was just a question of stalling him. In his heart, however, the boy knew that Diocles was another matter – he had still not given his answer to the owner of the mines.

To mark the Saturnalia, double rations were given to the slaves. In other parts of the Empire, slaves became the equals of their masters for the days of the festival; here, work schedules were simply cut by half so that the guards and overseers could take part in the revels thrown by Diocles on his estate. One evening, Aspar was summoned to the villa. Servants escorted him to the gates of the mine where a litter awaited to carry him the rest of the way. A team of slaves cleaned him thoroughly before teasing his hair into ringlets and perfuming and oiling his skin. During this process, the boy thought, not without some interest, of the debaucheries that he assumed were to take place. This was the Saturnalia, after all, the most unbridled of all the feasts of the year. Once they had completed his toilet, however, the servants dressed him in a long elegant toga of white wool, with a finely embroidered border, and led him into Diocles' triclinium.

To his surprise, the great dining room was empty but for the owner of the mine, also dressed in the formal toga, who gestured for the lad to take his place on an empty couch. The table was laid for a feast on embossed gold tableware.

'Wine, boy? It's vintage Falernian,' said Diocles. The man's morose manner and a slight slur in his speech suggested that he had already been drinking for some time. Aspar nodded and took the golden cup offered him by a servant. 'You're probably wondering why we're dining alone, and all dolled up like this.' He threw the boy a look of cunning through narrowed eyes. 'Seeing it's Saturnalia, I suppose you were expecting a drunken party and that I'd hand you over to my men for their pleasure. That's what you expected, isn't it? That's the kind of master you think I am, don't you?'

'I suppose I did assume that it would be much the same as usual,' Aspar admitted. 'What else did I have to judge by?'

'Well, I don't want them pawing you, see? I want you for myself, but I once said that you must come to me, remember? Then I thought: what do you know of me except what you've seen in the mines or the nights up here at the villa. You probably think I'm a brute. An ex-slave, and you a king, even though you're a slave now. So I haven't invited you for a party, or even to force you submit me. I want you to get to know me as a man. As someone who has worked to make something of himself. That's the great thing about this Empire of ours – we can better ourselves. I have. Look around you at this villa. Magnificent, isn't it? As fine as anything you would find in Rome itself. You can make something of yourself, too. You can have everything you had before – and more. That's what I'm offering you.'

'It's a very generous offer,' replied Aspar slowly, taken aback at the unsuspected depths of feeling Diocles had revealed. 'Yes, I am happy to get to know you, but you must get to know me, too. And you must understand that what I have lost is not just a question of gold and material goods. I have lost a way of life that cannot be replaced. You must give me time.'

Diocles looked cheered. 'Of course, I realise that it will take time for you to get to know me and trust me. You have brought out feelings in me, gentle tender feelings that I never knew I had. I have great wealth, but wealthy Romans have no respect for me: with you by my side it would be different. I could learn to be more refined, to be the kind of person you would expect to find in a palace.'

True to his promise, Diocles spent the evening with Aspar in conversation. Throughout the night, he did not lay a finger on the younger man. He showed a genuine interest in the boy's former life, and spoke of his own early life as the son of slaves, taken from his mother when still a toddler and sold illegally to a lanista who trained him as a gladiator for the arena. There he won his freedom. Aspar felt pity for him, and was touched by Diocles' earnest attempts to win his respect and affection. Whereas he had shrugged off Menander's advances, Aspar returned to the mines deeply troubled: Diocles was not going away, and there were no guarantees that some other youth would soon come along to distract him.

During the period of the Saturnalia, Aspar and his lover took advantage of the shorter working hours to spend as much time as possible alone together. Following his latest visit to Diocles' villa, the young king had shared his fears. Yet the sense of safety and strength that they had discovered in one another seemed to close off all outside threats. When they were together, the narrow confines of their rough secret chamber opened up to infinity: for them it meant freedom. Often, they would sleep there together after making love, rejoining the other slaves of Menander's team in the darkness before they were wakened. Sometimes, by the light of the roaring fire that Zosimus always built, Aspar would contemplate his lover while he slept. In the eyes of the young Dacian, the other man appeared to shrink in sleep and become like a child, vulnerable and pure.

Nevertheless, the two men resolved to be more cautious in

their movements: they would leave the communal cave separately, reach their private place by different routes, and each would return alone.

One evening returning home after work, Aspar recognised a herb growing by the path. He knelt and crushed a few leaves between finger and thumb. The sharp clean smell evoked memories of his mother and Dacia, and he held out his fingers for Zosimus to smell. The Ethiopian frowned and shook his head: the herb was unknown to him. 'My mother used this for healing burns,' Aspar recalled, sniffing at the crushed leaves.

'Do you remember how?' enquired Zosimus.

'I think I do,' mused Aspar, surprised at the clarity of his own memories. 'Although she never showed me, I watched her so often at work, I think I could recall.'

Not only did Aspar successfully reproduce his mother's preparation, but he had the chance a few days later to test its efficacy on Zosimus when he burned his arm while cooking.

'You see,' said Zosimus as his lover gently smeared the soothing unguent on his injury, 'yet again you have proved that the heritage of your people has not vanished, but is carried within you. Their past is your future.'

'You are a philosopher.' Aspar smiled up at him. 'You love to talk in paradoxes.'

The discovery of the herb undammed a stream of recollections which came back to Aspar with the detailed sharpness of the bas-reliefs which which the Romans loved to adorn their monuments. He examined the collection of herbs that Zosimus had stored in earthenware pots in their secret cave, carefully sniffing and tasting them. Many were familiar, and more of his mother's recipes came back to him as they experimented with these and other plants they found growing around the mine. The young king also remembered traditional songs, which he would sing softly to his

lover when they were alone at night. They also taught each other
the dances of their respective peoples and would perform them for
each other by the crackling firelight, or dance themselves into a
trance together, mesmerised as much by each other's presence as
by the movements and the incantations which accompanied
them.

Close to their hideaway was an opening in the rock near the
summit of a fanglike peak overlooking the eerie landscape of the
mine. The two lovers came to regard this as their private balcony.
If they sat within the mouth of the cave, they were too high up to
be spotted from below, and the path which had once led up to the
cave had long since crumbled away. Not only could they survey
the whole of the mine from this position, but it was also possible
to see far beyond the confines of their prison to open plains and
further still to range beyond range of mountains.

Sometimes, they would sit here and reminisce about their lives
past, at others they would make love or recount the sagas and legends of their gods and ancestors. More and more however, as they
gazed into misty folds of the distant mountains, their talk would
turn towards the future.

Zosimus had amassed a little store of pigments which he had
created from the many different hues to be found in the soil and
rock of the mines: warm ochres, earthy reds, sulphurous yellows,
coppery blues. One evening, the two used these colours to paint
long-remembered objects and scenes on the cave walls. With the
tip of his tongue gripped between his teeth, Aspar worked intently
on the figure of a Dacian warrior, a nobleman with a fine peaked
helmet, golden armour and brightly painted shield. Every now
and then, he would lean back to judge the overall effect, noting
with satisfaction how the golden winter sunlight added richness to
Zosimus' colours.

'A fine warrior,' commented the Ethiopian. 'No wonder the
Dacians proved a challenge for the Roman Army.'

'But in the end, we faced total defeat,' replied Aspar gloomily.

'But was it the end?' asked Zosimus softly. 'You are still here, and they have not conquered you in your heart.'

Aspar turned away from his work to gaze at the point where the endless planes of mountains faded into a bright infinity. 'Is it possible to dream of a time when Rome is no longer mistress of the world?'

'Egypt, Greece and Macedonia all ruled before Rome and now they pay her homage. Even now, to the east of the Empire, Parthia and other empires still further off have not fallen. But one day Rome herself will fall. There will be a time and a place where she no longer rules. Only the gods know when. Meanwhile, we must believe.' Now they both gazed into the distant haze. 'Let us promise one another that if we are ever separated –'

Aspar clapped his hand to his lover's mouth, stricken. 'Don't say that,' he hissed. 'Some jealous god may hear you and do what you suggest for spite.'

Zosimus gave a wry laugh and gently pulled Aspar's hand away. 'A jealous man is more to be feared than a god. And it is something we must at least think about, so that if it ever comes we might bear it. But if we are ever separated,' he continued, 'and one of us earns his freedom, let us make a vow that he will find the other and that together, in some way, however small, we will begin the fight for freedom from the Roman yoke.'

They swore the oath on the talisman of Aspar's mother: from that moment on, it symbolised their solemn pledge.

Dreams of the future began to occupy their conversations more and more. They imagined whcre they would go if they managed to win their freedom – to Parthia, where they would learn the skills that had inflicted so many humiliating defeats on Imperial generals in the past. Then at last to Dacia, with an army recruited from slaves, conquered peoples who would be only too happy to fight against the common enemy. After all, Aspar pointed out, tens of thousands of Dacians had been sold into slavery throughout the Empire. This band of skilled fighters could carry out constant lightning raids on Rome's frontiers, a tiny wasp tormenting the great ox of the Empire. Using coloured stones to stand for divisions of men, the two lovers planned the battles they would one day lead together.

Near the icy spring where they drank and bathed, a thorny bush grew in a rocky cleft. Aspar showed Zosimus how to tie strips of cloth to it, the way his mother used to, as prayers to the gods. Soon, its leafless branches grew festive with their hopes and dreams.

The bitter cold of winter gave way to the warmth of spring. The days lengthened and occasionally the lovers would return from their work in the mines before daylight had died. Without a word or a sign to one another, they would each make their way to their balcony, where they would stare over the mountains and share future plans. More daringly, they would rise when it was still dark and witness the first glimmer of day. Occasionally, they lingered too long and, by the time they reached the communal cave, Habinnas would already be waking the others. Although they took great care to arrive from separate directions, the youth would always glance suspiciously from one to the other.

Once or twice a week, Aspar was escorted to the villa to spend an evening in polite conversation with his master. On each occasion, the former gladiator awkwardly brought up lofty topics for conversation, such as a philosophical point from Plato or the works of Zeuxis, the artist. As these subjects would invariably peter out rapidly, Aspar suspected that Diocles was being coached beforehand by someone more knowledgeable than himself – a reluctant Menander, perhaps? Aspar had noticed a certain frostiness recently in the Greek's behaviour towards him, no doubt due to his awareness of Diocles' prior claim on the lad's attentions.

He dreaded these encounters with his master. Though he had declared that the boy should be free to choose, how long would his resolve hold? Fearing for his lover's safety, Zosimus suggested that he should feign submission, but Aspar refused, knowing that Diocles would immediately take him to live at the villa and make it impossible for the lovers to meet. Yet, in their hearts, both men knew that their enchanted existence must soon end.

Entering Diocles' triclinium one evening in March, Aspar immediately sensed that all was not well. Diocles was not waiting politely on his couch as he normally did. At first Aspar thought that the room was empty until he saw a movement in an unlit corner and noticed someone standing unsteadily by a pillar, a goblet of wine in his hand. As the man's huge frame emerged into the lamplight, Aspar saw purple winestains scattered down the front of his immaculate toga.

'So, boy, do you think you could make love to this former gladiator? Or am I too common, too ignorant for a king like you? Come here and show me,' he growled, swaying closer to the lad. Nervously, Aspar approached him. Diocles hooked his arm roughly round Aspar's neck, splashing wine from the goblet onto the boy's toga. He stuck his tongue into Aspar's mouth, his breath rank with drink. Aspar responded mechanically. The man tightened his grip. 'Not like that, boy. I said make love. Make love to me – like you do to him.'

'What do you mean?' stammered Aspar. The back of his knees tingled with fear.

'I mean the Ethiopian. I mean your lovers. You've been stringing me along all this time, making me believe that you could be mine one day, when all the time you were his.' He pushed Aspar away. 'Did you think I wouldn't find out. Well, you underestimated me, your highness –' he gave a mock bow and almost lost his balance, toppling onto a nearby couch '– I am a king, too, didn't you know that? Only unlike you, I have a kingdom – these mines. And sooner or later, I find out everything that goes on in my kingdom. I know all about you two. Even the things you say to one another when you make love.'

Then Aspar recalled Habinnas, always arriving at the cave at unexpected hours. Perhaps he had followed them to their cave – or the balcony. Who knows what whispered words and conversations he had overheard.

'So what does he have that I don't have? Can he give you all this?'

'What he gives me, you could never understand,' groaned Aspar despairingly.

Diocles clambered to his feet and grasped Aspar roughly by the shoulders. 'If you will not submit to me willingly, I am still your master and I can do what I will with you.'

'Yes, you can,' he breathed, bracing himself for the ordeal he had endured so often which was not without its pleasures.

At this, the former gladiator let out a roar like an enraged animal. He began to tear the toga from the young man's body and, thrusting him down onto a couch, ripped the flimsy tunic in two. Throwing off his own robes, he straddled the boy's throat and roughly shoved his erect cock between the full, curved lips. Aspar retched as the man rammed his long wide column into his gullet, the thick pubic bush pressed against his face, the heavy balls striking his chin. Diocles let out something between a groan and a sob of despair as he sank his long prick into the sweet mouth of the boy he had so long desired. He plunged the swollen organ in and out in a frenzy. He ignored Aspar's gagging and the boy flushed scarlet, tears streaming from the corners of his eyes as he tried to accommodate his master's prick.

Turning, Diocles crouched over the boy's face, pressing his arsehole to his lips, grinding it against the lad's soft pink tongue. He pulled roughly at the small tender nipples. Already half-smothered by the massive meaty buttocks, Aspar let out muffled cries of near-pain. Still riding the sweet young tongue with his lust-in-flamed anus, Dicoles leaned forward and began to twist Aspar's cock and balls in opposite directions. In reaction to the boy's writhing and grunts, Diocles wrenched the stiff white column more brutally than ever and swivelled his widening arsehole against Aspar's mouth. The mine-owner's face was distorted in a grimace of thwarted desire. He slapped and tugged at Aspar's help-less balls and tool until the skin was tight and shiny, the column a fierce red, cockhead and balls a raging purple. Striking the balls with blows of increasing harshness, Diocles smothered the lad's mouth with the heavy pressure of his now hotly aroused fuck-hole.

The ex-gladiator pulled Aspar's slender hips up towards him, trapping the lad's knees under his strong elbows. He pushed the golden arsecheeks apart to expose the pink pursed lips of the tight butthole. He kneaded it with rough thumbs, loosening the firm muscle-ring, then, drawing more muted gasps from the recesses of his own rocking hole, he pressed in first one and then two fingers into the unlubricated circle of flesh. With his other hand, he grasped the wide cock-root and, with a vicious turn of his wrist, bent the hard organ painfully against its natural direction. Aspar grunted. It was a pleasurable torment.

The mine-owner worked four, then five fingers into the hole, its pink edge now tinged with crimson. His legs firmly pinioned by Diocles' powerful arms, Aspar could do nothing but give into the throb in his burning hole and member.

Having worked himself into a fury of raging lust, Diocles swiftly turned, gripped the young king's ankles in his massive hands and used them as a lever to jam his manhood, already streaming with pre-come, into the boy's gaping red anus. Aspar groaned as he felt the older man's huge cockhead graze his sphinc-ter and plumb the depths of his anal canal.

'Tonight you're all mine, boy, and I'm going to fill every hole of your body with my load. You're going to be streaming with my cock-juice, boy – hear that – filled up with my come and piss – nobody else's. I'm going to make you taste my jism and feel my manpole so that you'll never forget it.'

'Take it,' he howled, as his intense fucking showered blended pre-come and pussy-juice in every direction from Aspar's loosened man-cunt. In a blind rage of passion, Diocles tugged and twisted Aspar's cock and balls without restraint, at the same time creating the maximum sensation in the boy's rectum with the ramrod action of his cock.

Diocles froze. His face and shoulders flushed, and from the mounting pressure in his bowels, Aspar knew the ex-gladiator was releasing a stream of hot piss inside him. After what seemed an age during which the ache in his intestines became excruciating, his master began to fuck frenetically, aroused by the sloppy feel of his own copious outpourings which streamed down the boy's back. The young king answered the man's thrashing movements with jerks of his pelvis, reaching such a pitch of stimulation that agonising white spurts of cock-milk shot rhythmically from his cock. The powerful clamping of his sphincter on Diocles' club of flesh sent the man roaring over the edge of pleasure into orgasm, discharging thick curds of spunk into the steaming yellow piss that already flooded the lad's insides.

Aspar's master made good his promise to possess him repeatedly in mouth and anus, in a desperate attempt to stake his claim to the boy. Hours later, Aspar lay on the couch, exhausted but sated, Diocles' bodily fluids gurgling from from both sets of lips.

Panting from his exertions, like a horse after a chariot-race, Diocles looked down at the boy with a sneer. 'You think yourself so grand – a king! You're nothing. You belong to me and I can do whatever I like with you. I can sell you if I want – and your friend the Ethiopian.'

Aspar paled. He wiped his mouth and pushed himself up to a sitting position. 'What does he matter to you? I'm the one who has offended you.'

Diocles roughly turned the boy's face towards him, looking into his eyes with longing for a moment: 'Because he has stolen what is mine and because by hurting him, I hurt you.' He averted his face. 'There is one way in which I can punish you both.' He turned back. 'Tomorrow I will send the two of you to the slave market of Tarraco. Dealers come there from all over the world. I will ensure that you are sold to masters at opposite ends of the Empire. When I return you to the caves tonight, say your good-byes, for you will never set eyes on each other again as long as you live.'

The separation did not come as swiftly as Aspar feared. The slaves of Menander's team were still deep in exhausted sleep when he was escorted back to the cave. He woke Zosimus and recounted the events of the night in an urgent whisper. Their first instinct was to head for the secret chamber, where they made anguished love, unable to hold back their grief. They watched as dawn broke over the distant mountains then, looking deep into each other's eyes, renewed the oath they had sworn there.

Aspar paid one last visit to the shrine by the spring and hastily attached new strips of cloth with fumbling fingers, each one a petition to the mother goddesses: that they would both be sold to kind masters; that one or both lovers would soon earn their freedom; that their separation would be short and that they would fulfil their dream of resistance to Rome in their kingdom beyond the mountains.

Soon after sun-up, Aspar and Zosimus were escorted by guards to the gates, where they were chained to other slaves also destined for the market: these were mostly sorry specimens, either too old or too weak to be any use in the mines. Several empty wagons were being sent to Tarraco under heavy guard to pick up supplies arriving from

Rome. This meant that the slaves would at least spend the journey riding in relative comfort, even though the vehicles were equipped for carrying goods rather than passengers.

There was, however, one rather more luxurious passenger carriage in the party. To his surprise, Aspar saw that this was occupied by Menander and his assistant. Diocles, it seemed, had been aware of Menander's attempts to win the young king's affections, and wished to rid himself of every painful reminder of his loss. The architect studiously ignored the Dacian, but, when his master's back was turned, Habinnas could not resist flashing a triumphant grin at his rival. His strategy had worked, even if it had also earned summary dismissal for his master.

Although the long journey to the capital of the province meant that they had several more days in each other's company, it merely extended the torment of parting, as each jolting mile brought Aspar and Zosimus closer to an unknown but divided destiny. Finally, they came in sight of the sea, a silver border on the horizon and, clustered beside it, the magnificent buildings of Tarraco glowing in the spring sunshine: the forum, temples, amphitheatre and circus. The large harbour already teemed with the first ships of the sailing season.

Diocles' stewards had orders to sell Zosimus privately to merchants from a distant province – preferably far to the east. They passed from ship to ship until they found interest from a merchant of Seleucia, the port of Antioch in Syria, and threw in the other slaves for free in order to clinch the deal. Aspar, however, was to face the indignity of the slave market. If he could not win the boy's love, Diocles was determined at least to make his money back and, perhaps, even a profit.

The slave auction was part of a busy market overlooking the harbour. Aspar was pushed into a pen along with a large number of others from every part of the Empire. Gradually, the compound emptied until he found himself alone with the guards. He, it seemed, was to be the prize lot of the day.

Stripped bare on the stone platform as the auctioneer introduced him, Aspar spotted Zosimus close to the front of the crowd, chained to the other slaves purchased by his new master. Once the auctioneer had identified Aspar as the Slave King and commended his breeding and looks, fierce bidding broke out.

The auctioneer started with a figure far in excess of the highest bids in the sale up to that point and soon he was gleefully calling out staggering sums. 'Remember, only a king's ransom will suffice to purchase a king,' he kept interjecting, clearly delighted with his own sales patter. Aspar screwed up his eyes to make out where the bids were coming from, but most of the interest seemed to be at the back of the crowd and the glare of the late afternoon sun off the sea was so intense that it was impossible to make out individual faces.

The auctioneer's gavel came down on his desk and the deal was done. Aspar was filled with sudden dread at what lay ahead. How did his future owner hope to be recompensed for his investment?

Descending the steps of the platform to his new master, accompanied by one of the auctioneer's servants, Aspar passed close to Zosimus. The two men's eyes locked, although they were not close enough to touch or even speak, but the Ethiopian clasped the wooden talisman Aspar had given him as a reminder of their oath. Aspar kept his eyes fixed on his lover's face for as long as he could, but, though he fought to hold them back, his vision soon misted over with tears.

'Stop that blubbering, boy – you'll spoil those lovely eyes. You should be glad to see the last of those mines, by Bacchus. Especially now you're destined for a life of luxury.' The voice, with its cultured Greek accent, seemed familiar and so did the jingle of trinkets which accompanied it. Wiping his eyes and streaming nose with the back of his wrist, Aspar stared with the shock of

recognition into the triumphant countenance of his new master –
Glaucus, the brothel-keeper.

Seven

A tall solitary figure emerged from the shadows of the Temple of Aesculapius into the warmth of the April sun. Lost in thought, the young man's head was still covered by the folds of his plain white toga, in the attitude of prayer. As he wandered onto the Fabricius Bridge, he looked up distractedly, squinting against the fierce white glare of sunlight reflected off the swift-flowing waters of the Tiber. Feeling the sun's rays on his skin, he pulled the covering from his head.

The long face had acquired the angularity of manhood. The lips were still full but were now firmly etched. The blond hair was no longer curled but cut short in a style that showed the strong shape of the head and the sinews of the neck. The chest muscles had thickened and the shoulders broadened, though, even through the folds of the toga, the hips and waist could be seen to be as slender as ever. Arranging the creases of his robe, Aspar decided he would take advantage of the lovely spring morning. He dismissed his litter and set out for the Forum on foot: he had a couple of hours to spare before his next appointment and needed to do some errands on the way.

As he wandered past the Theatre of Marcellus and onto the Vicus Tuscus, he returned the greetings of various Senators and other leading officials of the capital. The curtains of their litters were drawn back to let in the sunshine and they were accompanied by trains of handsome slaves: like Aspar, they were doing their shopping early to avoid the crush. 'Thinking up your next book?' asked one, noting the young man's pensive air. Aspar smiled and shook his head. 'I'm planning a supper for some of our more important literary figures: you must come,' the Senator went on.

Aspar bowed graciously in reply; he was not in the mood for conversation. In spirit, he was still in the semi-darkness of the Temple where he had just sprinkled wine on the sacrifice of a new-born lamb. It had become a custom for him to make an offering to Aesculapius each year to mark the anniversary of his arrival from Hispania. He had set himself a target of gaining his freedom within five years: this was the fourth time he had made the com-memoration, so he was still on target.

Each year, following the sacrifice, the haruspex would take the auspices, and each year they were favourable. Sometimes Aspar had a sneaking feeling that this was to ensure that the customary gift of cash to the temple would be generous, but he chose to be-lieve the words of the augurer anyway. Of course, he never let slip what his real intentions were in offering the sacrifice. He had se-lected the Temple of Aesculapius because he could only believe in a god of compassion, a god who saw all mankind, slave and free, high-born and low, as human beings in need of healing. And, as Aspar knew well, there were many different kinds of healing, both of body and soul. To him, Aesculapius and Zalmoxis – the healing god of the Dacians – were one and the same. Besides, his favourite dramatist, Sophocles, had been a priest of the god.

Since his arrival in Rome, he had continued to hone his skills in the healing knowledge he had first learned from his mother and which had later been deepened in his friendship with Zosimus. His hand went to his throat in an instinctive gesture. It still came as a shock to him, to not feel the warmth of his mother's rough wooden talisman, but the cold copy of gold and lapis lazuli he had had made shortly after his arrival in Rome. It was a constant re-minder of the only man he had loved and of the pledge they had made to one another.

The fine shops of the Vicus were open even at this early hour and the owners were busily swilling down their stretch of the pavement or setting out their wares to best advantage. The air was perfumed with delicious smells of baking bread and cakes from high-class bakeries and confectioners which had recently prolifer-ated as a result of a new Imperial policy. A small crowd had gath-ered round a bookshop. The seller was unrolling sections of scrolls from the latest publications so that readers could sample the most exciting passages and thus be enticed to purchase. With a flush of pride, Aspar noticed that one of the selected texts was his own *Shield of Gold*, which had just been issued in an edition of two thousand copies.

The fame of his sagas of gods and heroes, which had begun as a casual entertainment for the other boys and men in the House of Glaucus, had travelled fast. Soon his reputation as a storyteller had outstripped the appeal of his other charms, which neverthe-less remained much in demand. The bored Roman upper classes, with so much time on their hands, especially now in this period of peace throughout the Empire, were avid for novelty, and a gen-uine king who told stories, and good ones, was certainly that. Aspar was an honoured guest at Rome's top tables: he had even dined and told his stories at an Imperial banquet on the Palatine.

His many patrons had encouraged him to write and publish the sagas. It had taken him about a year to render a portion of the tales in Latin verse and a further twelve months for the publishing house to complete the laborious process of copying the manu-scripts. He had used the pen-name 'the Dacian', though the iden-tity of the author was no secret to most educated citizens. Even now, there was talk of a second edition and critical response had been excellent, with orders coming from as far afield as Athens, Alexandria and Antioch. Already, the second volume was almost complete.

Glaucus' reaction to the unexpected success of one of his most valuable slaves had been mixed. On the one hand, he was delighted at the attention Aspar had earned for himself and for his House. To all who complimented him on Aspar's presence in his establishment, he would take care to highlight his skill at spotting potential. He had paid a fortune for the Slave King and the young man had proved to be worth every denarius.

On the other hand, he was uneasy at the esteem in which Aspar was held by many leading figures in the Capital. They had begun to see him as a distinguished literary name, which somewhat diminished his value as a beautiful male prostitute. Worse still was the fact that Aspar was set on buying his freedom and, even though Glaucus had a rule that his boys could not accept tips in cash, he could not prevent clients from making lavish payments in kind. The luxurious private apartment which Aspar now occupied in Glaucus' House contained a small fortune in precious objects – more than enough to buy himself out of slavery. But the pimp stubbornly refused to let him go. The wily old Greek was only too well aware, however, that Aspar's influential friends would eventually bring so much pressure to bear on him – perhaps even petition the Emperor – that he would be forced to lose his most precious asset.

Aspar realised the strength of his position. He knew that eventually Glaucus would have to release him. In the meantime, he was amassing sufficient resources to buy not only his own freedom but that of Zosimus. With the publication of his book, he would also have further funds to finance their plans. He had learned patience during his sojourn in Rome: he was certain that if the schemes dreamed up with youthful enthusiasm by himself and Zosimus in Hispania were ever to come to fruition, it would only be as a result of careful planning.

As he strolled slowly along the Vicus, the young Dacian carefully scrutinised the valuable goods laid out in the windows of the stores: one specialised in rings, another in pearls, a third in carved ivory. He lingered outside a shop which dealt in rare cameos. Spotting a signed piece by Dioskourides, the designer of the Emperor Augustus' Imperial seal, he called the shopkeeper over. After a few moments haggling, they struck a deal and Aspar asked the man to deliver it to the House in Vicus Longus. He had been looking for a gift for his publisher whom he would be accompanying to the baths that afternoon; this would be perfect.

Nowadays his visits to the baths were for leisure and social purposes or for occasional business meetings, as was the case today. Aspar smiled to himself, recalling how different it had been when he had first returned to the city as Glaucus' glamorous new recruit. It was the policy of the old pimp that newly purchased slaves should work the public baths so that their charms might be exposed to the greatest number of potential clients. For this purpose, he permanently rented a row of luxurious rest-rooms at the Thermae Neronis in the Campus Martius, one of the oldest and most splendid of the city's luxury bath-houses. For the first few months of his employment in the House of Glaucus, therefore, Aspar spent most afternoons and evenings standing naked outside the curtained cubicle assigned to him. He never had to wait long between clients; the wily old pander knew that at the baths he would recoup his investment fast, as his boys could service numerous clients in a single evening. Many wealthy Romans remembered Aspar, the Slave King, from his first sojourn in Rome under the patronage of Valerius. This reknown, plus the fact that his charms had grown with maturity meant that his services were booked up weeks ahead. Hermes the Armenian, still one of the chief attractions of Glaucus' establishment, kept a watchful eye on the Dacian whenever they were on duty together. Any client planning to abuse the young man would soon change his mind when faced with the Armenian giant's menacing glare.

About six months after his arrival, Aspar was washing himself after the departure of a client, when his next appointment pulled back the curtain and entered the rest room. By the dim illumination of a single lamp, Aspar turned to see the burly outline of a soldier, small in stature, unhelmeted but in military dress, his chest glittering with medals: a centurion.

'Aspar?' The voice was familiar.

'Livius,' cried the Dacian as the man stepped into the light. The soldier had hired Aspar for the night, and the young king insisted on providing the services for which he had paid a substantial fee, although Livius was eager to assure him that this was not necessary. Aspar had not forgotten the soldier's kindness in the period he had spent with Valerius, and submitted to him willingly. Most of the night, however, was spent in conversation. As usual, Livius brimmed over with news, living up to his nickname of 'the oracle'.

The centurion explained how, disgusted at Valerius' treatment of his young hostage, he had applied for a transfer. He had been sent back to Dacia to join the tribune Proculus, who was engaged in the task of settling the country as a Roman province. Aspar steeled himself for news of his homeland and, indeed, it was depressing. The country had been divided into three and had been repopulated with Roman citizens from all over the Empire, while the former inhabitants had been sold into slavery. Livius was eager to point out, with a blush, that serving under Proculus he had learned to treat captives and slaves with respect. Aspar's eyes lit up when Livius casually mentioned that bands of Dacian rebels still eluded their Roman rulers in the north of the country, though they represented no real threat.

There was also news of Valerius. Although he had hired the best Greek surgeons, all operations to restore his looks had failed and the tribune had taken up a post on the eastern frontier of the Empire where several legions were permanently stationed to stave off the threat of Parthians and what was left of the Jewish resistance. He had vowed never to return to Rome, and his villa in

Latium was closed up while the palace in the Carinae district had been sold. Since then, nothing had been heard of him. His former clients, such as Glaucus, had been left to their own devices.

Livius had no regrets about parting with Valerius. On the contrary, he was delighted with life under his new commander. Proculus had just secured a post as tribune with the Praetorians, the Imperial bodyguard and the most prestigious corps in the Roman Army.

'I will be permanently garrisoned here in Rome, so I hope we can be friends. I have told Proculus much about you.'

Initially attracted by reports of the Dacian king's physical attractions, the tribune, a man of discernment, soon realised that Aspar had other, more intellectual talents, to recommend him. One evening, while dining at Proculus' Roman villa, at Livius' urging, Aspar began to tell the sagas of his forefathers. Since he had last recounted them to the soldier in the palace of Valerius, he had had much practice and had refined his story-telling technique. Proculus was spellbound and demanded more, becoming Aspar's first patron in Roman society.

Stepping out of the shade of Vicus Tuscus, Aspar began to feel the weight of his toga as he strode across the brilliant sunshine of the Forum towards his destination.

Even if he had wanted to, it was impossible for anyone living in Rome to forget Trajan's Dacian triumph. Five years after its victory in the north, the Imperial capital was still basking in the fruits of its success. The gold looted from Decebalus and his allies, which had become the personal property of the Emperor Trajan, made him richer by far than any of his predecessors. Wisely, however, he had used this wealth to benefit his people, providing games and festivals and initiating charitable schemes in favour of the Empire's numerous poor citizens.

The most spectacular example of Imperial munificence, however, was the vast programme of public works which had turned the centre of Rome into a vast building site. The recently completed Thermae on Mount Oppius overshadowed and dwarfed the Baths of Titus which, up to that point, had seemed an architectural marvel. Aspar now approached the most ambitious of all the Emperor's projects – his new Forum, not yet complete, although parts of it were already in operation. It was a public complex on a scale never before seen in Rome, comprising a law court, two libraries – one for Greek and one for Latin manuscripts – and, most popular of all, a five-storey, semi-circular covered market. Each day, more of the scaffolding which concealed the structure was dismantled, revealing the splendour of its design and ornamentation.

As he wandered past the shops of the lower gallery of the market, overflowing with colourful displays of fruit and flowers from many parts of the Empire, Aspar was distinguished among the milling throng only by his looks and his bearing. He hardly shared their enthusiasm for the new building, however – although he hid his feelings skilfully, the new Forum, which had been under construction since his return to Rome, was a constant reminder of the crushing defeat the Empire had inflicted on his people. The cynical words which Trajan had had engraved in massive letters on the four walls of the law Court were also etched in his mind: E Manubiis – From the Booty.

Aspar's apparent compliance with the role assigned to him by his Roman masters had aroused bitter criticism among sections of the large Dacian slave population of the capital. In the fluid social order of Rome, the status of former Dacian citizens had been scrambled. A handful of Aspar's former subjects had already been manumitted and ran their own businesses under the patronage of their former masters; others occupied positions of influence in wealthy households. Their king, on the other hand, though celebrated, had the status of a male whore and a slave.

Shortly after his arrival, Aspar encountered a former bodyguard of his father's, now a slave in the household of one of

Glaucus' distinguished clients. After an exchange of pleasantries, the man broached the subject which really concerned him – revolt against Rome. 'Many would be ready to fight – what they lack is a leader. They would follow you, my king.'

'What with the Praetorian guard and the other legions garrisoned here, crushing a slave rebellion in Italy would be like swatting a fly. No, another kind of warfare is necessary: a sustained assault where the Empire is weakest – on her borders. And for that an alliance between her enemies is needed.'

The man nodded slowly.

'And how many of the Dacian slaves would be ready to fight? Remember: most of them live more comfortably here than they ever did as free men in our own country. The Empire's strength lies not so much in its cruelty to opponents in war but its kindness to enemies in defeat.'

The other man averted his gaze in embarrassment. 'My king,' he began, hesitantly, 'some of our people say that you have capitulated to the enemy. They wonder how you can submit to... this kind of life.'

'As a whore to Rome?'

'Yes,' replied the man dully, dropping his eyes to the mosaic pavement.

'And if I were to rebel, or to attempt escape, what good would it do? How far do you think a renegade slave would get in an Empire that stretches thousands of miles in every direction – especially a slave as well-known as I, one who is on nodding terms with the Emperor himself? No, my plans are based on the long view. I have gained the confidence of my Roman masters. I have learned much about the Roman mind. I am respected and one day I will be able to buy my freedom, perhaps achieve riches, have liberty of movement throughout the Empire. Only then I will make my move.'

The other man looked up. His eyes shone. 'So you have not given in to Rome, as they say?'

'No, my friend.'Aspar smiled. A distant look came into his eyes. '"It is in the uncertainty of the outer world that we find inner strength." However it might appear, in my heart I am still free. My father told me that I must live, even if that meant apparent submission to Rome. There was a moment, years ago, after I was sent to the mines of Hispania, when I lost hope. But the gods were with me: they sent me someone who restored my belief in the future and renewed my resolve.' He paused for a moment while the other Dacian hung on his words. 'The memory of that man has sustained me throughout these years in Rome,' he continued. 'I have never lost my dream of freedom – not just for myself, but for our people, for all those crushed by Rome.'

As Aspar reached the centre of the semi-circle of shops, he spotted Livius striding towards him, grinning broadly, decked out in the colourful scarlet and gold uniform of a Praetorian. The soldier's jaunty walk had not changed since the day Aspar had first seen him in his father's chambers in Sarmizegetusa.

'Am I late?' asked Livius breezily, linking Aspar's arm as they continued to walk around the curve of shops.

'In good time, as always: I heard the fifth hour sounded as I passed through the Forum.'

'So where shall we go to talk? A tavern? Or are you hungry? Perhaps we could have a bite to eat at one of the kiosks here in the market – I hear there is one that serves delicious new dishes from Mauretania.'

'First, I have something to show you – it's up here on the fifth floor of the market.'

The two men made their way to the broad stairways that allowed huge crowds to flow freely throughout the building. Livius chatted excitedly as they went. The purpose of their encounter was to discuss Proculus' latest project. In common with Livius' former commander, he was a reknowned party-giver in the capital. He had been invited to stage an evening's entertainment for the imminent opening of the Emperor's new Baths, the Thermae Traianae. The tribune had great faith in Aspar's artistic gifts and had asked him to collaborate with Livius on a theme for the revels.

As they made their way to the upper level of the market, Aspar, not for the first time, was conscious of the irony that the greatest kindness he had received in Rome had been from this man and his commander, both of whom he might one day have to face in battle. Indeed, private dinner parties between the three men had often ended in enthusiastic discussion between Aspar and Proculus on the strategies employed by the Romans in the various campaigns in which the tribune had taken part. Jugs and platters became siege weapons and formations of men, as they illustrated their ideas.

In this way, Aspar learned a great deal about the Roman military mind. Proculus, for his part, was impressed by the freshness of Aspar's ideas and particularly his insistence that the great mistake of the Dacian leaders had been to meet the Romans head on in battle. The young king was now convinced that they would have had greater success if they had split into many groups and made sorties from remote mountain hideouts. Then, the Romans would have been forced to divide their forces and to fight on unfamiliar terrain in which many of their battle techniques and weapons would have been useless. Certainly they would have been unable to obtain an outright victory and might eventually have decided it was better to give up this drain on their resources.

Proculus also listened intently to Aspar's ideas on the vulnerability of the Empire, how easy it would be to attack on several borders at once, if only its enemies were able to forge a workable alliance. He was quick to point out, however, that apart from the Parthians to the east and some of the northern tribes, most of Rome's potential enemies had either been crushed or had reached an accommodation with the Empire.

Sometimes in these discussions, Aspar experienced an inner conflict. He felt himself in the position of a spy, intent on extracting knowledge from these men; yet at the same time his affection for them and appreciation of their personal qualities continued to grow. After a while, he felt that there was an unspoken understanding between himself and Proculus. At the conclusion of one of their discussions, the tribune's animated features had stilled into seriousness: 'If the Dacians had followed your strategy, perhaps they would still hold their territory today. Certainly you would make an honourable opponent, Aspar.'

The two men had now reached the fifth storey of the covered market. One of the wonders of the new development, it was wholly dedicated to the selling of fish, most of them live. Aspar and Proculus inspected the astonishing variety on display, gathered from all over the Empire. Freshwater tanks were supplied directly from an aqueduct, while other tanks were replenished daily with sea water from Ostia.

As they watched customers selecting their purchases and the merchants catching them with nets, Aspar turned to Livius with a mysterious smile: 'This is my idea for Proculus' party.'

'What?' asked Livius blankly.

'This,' insisted Aspar, looking back into the pond of teeming sea creatures.

'Only you could have conceived of such a fabulous spectacle,' breathed Proculus as he watched the throng of illustrious guests process from the dressing rooms of the Baths and into the soaring caldarium. 'Look at them,' he whispered to Aspar. 'If they are impressed now, wait until they see the wonders you have prepared for them.'

The crowd of rich young Roman males preened themselves, twirling and posing to show off to one another the extravagant costumes of sea gods and monsters with which they had been fitted out by their host. Long stiff fish-tails, fins and headdresses sewn with glittering semi-precious stones and exotic feathers complemented flowing robes in shimmering translucent tones of turquoise and sapphire, shot through with threads of silver and gold. The costumes were designed in such a way as to show off the attributes of muscular naked bodies and also to ensure comfort in the heat of some of the halls. Aspar and Proculus joined the procession of Tritons, crocodiles, crabs, octopuses and river deities. The Dacian was costumed as the Nile god and Proculus as Tiberinus, the spirit of Rome's own stream.

The excited comments rose in volume and fractured into a thousand echoes as the men entered the domed caldarium and took in its wonders for the first time. Great gilded candelabra lit up the gold coffered ceiling, the sparkling mosaics of the walls and variegated marble of the pavement. Cast in gilded bronze especially for the occasion, the base of each lampstand rose to the height of three men and had been shaped to represent a sea creature, real or imagined. The great branches that sprouted from the top of each stand, spreading out like the foliage of a young tree, carried hundreds of hanging lamps. There was also a hint of the nature of the forthcoming entertainment – as if it were needed for this carefully chosen company – each lamp was in the form of an erect phallus, cast from life.

'I think you should come and check the preparations in the frigidarium,' panted a sweating Glaucus, as he waddled up to Aspar. The flowing fronds of the old pimp's costume were beginning to wilt and, with the great quivering folds of white flesh visible beneath, he resembled nothing so much as a large jellyfish.

'Have the costumiers and make-up artists finished their work?' Aspar asked the brothel-keeper.

'Yes.'

'And have the gantries been greased?'

'Yes.'

'And the scene-shifters are all at their posts?'

'Yes.'

'Then there is no need for me to come.'

'But will it work?' whined Glaucus, wringing his hands anxiously, numerous bangles jangling. 'I'm afraid my poor boys will get hurt. They have no idea what to expect. All my best lads are up there.'

'The equipment has been thoroughly tested and no one was hurt in the rehearsals. There is no need to worry. But it is important that neither the boys nor the guests know what to expect or half the impact of the moment will be lost.'

'I suppose that's right,' muttered Glaucus, chewing his lip.

'And just think what lustre this will bring to your house, Glaucus,' urged Proculus. 'This will be an evening that men will talk about for years to come, and your boys will be the wreath that crowns the event. Not to mention the genius of Aspar which brought it into being.'

'Yes, your lordship,' grunted Glaucus grudgingly, with a sideways glance at his celebrated slave.

'You'd better get back to your position, Glaucus,' Aspar gently encouraged his master, 'and wait for my signal. Serve the boys with wine: keep them relaxed.'

The last stragglers among the guests were now making their way into the caldarium. At a signal from Aspar, a group of musicians sounded a fanfare on rasping buccinae, which drew instant silence. A curtain embroidered with sea-scenes in shimmering colours was whisked upwards to reveal the circular pool in the centre of the vast chamber. At the same time, great chandeliers descended from the ceiling. They bore lanterns of coloured glass – emerald, amethyst, agate – which cast their gem-stained sea-shades through the mist that hovered over the surface of the water. A fine spray descended from above the pool, a translucent curtain, catching rainbows in its mesh.

Unearthly watery music of massed lyres drifted down from a balcony in the dome and a reciter announced the theme of the evening: The Gods Go Fishing. In verses Aspar had composed especially for the occasion, he proclaimed the arrival of the sea-gods. One by one, these spirits rose from the water, accompanied by young lads dressed as naiads and nereids, in scraps of filmy material that only served to emphasise their nakedness. The gods, on the other hand, had been selected for their impressive stature and masculine characteristics. Some were actors and mimes, others carefully chosen by Aspar from Glaucus' exoleti – the hairy, muscular, well-endowed members of his stable.

The audience gasped at the scenic effects as the gods appeared, one in a giant shell, another astride a dolphin, a third on the back of a giant crab. The naked body of each of the divinities was painted a different colour – pale purple, green, blue, yellow, silver, gold. They wore long glittering wigs of a matching shade, while their body hair was picked out with coloured spangles. Make-up lent a god-like power to their facial expressions.

Oceanus, Nereus, Glaucus, Proteus and Triton emerged from the water and appeared to hover above it. Blasts from bands of bronze buccinae rang out from numerous points above the heads of the audience, from the dome and the balconies halfway up the mighty pillars which supported it. The effect caused the audience to start and, as they looked up, broad columns of water shot down from the dome into the pool. At the same time, fountains soared into the air at points all around its circumference as from its centre a silver Poseidon, god of the sea, reared streaming from the water in a glittering horse-drawn chariot.

The audience gasped and applauded, but before they could recover from this effect, the figure of Poseidon began to glide over their heads in the direction of the tepidarium. The voice of the narrator bade the audience follow as curtains slowly opened across the arches that gave onto the great rectangular space. The vehicles of the other gods were manipulated by hidden stage-hands into various positions in the second hall. The naiads and nereids, meanwhile, spread out across the inlaid marble pavement and stretched giant webs of sparkling seaweed between them. They moved smoothly into the sinuous movements of a ballet, made more erotic by the fact that they barely wore any clothing. The dancers closest to the audience needed all their agility to avoid lunging hands, though some unfortunates disappeared into the crowd with a wild flailing of slender legs and arms.

The narrator announced the subject of the next section of the entertainment: the love of Poseidon for the beautiful youth Pelops. The chariot of the god glided slowly down the great hall where different scenes had been laid out, starting with the abduction of Pelops and climaxing with the rape of the youth by the god. This was not mimed but enacted by the performers before the large audience. The actor playing Poseidon was able to produce an erection on cue, so gargantuan that it could be clearly seen by every member of the astonished crowd. The howls and contented grunts of Pelops as the god entered him and began to thrust with his divine member were also genuine, as no man in the audience doubted, and a hush of mingled awe and lust settled over the crowd as the echoing cries of god and mortal signaled the ascent to climax. The roars of the pair as they shed their seed drew more than a few involuntary moans of orgasm from overexcited members of the audience. Aspar smiled to himself: he had anticipated this effect when he had cast Hermes the Armenian in the role of the Sea God.

A musical interlude gave both audience and performers a few moments' breathing space before the reciter proclaimed the crowning moment of the evening: the Creation of the Sea-creatures by the god Proteus.

As the crowd passed into the frigidarium, the low hum of conversation rose to a rumble of distant thunder, magnified by the walls that soared like multi-hued cliffs on all sides; this was the largest of the Thermae's chambers. The comments of the guests were stimulated not only by their first sight of the lavishly decorated bath-house and its great pool, but also by the scenic effects that Aspar had dreamed up.

He slipped through the crowds, closely followed by Proculus, to the position from which he would give Glaucus the crucial signal. The men exchanged satisfied glances as they observed the reaction of the audience. They stared mesmerised, jostling for poolside positions as Proteus, mounted on a huge undulating sea-serpent, skimmed across the rippling surface, flanked by a shoal of mermen on sea horses. The colourful creatures swooped over islands dotted round the pool, replete with real exotic trees and foliage imported from Africa, and sliced through the spray of waterfalls that plunged from rocky eminences towering into the shadows of the vaulted roof. A full orchestra accompanied their passage, including the ringing tones of a battery of water-organs which Proculus had shipped from Alexandria.

With gestures of his arms, the god invoked a storm. Claps of thunder were heard and slaves worked great wind and wave machines at either end of the pool. The audience were spellbound by the realistic effect, as trees bent in the gale and the islands were lashed by white-crested breakers. Above their heads, clouds of dark blue and purple silk covered the whole of the roof, billowing and seething.

Aspar followed the actions of the god intently. So far, the complex mechanical systems of wires, tracks and pulleys, aided by an army of stage-hands, had worked without a hitch. Would the climax of the evening come off with equal success? Proteus was now moving to an island at the centre of the pool, surrounded by his train of young men. Proculus was as caught up in the action as his guests, his excitement intensified by anticipation. Aspar looked up: he could see Glaucus peering down anxiously from the edge of a cloud. He glanced back to the action over the pool. The storm was at its height. Proteus hovered over the island. He raised his arms towards the clouds in a dramatic gesture.

'Spirits of the sea, come forth!' he called out. Fanfares and thunderclaps echoed all around as a gap opened in the clouds overhead and forks of lightning rent the sky. The guests began to applaud. Aspar looked up at Glaucus and gave a decisive nod. The old man's face disappeared behind the cloud-curtains. Aspar and Proculus experienced a moment of suspense and then a chorus of shouts drowned out the applause of the audience as a torrent of beautiful young men cascaded from the clouds and tumbled down the waterfalls, turning the pool into a frothing mass of bodies.

It was difficult to say who was more surprised, the boys who fell or the audience who watched. The applause grew, accompanied by shocked laughter. Aspar saw that his system of gantries that turned into chutes had functioned perfectly, in spite of the old procurer's misgivings.

Glaucus' boys, variously dressed as brilliantly coloured sea-anemones, fish and nymphs, had not been informed about what was to happen, but they did know that their task was to draw the audience into the melee. Those who recovered quickest, therefore, made their way to the sides of the baths and, slipping out of their costumes, turned somersaults in the water in order to display their charms. Meanwhile, slaves dressed as fishermen were moving among the audience and offering them every variety of fishing net with which to catch the creatures called forth by the god. Groups of guests cast great nets woven from gold and silver threads, while others pursued individual 'fish' with outsize versions of shrimping nets at the end of long poles.

Soon the islands and the caves that had been constructed in cliffs surrounding the pool were filled with writhing bodies, gorgeous costumes giving way to bare flesh, and the stately pageant was transformed into a landscape of unbridled license.

Aspar and Proculus wove their way through the crush of bodies that lined the sides of the pool as guests landed their 'catch'. They watched in amusement while a slippery haul of struggling arms and legs was pulled ashore at their feet. Aroused by the preceding spectacle and by the gyrations already taking place around them, the 'fishermen' grabbed at the anemones, water-sprites or fish that caught their fancy – sometimes two or three were bagged by one man, or else shared by a group of friends.

Faced with these scenes, Aspar and Proculus felt their own flesh begin to stir. One of the boy-nereids in the net had caught the eye of the tribune. Ripping off his own river-god costume, Proculus shoved the head of the youth towards his crotch, where the broad upward swoop of his member was already bobbing with anticipation. The lad looked up, eyes bulging with astonishment, as Proculus forced his cock down the tight corridor of the boy's throat. A professional, the young man fought back the urge to gag, even when Proculus grabbed handfuls of his long dark curls and began to batter roughly at his tonsils.

Aspar noticed one of the guests, a tall gangly youth, the son of a noble family no doubt, eyeing him lasciviously from an archway. When he returned the look with an encouraging raise of his brows, the lad, already stripped naked, hastened towards him and fell to his knees. He was transfixed by the young king's fabled pillar, its glistening mouth already aimed towards the ceiling, the large balls tight with arousal. Although his build was slight, the young man's muscles were hard and sharply delineated. Aspar gently placed his hands on the tight dark curls and the youth licked a drop of love-juice forcing its way from the slit. The full, loose foreskin had retreated a little, baring a perfect hemisphere of shining cockhead. Wetting his lips, the boy inserted the tip of his tongue between foreskin and glans, savouring the looseness of one and the glossy firmness of the other, pushing it down to meet the smooth furrow where they joined, running it to and fro. His own long slender appendage was already beating a lustful rhythm between his thighs, as he opened his throat and pushed remorselessly down until it wholly engulfed Aspar's hardness, releasing a hoarse sigh from the king.

Through half-closed eyes, Aspar saw that the boy's move had drawn others and he felt lips clamping onto his nipples and a slippery tongue teasing the velvety creases of his anus. Proculus' powerful form swayed an arm's-length away as the long-haired water-sprite sucked hungrily at his cock, broad and firm as a sea-cucumber. Somehow the lad's throat had miraculously accommodated itself to Proculus' outsize dimensions. The tribune reached over to Aspar and pulled the Dacian's mouth towards his own. As their tongues sparred fiercely, Aspar surrendered to the ministrations of the mouths feasting on his body.

Over Proculus' shoulder, Aspar spied a shimmering mountain of a man approaching, whom he recognised as Hermes in the guise of Poseidon. He felt the pressure on his rock-like manpole intensify and the speed of the strokes rapidly increase. He was aware of the sound of muffled screams and felt their vibrations against his member. Pulling away from Proculus for a second he saw that, with a meaty hand gripping each thigh, Hermes had pulled the gangly young man's arse up to the level of his own giant manhood so that his body was lifted clean from the marble pavement, while his mouth remained clamped to Aspar's column of gristle.

The Armenian had only managed to insert the fist-like head of his dick into the tight virginal arsehole. At first, the young man's legs kicked in helpless panic, like a trapped animal's, as he tried to accommodate such a huge cock. But then he pushed his hips back against the intrusion to facilitate total penetration. Grunting and thrusting his mighty buttocks, Hermes' monster inched into the boy's guts with agonising jerks, matched by the rising notes of the lad's screams of pleasure. It seemed that the process would never end until, with a final determined shove, the last of the huge bulk disappeared, and Hermes released a long sigh of satisfaction. The boy, incited by the delicious torment in his hole to suck ever-harder at Aspar's appendage, continued to whimper. His lusty moans grew louder again as Hermes began to bore into his hard butt-cheeks with all his considerable strength.

All around him, Aspar could hear the moist sounds of sex: wet lips sucking at his nipples, tongues slurping at his armpits or lapping up the juices of his rectum, the saliva of his own mouth mingling with that of Proculus. From all over the hall, similar sounds could be heard: a hundred pricks sloshing in the wetness of throats and loose, sloppy, man-cunts. In this watery setting, the flow of torrents of human secretions threatened to drown out the splashing of pools, fountains and cataracts.

Proculus pulled away from Aspar and turned the broad triangle of his back towards him, pushing his narrow hips out till the pert arsecheeks parted invitingly, the single pink eye of his anus staring up entreatingly. Aspar bent down to inspect the twist of flesh he had so often impregnated. He licked it with the flat of his tongue, the ripples of aromatic skin stimulating his taste-buds.

As Proculus began to groan, he tantalised the folds with his tongue-tip, darting it across the surrounding smoothness then flicking it directly over the sensitive opening. The tribune rubbed the star of his anus longingly over the Dacian's tongue and Aspar knew that it was time for him to join the quickening flow of man-juice that was coursing though the great Baths, just as tiny springs feed the sacred waters of the Nile or the Tiber.

Grasping the hardness of Proculus' hips, he plunged his tool into the satiny smoothness of the man's rectum with a feeling of infinite sweetness. This drew a heart-rending moan of pleasure from the tribune, as though Aspar had not only pierced his guts, but his soul. The gangly youth, still held aloft on the spit of Hermes' tree of life, had by now positioned his mouth around Proculus' pole and was sucking on it purposefully, thirsty for manseed. Aspar glanced towards the Armenian and saw that his dark eyes were fixed upon him. In a rush of tenderness towards the sweet-natured giant, Aspar leaned across Proculus' muscular back and thrust his tongue into Hermes' mouth. The Dacian saw tears of gratitude start into the wide eyes and heard a deep rumbling rise in the other man's chest.

Startled gasps came from Proculus as Aspar pounded his streaming pussy and the lad's throat polished his broad dick with its hard smoothness. Hermes pulled away from Aspar, throwing his head back and uttered cries that cut through the din of moans that grew in volume by the second. Each cry was accompanied by a fierce lunge that shook the slight frame of the lad that hung from his fuck-rod, as a torrent of semen catapulted into the youth's flaming back-passage. Hermes' cries tipped Proculus into orgasm and as hot gobbets of semen streamed down the young man's throat, the tribune's rectum bore down heavily on Aspar's vertical column. The young king felt his love-meat clench in an ultimate spasm before it shot liberating floods of life-giving fluid into Proculus' avid hole. Aspar was aware of cocks on every side disgorging their fertilising loads in mouths and arseholes, or simply shooting over faces and bodies, and he felt a profound satisfaction as his own juices joined the flow.

The tops of temples and palaces blushed pale-rose in the first light, as scores of litters jostled outside the Baths to transport the exhausted partygoers home. Proculus insisted on dropping Aspar off at Glaucus' House. It was only a short distance, but they made slow progress, weaving their way through heavy carts stacked with building materials, hurrying to their destinations before the first hour of day, when wheeled vehicles were banned from the city centre.

Proculus settled back against the silk cushions with a satiated sigh. 'Years from now, the men who attended tonight's party will still be saying "Do you remember that party Proculus threw for the opening of the Baths". And it's all thanks to you, Aspar, my friend.' He pulled a purse from his belt. 'I want you to have this.'

'No, no,' said Aspar embarrassed, gently pressing the tribune's hand away. 'I have much to thank you for. What I did was for the sake of our friendship.'

'Take it,' said Proculus firmly, placing the leather pouch in the Dacian's lap. 'I think you'll find that it contains more than enough to buy your freedom. Certainly sufficient to stimulate Glaucus' greed. And if he has any objections to a gift of money, tell him to address them to me – I am one of his best customers, after all. And the payment is in recognition of your contribution as an artist and not for the services in which Glaucus' establishment specialises.'

Like the other weary members of the household, Aspar spent most of that day sleeping. Towards evening, he made his way to Glaucus' study, through the yawning boys and men straggling out of their cubicles towards the villa's bath-house.

'Well done, my boy,' said Glaucus effusively, waddling up to Aspar as he entered the room. He clapped the young man on the shoulder, his wrist clanking with even more baubles than usual, and led him by the elbow to a couch. The pimp sat down at his desk. 'Last night's splendid entertainment was the start of a new era for the House of Glaucus. I admit I had my doubts whether it would work or not. But now I'm convinced. I haven't been able to rest yet; so many clients have dropped by requesting your services to stage similar events.'

'That's just what I want to talk to you about,' began Aspar, moving to the edge of the couch.

'Good, good,' encouraged Glaucus. 'I have every faith in any ideas you suggest.'

'But there aren't going to be more ideas,' protested Aspar.

The pimp stared at him blankly, his heavy lower lip hanging open, dewlap aquiver.

'You know that I have asked you many times before to allow

me to buy my freedom, as is my right. Well now, as a "thank you" for my assistance with his party, Proculus has made me a generous cash gift that I think you will not want to turn down.'

'How dare he make a payment directly to you? And how dare you think that, at such a turning point in the fortunes of my establishment, I would be prepared to sell you? Why, I would be no businessman at all if I were to do that. It would be sheer financial folly.'

'I wonder what the Emperor would have to say about that. He is acquainted with my work. No doubt he will hear about the party, too, if he hasn't already.'

Glaucus hauled himself to his feet, folds of fat trembling with rage beneath his capacious tunic. 'Don't hold a knife to my throat, boy. I, too, have ties with the Imperial household. In fact, I have already received visitors from the palace today, inquiring about our involvement in a forthcoming banquet. I am prepared to allow you every privilege: a villa of your own, a place in the country. I will not even oblige you to carry out the duties expected from every other member of my household – but freedom is out of the question.'

Shaken by Glaucus' rebuff, Aspar walked back to his quarters without returning the excited congratulations of the colleagues he passed in the corridors. One young servant caught him by the arm outside his room. 'A gentleman is waiting to see you. An old friend, or so he says.'

Aspar brushed him aside. 'I am in no mood to meet anyone at the moment, whoever they claim to be.'

'Aspar, I –' protested the youth. But the young king had withdrawn into his chambers, slamming the door firmly behind him.

One of the servants had already lighted the lampstand by his writing-desk. Aspar slowly crossed the room and stared at a roll of parchment which lay open on his desk. He frowned uncomprehendingly. A familiar object lay across the last words he had written.

Without thinking he reached out and tenderly stroked the comforting warmth of the wood. His mother's talisman – the one he had given to Zosimus at their parting. How did it get here? He was filled with sudden fear. What did it mean? Could Zosimus be in trouble? Worse still, was he dead?

Aspar turned abruptly as he heard a noise behind him. In the penumbra behind the door was the silhouette of a man. The richly embroidered toga marked him out as a wealthy eastern merchant, yet there was no mistaking the strong outline of the shaved skull.

Eight

Aspar mouthed his lover's name and stumbled back against the desk.

Zosimus had scarcely stepped away from the door when the Dacian collided roughly against him, pressing his mouth fiercely to the soft lips of the Ethiopian, clutching at the firm arms and shoulders of his friend as though desperate to convince himself that this was not a trick of the imagination.

'I'm here to fulfil the pledge we made all those years ago,' said Zosimus, gently pulling away.

'But how did you find me? Not a day has passed when I haven't thought about you and wondered what had become of you.'

'Your fame has spread throughout the Empire,' smiled Zosimus. 'Even in Antioch we have heard of your book – my master has his own copy. Of course, as soon as I read it, I knew it was yours, even though your identity was disguised.'

'But how did you get here – and why are you dressed like this?' Aspar laughed, standing back to admire his friend's splendid garb. 'Are you a freedman?'

'Strictly speaking, yes. My master freed me last year when he made me his chief steward. I have a villa of my own in Antioch.' Zosimus took Aspar by the shoulders, his eyes shining. 'It's a wonderful place, Aspar – full of glorious buildings spread over steep hills. At night, the streets are as bright as day; not like Rome. They call it the City of Lights. One day soon, you will see it, too.'

'What sort of host am I?' cried Aspar, taking Zosimus by the arm and leading him into his luxurious triclinium. He gestured towards a couch. 'Make yourself comfortable. Do you need to bathe? Should I order supper?'

'I arrived yesterday at Ostia and spent the night at my master's villa here in the capital. I have just come from the baths. But I would welcome something to eat.' Zosimus stretched himself out on the couch, without taking his eyes off Aspar. 'My feelings for you have never wavered and now I am with you again, I realise they have only grown.'

Aspar smiled. 'It is the same for me, too.' He rang a bell and ordered supper. 'This is a high-class establishment,' he assured his friend, with a grin. 'The food is very good.'

'Yet how different everything is for both of us,' said Zosimus, suddenly serious. 'Here am I, a freedman, rich, with my own villa. The Empire has given me much. And you, Aspar –' he looked around at the lavish frescos and heavy tapestries adorning the walls '– this is a world away from our life in the mines. It seems Rome has been generous to you, too. You are a famous writer. What has brought us to this point? What thoughts and emotions have we experienced these last five years? What has it meant to you to have existed in this place? I'm sure you must have changed in your spirit. I certainly have.'

'You still haven't told me what you are doing in Rome,' repeated the Dacian impatiently.

'I am here on my master's behalf, accompanying his fleet with a cargo of rare goods brought from the east by the caravans of Arabia. But I also came to find you. I have brought money with me to purchase your freedom.'

'I am afraid that is impossible,' said Aspar with a sad smile. 'Not even all the freight from your master's ships would be sufficient.' And he explained to his lover how valuable he had proved to his master.

When the supper arrived, the two men found they had little appetite for food. Aspar bolted the door of his quarters and, tearing their clothes off in eagerness, they fell upon each other, consumed with an urgent need to rediscover one another's body and fill the gap of empty years. Aspar pushed the Ethiopian back onto his desk and stooped to take the long dark member between his lips. He sighed deeply as he slipped his tongue into Zosimus' foreskin and tasted the fragrant cockhead. Bending further, he received the full length of the weapon effortlessly into his throat, feeling the hood slip smoothly away so that the sensitive sheen of the glans caressed his gullet. Now it was Zosimus who exhaled, as though a soothing balm had been administered to an ancient pain. Aspar constricted his throat, making slow circular movements of his head so as to stimulate every part of his partner's prick. Zosimus gasped, arching his back and pressing his crown against the wall.

'How I've missed that – you,' Zosimus whispered.

Drawing his head back, Aspar sucked hard on the glossy head, further engorging it until it was marble-firm. Zosimus groaned with the pleasurable ache. Pushing his throat down again over the twitching organ, Aspar let its hammer-head click firmly over the threshold of his throat again and again, sending a shudder through the other man's body each time. Releasing Zosimus' cock from his mouth, Aspar knelt and began to tease the sensitive skin of the Ethiopian's groin with his tongue. His saliva spurted as he tasted and smelt the other man's musky scent and trickled down Zosimus' velvety scrotum.

Aspar pulled with his lips on the skin between cock-root and thigh, sliding his tongue firmly along the trapped fold of flesh. Zosimus began to writhe, eyes closed in ecstasy, rubbing his head against the wall. With one hand sliding the loose satiny skin over the proud erection, Aspar moved his head to the other side, running his tongue lightly over the testicles, and began gorging on the skin of the groin, inflamed by the spasms he caused in his partner's body.

Aspar stood, pulling Zosimus' hips towards him and pushing back his knees so that his dark anal star was poised on the desk's edge. Bending to inspect it lovingly for a moment, Aspar began to attack it with darts and swoops of his tongue. He spat hard, and then spread the glistening blob across the dark-pink crater of wrinkles with his tongue-tip. Clasping his mouth around the circle of loosened skin, Aspar began to stab hard at its opening with his tongue.

His own cock stood white and rigid between his parted thighs and the cool of its juice streamed down its length. Feeling the urgent thrusting of his lover's pelvis, he knew he could hold back no longer and, pushing himself to a standing position, skewered the man's vitals with his pole. The long groans that escaped from both men's throats were expressions of pure pleasure and the movements of their hips as they thrust towards one another in perfect rhythm showed that a single will united their bodies.

Aspar felt Zosimus' arse-juices flooding round his lunging prick as he rampaged towards an unstoppable climax. Powerful jets of spunk catapulted from his slit into his lover's vitals again and again, matched by the thin white strands hurtling across the hard abdomen from his lover's rampant manhood.

For some minutes, they stayed as they were, spent but unable to bear the ache of breaking this intimate position, feeding gently from each other's mouth. But after its short repose, Zosimus' long dark manhood was already rearing up and unsheathing the glossy plum of its glans. Without a word, Aspar disengaged himself from his partner's vitals with a generous outpouring of mingled love-juices. Taking Zosimus by the arm, he crossed the room to his low bed and, turning his back to the other man, squatted on its edge, leaning his palms against the walls and thrusting his spread anus outwards.

The hole was already rosy and moist as a sea-anemone and Zosimus' man-pole, still sticky with its own spurtings, slid comfortably into it. Zosimus pressed his abdomen to Aspar's muscular back and thudded fiercely, as though he needed to reassure himself with the intensity of the feeling that the reunion was truly taking place. Leaning back in order to see his rod going into his lover's body, he withdrew its full length and froze, watching the hole gaping and drooling in anticipation. Aspar, knowing what Zosimus wanted without being told, pushed back onto the horizontal weapon until it was fully embedded, repeating this again and again until the madness of Dionysus descended once again on the two men and they soared towards climax.

Zosimus emitted staccato shouts as a second, even more intense orgasm, edged with pain this time, overwhelmed his strong frame. As he sluiced his lover's innards with heavy ballfuls of come, it was as if the sap was rising not from his groin but his mind and, as the scalding libation drained into the other man, so did his consciousness. Transfixed by the sensation of Zosimus' essence coursing through his guts, Aspar's cock began to leap convulsively, splattering the wall above his bed with skeins of spunk. As the two men collapsed onto the bed, Aspar clasped Zosimus to him. Silently, he watched his own semen refract the bright colours of the fresco as it clarified and thinned, slipping down across them, and he wondered if he could face a second parting.

Although over the next weeks Aspar fulfilled his duties in the House of Glaucus – which now mainly consisted of planning banquets for wealthy clients and various administrative duties – he snatched every moment he could with Zosimus. The two men spent most of their nights in Aspar's quarters and each afternoon would attend the baths before dining alone together. Zosimus had planned to spend most of the summer in the capital, returning to Antioch before the end of the sailing season. This was still a long way off, and Aspar preferred to concentrate on the present.

One morning in July, the two men were browsing among the stalls of the many scroll-vendors of the Vicus Sandalarius on their way to Aspar's publisher – whose factory was situated on the Esquiline Hill, close to the vast papyrus and parchment warehouses. Although it was still early, the sun beat down remorselessly. The two men pored over a new map of the Empire. It was one of the first to feature Dacia, now carved into three provinces.

'Remember the plans we used to make in the mines?' said Aspar, glancing up at Zosimus. Zosimus nodded solemnly.

'I have never lost hope that we would win our freedom and fulfil those dreams. But in spite of everything, they are still beyond my grasp.'

'We will find a way of securing your freedom, Aspar. I live for the day when you will join me in Antioch. And until then, I will visit you here.'

'And then from Antioch, where will we go?'

Zosimus placed his hand over Aspar's. 'First, let us win your freedom.'

They continued up the hill arm in arm, dodging passers-by in order to stay under the shady awnings of the shops; the Empire was at peace and the city was flooded with soldiers on leave. 'I find you much changed in these years,' said Zosimus. 'I was right when I said that your spirits were strong with you. You have grown inside: you are more sure, yet you have learned patience.'

'I only feel impatient at the thought of losing you again. I have to admit, though, that being alone these years, I have had to find strength in myself. I learned so much from you in Hispania. But we needed to part so that I could make that wisdom my own. However,' he added hurriedly, with a laugh, 'now I have absorbed those ideas, being together is certainly better.'

Aspar found his patience tested to the limit that night. Now that he was no longer required to service Glaucus' clients, he had been assigned other obligations. Glaucus had secured the franchise to provide boys for hire in the new Baths of Trajan. Some evenings, Aspar was required to supervise the operation. Tonight, he was seated in his cubicle at the end of the row where Glaucus' team were lodged. He had had a small table installed and would take a manuscript with him so that he could while away the hours working on his new book. The boys brought him the money after the departure of each client, which he placed it a cash box and noted in the ledger.

He had a single lamp burning; clients preferred this area to be dimly lit. Although he had every intention of working on his new publication, now nearing completion, all he could think of was his appointment with Zosimus later that night. The curtain of the cubicle was open a chink so that he could keep an eye out for trouble in the corridor. There was continuous movement of naked bodies and a padding of footsteps as customers paced up and down, idly inspecting the merchandise. Aspar was staring blankly at this endless procession when something caught his eye: a phallus of unmistakable shape – long and curved downwards like a bow. He looked up towards the face of its owner, but it was masked by a gold helmet that completely concealed the wearer's identity. From the symbols and sculpted scenes that adorned it, Aspar recognised the helmet as an image of the god Vulcan, the god of fire, disfigured by his lameness. It confirmed Aspar's suspicions. He quickly snuffed out his candle. He had dreaded this moment, as indeed had his master, Glaucus: the tribune Valerius was back in Rome.

It was many years since Aspar had incurred his wrath and been despatched to the mines, but the Dacian suspected that Valerius' desire for vengeance had not abated. It was not difficult to predict his reaction on discovering that the youth who had put paid to his lofty ambitions had not been languishing in the gold mines of

Hispania all these years, as he had supposed, but living in relative luxury as the protégé of his own former slave, Glaucus. Hermes was on duty at the Baths that evening and, when he came to Aspar's cubicle to hand over his earnings, the young king hurriedly explained what had happened and asked him to take over the supervision of Glaucus' boys.

Anger flashed across the face of the Armenian. He clenched his fists and the muscles of his arms knotted like stout tree branches. 'Where is he? He won't harm you when I've finished with him.'

'That would not be a good idea,' said Aspar soothingly. 'The penalty for a slave who assaults a soldier, and a tribune at that, is death. No, I need to disappear, and quickly.'

Despite the oppressive heat of the summer night, he wrapped a cloak around his head and slipped out of the cubicle. Once outside the Baths, he ordered his litter-bearers to travel quickly to the the Vicus Longus where he knew Zosimus awaited him.

But when he entered the triclinium, he saw that Zosimus was not alone. Proculus and Livius were also present and Aspar could tell from their expressions that they had been engaged in serious conversation. Zosimus rose anxiously to his feet as his lover entered.

'You know Valerius has returned,' said Aspar as soon as his eyes met the other man's.

'He came to my villa looking for Livius this afternoon, to see if he had news of you,' Proculus interjected. 'Rumours from Rome had reached him. He is here to find you.'

'So his anger has not faded.'

'He's more bitter than ever after all these years in exile, Aspar. He means to destroy you, whatever the consequences.'

'Of course we told him nothing,' added Livius. 'In fact, we tried to deliberately throw him off the scent. But it's only a matter of time before he tracks you down. He probably already knows where to find you.'

'He was at the Baths tonight. I'm not sure whether he was looking for me there.'

'You must come with us now,' said Proculus. 'You can take refuge in the villa until we can smuggle you out of the city.'

'I will be able to arrange passage on a ship from Ostia,' put in Zosimus.

'Wait,' Aspar protested. 'You've forgotten one important thing: I am not free to go.'

Zosimus took a step towards him and clasped him by the shoulders. 'You are now,' he said softly. 'I have spoken to Glaucus and he is only too willing to get you off his hands. I have paid for your freedom. There are the documents,' he added, indicating sealed tablets on a bronze table. 'Now he's desperately trying to think up what to tell Valerius when he catches up with him,' he chuckled.

'Why didn't he just hand me over and let him do his worst?' said Aspar gloomily.

'He's decided to lie low, hoping that Valerius will give up the search. To have a murder on the premises would be very bad for business.'

Zosimus had already packed a few things that Aspar would need over the next few days. He assured him that he would attend later to other matters, such as the valuable goods that constituted the Dacian's considerable wealth, which he would certainly need wherever he was to take refuge in the Empire.

In spite of the differences he had had with his pimp, Aspar insisted on taking his leave of the old man. He found Glaucus pacing up and down in a state of acute anxiety, starting at every noise. Understanding that the old Greek just wanted to be rid of him, Aspar kept his farewells brief. Afterwards, as he hurried through the corridors to the tradesman's entrance, many of the boys and men of the House pressed gifts of precious objects and money into his hands. Proculus exited first and, once he had checked that the street was empty but for his litters and retinue of slaves, he called softly for the others to follow.

Aspar came last, but, just as he was about to slip through the door, he felt a heavy hand on his shoulder. Glancing up, he recognised the great bulk of Hermes. In the gloom, he could just make out that the giant's cheeks were wet with tears.

'Here,' came Hermes' rumbling voice, 'take this.' He thrust a bulging leather purse into Aspar's hands. From the weight, it was clear that it contained a considerable sum in gold coins. 'You will need it.'

'But, Hermes,' protested the Dacian, taken aback. 'With this you could buy your freedom.'

'Who would that benefit?' asked Hermes. 'You will put the money to better use. I have observed you carefully all these years, Aspar, and I know that you have not forgotten that you are a king.'

Aspar stared back at the Armenian for a moment. 'I know what I could make use of, Hermes,' he said rapidly. 'You. You speak the languages of the east – Armenian, Parthian – don't you?'

'Yes,' replied the other man, mystified.

'Why not come with me and help me with the task I hope to fulfil? My first destination will be Parthia. It will be an arduous journey and I could do with a bodyguard.'

The man's eyes widened. 'How could that be possible?' he asked, wonderingly.

'Wait here,' said Aspar and quickly conferred with Proculus.

The tribune, with Hermes' money in his hands, hurried back along the corridor to Glaucus' office and returned a few minutes later, beaming. 'I think he'd agree to anything, just so long as he's rid of you,' he whispered to Aspar and looked up at Hermes. 'You're coming with us. I'm returning tomorrow for the documents. Oh, here's your money back. I negotiated a special fee. But this is on one condition,' he added raising a warning finger. 'That you guard this man with your life, because many lives may depend on him.'

'If anyone as much as touches him –'

'Hurry up and get your things,' urged Aspar. 'We must leave.'

Over the next few days, reports reached Proculus' villa of Valerius' enquiries. The tribune now had few friends left in the city, so his progress was slow. There had been terrible scenes at the House of Glaucus, where the guards had had to physically restrain the tribune. Now they were posted at every entrance, day and night. Glaucus announced a holiday for his staff and disappeared from the capital.

In the meantime, Aspar discussed his travel plans with Zosimus.

'I would suggest Antioch, of course,' said the Ethiopian, 'but Valerius is certainly likely to pass through there if he returns to the eastern frontier. He might even be posted there, as it's the closest important city to the border.'

'But Zosimus,' protested Aspar, 'now the way is open to achieve our dream. Not Antioch – Parthia. The Parthians are still the most effective enemies of Rome; even now, there are rumours of a war, and they are former allies of my country. That is where we can learn the skills we need before we head for Dacia. Could you arrange a safe passage for me there? Then, on your return to the east, you could join me.'

'I could arrange it, I think,' replied Zosimus uncertainly. 'The overland trip to Parthia would be dangerous – you may have to convince their border troops that you are genuinely an enemy of Rome and not a spy.'

'Hermes could be of help with that.'

Zosimus took his lover's hands in his and fixed him in the eye. 'Are you sure that this is what you want? Would it not be better if you were to wait for me in Antioch, or nearby, and then we could decided what to do next?'

'No!' Aspar shot back, with a firm shake of his head. 'Thus far I have had to be patient: now it is time to act. Think of it – our chance to be together and do what we promised each other we would do.'

Aspar left the city a few nights later in an empty cart which had just discharged its load of masonry; it would be unlikely to attract suspicion as it left the gates used for deliveries at the rear of the villa. Aspar took his leave of Livius and Proculus in the courtyard of the villa. 'I won't ask where you are bound,' said Proculus as he embraced the Dacian. 'But I think I have a good idea. If we meet again, whatever the circumstances, remember that I have always admired you. You are truly the son of kings.'

Zosimus accompanied Aspar and Hermes on the bumpy jour-ney to the port. He had secured relatively luxurious quarters – a wooden cabin, in contrast to the flimsy tents of the other passen-gers – on a merchant ship bound for Seleucia, the port of Antioch. From there, the two men would take the overland route to Parthia with a merchant caravan.

Once Aspar's boxes had been loaded onboard, he descended to the dockside. This was the moment he had dreaded – separation from Zosimus. Who knew for how long?

Aspar clung fiercely to his friend, as though wishing them to be as fused physically as they had become in spirit. 'Let this separa-tion not be for too long,' he murmured. 'I will send word to you in Antioch so that you may join me.'

This met with silence. He felt the other man's chest heave in a great sob, and experienced a flutter of panic. Pulling away from Zosimus, he shook him roughly. 'What is it? Why don't you an-swer me?' For a moment his friend remained silent, his eyes down-cast. Then he looked up at Aspar and the trapped tears cascaded down his cheeks.

'Aspar, I can't join you. I kept the first part of our pledge and came to buy your freedom, but I cannot keep the second. For the first time since I can remember, I am a free man, doing work that I enjoy for a man I respect. I cannot return to the life of a renegade, little better than the slave's existence I led in the mines. I was hoping that, with time, you might have changed and that you would be satisfied with a life together. I found that you had indeed changed, but you had only become more determined. You have outgrown me.' He gripped Aspar's arms with painful firmness. 'You know what you have to do. But I cannot follow you.'

The sailors were casting off and the captain was calling impatiently to the passengers to cut short their farewells and board.

Aspar could not find the words to express what he felt. He had thought that all his hopes were about to be fulfilled and now the thing he had wanted most of all – a life with Zosimus – had been snatched from him. He clung hard to the Ethiopian. Then, tearing himself away, he hurried up the steep gangplank to where Hermes stood silently on the deck. Fighting the sharp pain in his throat, Aspar watched Zosimus, who stared motionless on the dock until the ship pulled out of the port and penetrated the veil of darkness suspended across the harbour mouth. Still, Aspar remained by the rail, his eyes fixed on the great fires that burned day and night atop the twin lighthouses flanking the harbour. Finally, these dwindled to guttering red specks before they were snuffed out by the night and the ship sailed on alone, cocooned in blackness.

Nine

For much of the long sea journey east, the ship ploughed a solitary course out of sight of land, making slow headway against opposing winds and currents. For Aspar, its inexorable progress only served to widen the breach between himself and Zosimus. Their parting in Hispania had been merely physical. This severance cut far deeper. The Dacian king felt as though a vital organ had been torn from his body by some form of barbaric waking surgery. In endless rambling mental dialogues, he berated his lover for betraying the pledge they had made in the mines. Despite the humiliating existence he had been forced to endure in Glaucus' house, he had managed to keep the flame of that dream alive. Why had Zosimus not been able to do the same?

Yet what his head knew to be true – that a decisive break had taken place – his heart was unable to grasp. Sometimes a thought would come to him and he would turn eagerly to share it before he remembered that Zosimus was no longer there and the words would wither on his lips. Each time the realisation came with re-newed pain, a wound reopened by a fresh blow. Hermes left him alone with his thoughts, but was quietly attentive to his physical needs: ready with a cloak or a counterpane against the stiff sea-breezes; preparing hearty dishes with the generous supplies pro-vided by Proculus.

Sleep was his only relief, and Aspar spent much of the journey in his berth, by day and night, even though, in his dreams, Zosimus was always present. He was oblivious to the cries of the sailors as they called the watches or lustily sang bawdy shanties when they trimmed the sails. He missed the glories of Rhodes and the shimmer of the acropolis crowning the cliffs over Lindos. By the time they docked at Myra in Asia Minor, the last stop before Seleucia, time and endless hours of unconsciousness had dulled the acuteness of his pain, just as the ship's wake had faded in the ceaseless churning of waves and currents.

Disembarking at Seleucia, they travelled up the Orontes to Antioch, where they joined the caravan belonging to Zosimus' merchant master. The stewards and slaves enquired eagerly after Zosimus' health. Aspar left it to Hermes to reply. These men would be the guides with which they would travel overland on the trade routes that crossed the Parthian Empire. Now, slowly, Aspar's thoughts began to turn towards his future plans. After so many years of setbacks, he was in a position to fulfil his father's last wish. And though nothing could alleviate his sense of loss, this goal became his lodestar, the one thing that could give his life meaning.

The summer was now over and Aspar had determined to make for Ctesiphon, Parthia's winter capital. There, he hoped to gain admission to the circle of the Parthian King of Kings, Osroes, Brother of the Sun and the Moon. At Carrhae, Aspar and Hermes left the caravan and journeyed south by camel, along the banks of the Euphrates. On this last leg of the journey, the gentle Armenian proved invaluable. He knew the best times of the day or night to travel and was able to avoid the dual dangers of desert journeying – bandits and dangerous terrain – which always had proved fatal to wandering foreigners. To Aspar's surprise, many of the inhabitants were of Greek descent, and indeed most of the educated Parthians spoke the language. Nevertheless, the simple populace only spoke Parthian, and Hermes was able to barter with them for the necessities of life.

As they passed through towns and cities en route, Aspar gained a sense of the size and sophistication of this Empire which had decisively repelled the challenges of some of the greatest Roman generals. Dacia was indeed a backwater compared to this. Gradually the desert wastes melted into the fertile plains of Mesopotamia, irrigated by a network of broad canals along which dhows floated serenely like huge white birds. Peasants busily harvested abundant crops of fruit and grain. What ingenuity, thought Aspar, that could transform a landscape, and what a cornucopia of riches had resulted.

When he glimpsed the red walls of Ctesiphon, towering over an ocean of lush green palm-groves, he felt that here was a capital that bore comparison with Rome itself. Documents provided by Zosimus, giving the two men the status of merchants, gained them admission to the capital as they had granted them passage through the Empire so far. Traders were welcome here, much of Parthia's wealth stemming from taxes imposed on the caravans that travelled the country's vital trade routes.

Once inside the walls, Aspar pursued the plan that he had had in mind from the start – to trace the family of Prince Surena, the companion of his youth. He knew that Surena's father was a member of the royal household and that therefore there was a chance that he would be present in the city.

Hermes found them lodgings in a rough inn of mud bricks. The owner was a sharp-eyed old widow who demanded a week's payment in advance for a pokey airless room with a stinking pile of straw for bedding. While she counted their money, the old crone recited a long list of house rules. Aspar and Hermes began their search, hampered by the fact that one of them had to remain behind at the inn to keep an eye on their luggage. In the shadow of the city's mighty temples and palaces snaked a maze of dark, narrow alleyways. They soon realised that the society it contained was equally labyrinthine. The king was rarely glimpsed by his people, dwelling with his court behind a carefully maintained veil of mystery.

At first, it seemed that every member of the population could claim intimate friendship with the family of Surena, but once bribes had changed hands, little information was forthcoming. On a number of occasions, Hermes or Aspar would follow garrulous guides through the honeycomb of twisting lanes, facing constant demands for more money in order to reach their destinations. Once their informant was certain that they had no more cash about their person, they would suddenly find themselves alone and back in front of the lodging house. They did learn, however, that Surena's father had been dead some for some years and that he had been succeeded by his son. As to his whereabouts, all enquires proved fruitless.

By the end of the first week, Aspar was beginning to lose heart. Alone in the grimy room, as he waited for Hermes to return from another round of questioning, he pondered what other means they could employ to gain access to the king. The old hag chose this moment to demand another week's money and to exchange the filthy pile of straw for what appeared to Aspar to be another equally dirty heap. He waited on the balcony overlooking the courtyard of the inn, while she staggered in and out of the room with armfuls of the foul stuff, wheezing and coughing in the clouds of evil-smelling dust she raised.

Hearing a commotion below, Aspar peered over the parapet and was surprised to see a band of mounted noblemen crowding into what passed for a courtyard, their glittering splendour emphasised by the squalor of the surroundings. Horses and riders were decked out in brilliantly coloured silks with headdresses and weapons of gold – Aspar recognised the costumes as those of light cavalry. The widow darted onto the balcony by Aspar's side. With an alarming shriek, she grabbed a broom and rushed downstairs. 'Get those horses out of here,' she yelled, dealing out hefty blows to right and left. 'I won't have them doing their business in my nice clean yard.'

The horsemen roared with amusement. 'I'm more concerned about what they might pick up here than what they might leave behind them, old woman,' laughed the commanding figure, who was clearly the leader of the group. 'Our horses take more baths in a week than you do in a year.' The young nobleman cut an impressive figure, his broad, hard frame visible under the light robes. He was bare-headed, but for a thin pearled diadem of gold filigree. His dark hair and beard were oiled and curled in an elaborate style and his eyes, brows and mouth were dramatically emphasised with make-up.

'I run a spotless establishment, and I won't have it said otherwise,' shrilled the widow, striking out at the horses and riders, who laughingly ducked her blows. 'I'll appeal to the judges, if I have to.'

The lead rider looked up as Aspar craned over the balcony in order to see better. His face broke into a broad grin of recognition and he leaped from his horse and darted into the inn, racing up the stairs three at a time. The Dacian was lifted from his feet and spun round in the young nobleman's tight embrace. The dark-red lips pressed hard against his. Then he was deposited shakily onto his feet.

'Aspar – it really is you!' cried the man in Greek and, clasping the king to him, span him round again. When he had regained his balance, Aspar peered into the handsome face. This was no longer the slender, pretty youth he had known back in Dacia, but a sturdy, vigorous warrior. Still, though the years had wrought much transformation, the warmth of Surena's smile remained unchanged.

'Yes, it's me,' laughed Aspar, grabbing his friend's arm to steady himself.

'It's taken me days to track you down,' cried Surena, clapping his palms to Aspar's cheeks. 'Rumour flies swifter than an arrow in Ctesiphon. But finding the archer is a much slower business. We must have ridden the length of the Euphrates, twisting and turning round the lanes of the city.'

'And we did the same in search of you,' smiled the Dacian. 'Two people could spend a year trying to find one another in this place and their paths would never cross.'

'Little Aspar,' grinned Surena, playfully mussing his friend's blond hair. 'How you've grown. A man now – and a king I hear.'

'You, too – I hear.'

'I never thought I would see you again,' said Surena, suddenly pensive. 'We heard of Decebalus' defeat, the fall of Dacia, the thousands executed or sold into slavery. My father tried to find news of you, but without success.' He clutched Aspar's hand. 'Many Dacian slaves were shipped across the Pontus Euxinus to Bithynia and Galatia, but all they could tell us was of the outcome of the war. From our spies in Rome we learned of your father's brave death in the arena. But of you we heard so many conflicting rumours: some said you had become the concubine of a tribune, others than you had perished as a slave in the mines. Then, recently, I received a report from one of our Roman informers.' The young man's brow darkened and his tone became angry. 'I didn't believe a word of it, of course – I threatened to have him killed unless he denied it.'

'And what did he say?'

Surena scowled at the beaten-earth floor. 'That you had become rich as a Roman whore.'

'I am touched by your constancy, Surena. All of those reports are true – and none of them. The real truth is that, before he died, my father told me to survive and fight to restore the fortunes of our people. That is what I have done these many years. And that is why I am here.'

'I knew it!' exclaimed the Parthian in delight, flinging his arms around Aspar's neck so tightly that he nearly choked him. 'And you have become more handsome than ever, my little king,' he whispered in the Dacian's ear so that only he might hear.

Surena insisted that Aspar should come with him at once to his palace; his men would await Hermes and arrange for the transfer of their luggage. Aspar and Surena rode together on the prince's horse, as they had done as boys returning from manoeuvres in Dacia so many years before. The widow was still screaming curses and waving her broom as they headed for the gate, but when Surena threw a handful of gold coins into the dust at her feet, her threats to sue for damages were abruptly cut short. As she grovelled among the refuse that littered the yard, hunting for the coins, she demonstrated a diligence that she had never bothered to waste on the care of her establishment.

After threading their way through endless tortuous alleys, Surena and Aspar passed, without dismounting, through heavily guarded gates in several concentric walls before taking a broad zigzagging path up what appeared to be an almost sheer cliff but was, in fact, the man-made base of the palace. As they cleared the high walls, Aspar could see over the low dwellings that constituted most of the city. Amidst these loomed colossal structures similar to Surena's palace, each built on a perfectly square base. Surena explained that the palaces belonged to the many noble Parthian families; the largest palace and temple complex, which towered over the others in the very centre of the city, was that of Osroes, the King of Kings.

As they entered the palace itself, Aspar was dazzled by the scale: tier after tier of gardens, courtyards, pavilions and great open halls. Here the din of the streets faded into the rustle of fountains, and the dust and stench gave way to the intoxicating scent of jasmine. Servants escorted the Dacian king to a suite of airy rooms, where he bathed and dressed in a short crimson tunic delicately embroidered with gold thread. They accompanied him to an open marble court where, under an awning, refreshments had been laid out on a table surrounded by couches in the Greek manner. Surena sprang to his feet as he saw Aspar approaching.

'That colour suits you,' he exclaimed. 'I thought it would – I chose it myself.' His Greek was excellent, with hardly a trace of an accent. He spoke in a rapid staccato fashion, as if to show off his proficiency in the language. Surena flung himself on a double couch and patted the space beside him, indicating where Aspar was to lie. The Dacian gazed around him in awe. On three sides of the courtyard rose vaulted halls, richly decorated with coloured tiles. Silk tapestries adorned the walls and intricately woven rugs covered the floors. The fourth side of the courtyard was open and afforded a magnificent view over the vast expanse of the city with its soaring palaces and gardens. Beyond the walls, the crumpled desert mountains glowed red in the late afternoon light.

Surena rolled over on his back and laughed delightedly at Aspar's awed expression.

'Now I understand why Rome fears Parthia – and covets it. This is a great empire that presents a real threat to Roman expansion,' said the king, turning to Surena.

'That may have been the case once,' replied Surena moodily, 'but now I fear we have too many internal divisions to be able to face Rome with the necessary strength. Many of the noble families ruling different parts of the empire are no longer loyal to the King of Kings. Rome is expert at exploiting divisions. Take Armenia, for example. Easily approached from the west. A treaty was made with Nero almost a century ago. If the Emperor can hold the present ruler to that old agreement, a large chunk of Parthian territory would be split off. That would provide an ideal base for attacking other parts of the Empire.'

'But your fighting methods have proved more than a match for Roman armies in the past,' insisted Aspar, sitting up. 'I have not wasted my time in Rome. I have learned a great deal about the Roman military mind. The Roman army is deployed as a single vast machine. Parthian tactics make use of many small groups, teasing and worrying the great Roman beast. This has confused their generals in the past and it could again. That is why I am here. Remember how you tried to teach me the skills of a Parthian archer? Well, now I want to become truly proficient in your kind of warfare. Then I will return to Dacia and train a rebel army, fighting from remote mountain areas. I am sure that a grand alliance between Rome's enemies could one day beat back her domination.'

Surena, who had listened to Aspar with a serious, steady gaze, now broke into a smile. He pulled the Dacian down towards him. 'You haven't changed much after all. Still as serious and enthusiastic as ever. I would be glad to train you – I'm sure you will make an excellent archer. Osroes is aware of your presence in the city and wants to meet you –' he pouted '– but all that will have to wait. First, I am going to be greedy and keep you to myself for a while.' He drew Aspar's mouth to his and, parting his soft lips, kissed him languidly.

Pulling away, Aspar began haltingly: 'Surena, I should tell you –'

'No,' interrupted Surena swiftly, placing his palm over Aspar's mouth. 'Let's not spoil it by telling. Why don't we just take up from where we left off? I would love to have again the passion I felt for you.'

Surena rolled Aspar onto his back and began to cover his face with soft kisses. The king felt the warm feelings of his youth rekindled. They came as a healing balm for recent wounds.

'I will never forget how you kept a homesick young Parthian warm on those cold northern nights,' smiled Surena, pausing for a moment. 'Before we went to sleep, you used to tell me those old stories you learned from your mother; even now, I think of them sometimes at night as I'm dozing off. Do you still remember them?'

Aspar chuckled. 'They have been my fortune these past few years.'

A thought occurred to the Parthian. 'One night, I will organise a banquet for the nobles of the court – perhaps even Osroes himself will honour us with his presence – and you can tell them your stories. Parthians love a good tale and they are always eager to hear new ones. But that must all come later. Tonight I have planned a feast in your honour, just for us.'

The intimate dinner party did not turn out quite as Aspar had envisaged.

He and Surena bathed together in the palace baths, which rivalled some of the smaller thermae of Rome in size and ornamentation. Slaves oiled and scraped their bodies, and coaxed Aspar's short hair into something resembling a Parthian style. After the two men had been anointed with perfumes that made Aspar dizzy with their sweetness, Surena insisted on selecting magnificent robes for them both from his own vast wardrobe. For Aspar he chose a tunic of peach silk, its wide border of gold set with amethysts. Over this Aspar wore a long cloak of the finest cloth-of-gold, held with a fibula in the form of an Imperial eagle. Surena himself picked a pale blue tunic whose silver border was scattered with garnets. His cloak was of spun silver. Both men wore wide belts in the Parthian style, of silver and gold encrusted with precious gems of every hue.

They were to dine together in one of the vaulted halls that flanked the courtyard. At least that was what Aspar understood. When they arrived at the archway which led into the central hall, however, he found that they were at the head of a procession of handsome, finely robed young aristocrats that stretched back into the shadows of a long high corridor. Surena led Aspar through the arch and the nobles paraded behind them. The Dacian saw that the hall was filled with numerous double couches, each with its own table laid with food on golden platters. Over the couches hung canopies of tapestry emblazoned with horses and riders in various military manoeuvres.

Surena and Aspar occupied a couch overlooking the courtyard. Around it were set a score of towering bronze lampstands, which Aspar had not noticed earlier. They represented the monstrous, many-headed Hydra that Jason fought in Colchis. Fire blazed from the open mouth of each head, bathing the courtyard in brilliant light. Beyond, the palaces and temples of the city were picked out by flickering torches. As he took his place on the couch, Aspar saw that not only their hall, but the two others on the second and third sides of the courtyard had also been similarly arrayed with couches and tables. Processions of young noblemen were taking their places there, too. Behind them, the couches of their own hall were filling up, but even these vast spaces had not been sufficient to accommodate the prince's companions-in-arms; at the foot of the steps that led down from each of the halls, more rows of tables and couches had been set out. Seeing Aspar's expression of bemusement, Surena shrugged. 'These are my men. We always do everything together – that is the Parthian way. Don't bother about them – they are family. Act as though we were alone.'

To the sound of fanfares, food was carried in on enormous platters by processions of naked slaves. They served chilled palm wine from golden jugs. The men drank with gusto from golden rhytons, drinking horns in the shape of legendary beasts or dancing boys. The wine issued in a jet from the narrow end of the horn – the mouth of the beast or the erect phallus of the boy – and Surena watched gleefully as Aspar gave himself a thorough soaking in his attempts to master it. During the meal, dancers performed among the diners. Aspar guessed that they were slave boys from Hispania: they performed the characteristic gyrations of the dances of Gades, bending backwards almost to the ground as they undulated their limbs.

Afterwards, at a signal from Surena, actors in masks ran into the courtyard and one of them announced in Greek a performance of

Aristophanes' comedy *The Knights*. The noblemen at the back of the halls crowded forward excitedly to seat themselves on the steps bordering the courtyard.

'They're a touring company from Greece,' Surena whispered to Aspar, throwing an arm over his friend's shoulder as he settled down to watch. 'I requested this especially for you. It's hilarious.'

'I know. It's a favourite of mine, too,' Aspar muttered back.

The audience was an appreciative one. They applauded spectacular moments, such as when one of the leading characters was borne in shoulder-high by a bevy of muscular Nubian slaves painted gold from head to toe. They roared with laughter at the antics of comic characters in the guise of ithyphalloi, sporting enormous fake penises. Surena clapped and laughed louder than anyone, throwing frequent sideways looks at Aspar to make sure that he was enjoying the performance. At one point, he was so overcome with delight at the success of the evening that he rolled on his back and kissed Aspar full on the lips. At first, the Dacian glanced around in embarrassment, but the other men were too absorbed in the play to pay them any attention.

When the actors had taken several bows in response to the wild applause at the end of the comedy, the men were left in high spirits. Aspar had noticed that the pairs on the couches appeared to consist of an older and a younger warrior, and guessed that these were lover and beloved as was the custom among his own people. Soon, this impression was confirmed as more and more of the couples grew amorous, kissing and caressing one another as though they were alone in their bedchambers. They began to shed their clothes, so that the halls were quickly filled with naked bodies absorbed in tender, passionate love-making. Slaves moved noiselessly between the couches, drawing curtains of coloured gauze around each of them. Although these concealed nothing, they symbolised the fact that each of the couples was oblivious to its neighbours.

Surena motioned Aspar to sit up on the couch and slowly removed the Dacian's light clothing, his deep eyes drinking in each part of his friend's body as it was gradually revealed. Once Aspar was naked, Surena shed his own robes, keeping his gaze fixed on the other man's face. He stretched out his long lithe body upon the silken couch, with the sensuousness and coiled strength of a tiger. He let out a deep purr of pleasure as he felt Aspar's naked body slide along his own. Slipping an investigating tongue into his friend's mouth, he curled his legs about his body, eyes narrowing in ecstasy. 'How many times I have dreamed of this moment, Aspar, though I thought you were lost to me,' he sighed, running his fingers lightly over the taut muscles of the Dacian's back and thighs.

Rolling the other man over onto his back, Surena pinioned his hands behind his head and began to kiss him hard, chewing his lips roughly until they were dark as over-ripe strawberries. He ground his hips against Aspar's, their stiff members rubbing over one another like two logs in a hearth. Their testicles, too, knocked roughly together like seed-heavy pomegranates in a basket. The growing ache which coursed through their loins formed a bond between them, sweet and mysterious.

Still restraining Aspar's wrists with his strong hands, Surena pulled himself up so that his slender brown manhood beat urgently against Aspar's parted lips. For a moment, the young king observed the delicate helmet, edges purple-tinged and thin as silk, pulling back from the bulbous head. Copious love-juice was already dripping from the gaping slit. As Aspar watched, the foreskin eased all the way back, stripping naked the broad mushroom head. He tasted the faint saltiness of pre-come as it dripped on to his tongue. His hunger pricked, he embraced the member with his mouth and thrilled as the bulky glans clicked into his throat, pursued by its elegant curved stalk. Head thrown back so that his expression was hidden from the young king, Surena emitted a long sigh.

Aspar sucked greedily on the appendage, saliva pooling under his tongue, drawn out by the delicate flavour of pre-come and the unique shape of Surena's endowment. The Parthian king rode Aspar's' mouth with increasing abandon, as lavish pourings of love-juice stimulated the Dacian's appetite. Aspar let the prick slip from his gullet and watched it throb in front of his face, streaming with his spittle and Surena's own secretions. Pushing himself under the other man, he took first one, then both, date-shaped balls in his mouth and sucked hard on them, feeling with his tongue the wriggling mass of vessels harbouring his friend's seed. Surena squirmed at the agonising pleasure. Aspar dragged himself down still further so that his mouth was poised directly under Surena's spread arsecheeks. Inhaling the mingled sweetness of exotic perfume and the Parthian's own manly scent, Aspar raised his tongue to tantalise the dark-red full-moon of the tender lovehole.

Surena pushed down onto his partner's mouth and the petals of velvety skin opened like a rose at the probings of Aspar's tongue. The Parthian swivelled his body around the fixed axis of his hole so that it hovered, firm as the Great Star, over Aspar's lips. Now he faced the other way and leaned down, at the same time tilting the king's buttocks towards him until he, too, was able to insert his eager tongue into Aspar's arse-lips, which already pouted with arousal. The two men feasted deeply on the silky sweetness of their most intimate parts. Waves of pleasure radiated out from their loins until the tingling waves reached their extremities.

Again, Surena changed position, with the speed and grace of a mountain cat. He rubbed his spit-slicked hole against Aspar's marble-hard pole. Then, tilting the phallus into a vertical position sank down on it until it ran full-length into his vitals. The bodies of both men were racked by a shudder of pleasure. Slowly, so as to savour every inch of Aspar's pole with the sensitive lining of his manhole, Surena began to ride his partner with all the control of an ace horseman. He gasped each time the clenched head bumped against the smooth chestnut of his prostate. Surena's eyes were filled with a wondering expression and never moved from Aspar's face, as he rode the Dacian's cock inexorably towards climax.

When at last the floodgates broke, it seemed to Aspar that somehow the Parthian had gained mastery over the very mechanism of his genitals, slowing its action so as to extend the sensation to maximum length. Surena's erection reared up several times, pausing at its zenith on each occasion, the huge head almost obscenely provocative on its curved shaft. Then its milk seemed to arch motionless in a long trajectory, each stream separated by a painful pause. Aspar felt the hot spouts slash across his chest and strike softly against his lips. The spasms of the other man's rectal muscles milked his own dick mercilessly until he felt the juices brimming over, toppling into a powerful orgasm. His cries of pleasure, signalling the launch of his seed into Surena's ravening man-cunt, provoked the prince into even louder bellows of satisfaction.

As they lay together for a moment of satisfied recuperation, Aspar became aware of the sighs and exultant shouts that filled the hall, although he had been oblivious to them until now. Stirred by this tide of pleasure, the two noblemen were soon entwined in a writhing embrace. Now Surena was pushing Aspar's ankles upwards until his thighs lay along his chest and the clump of flesh that crested the Parthian's phallus was knocking impatiently at the entrance to his partner's fuckhole, a divining rod furiously signalling the source of pleasure and sustenance. The Dacian squirmed ecstatically as the huge dickhead stretched his sphincter to its widest. He gasped as his hole swallowed the indecent glans with a gulp.

Sheathing his cock in the scabbard of Aspar's arse, Surena began to pound away, adjusting his position to explore Aspar's bowels with his battering ram. Pushing his friend's feet beyond his shoulders so that his anus was aimed directly upwards, Surena raised himself into a crouching position, enabling him to delve deeper. Placing one foot behind Aspar's head, he fucked him at right angles. The Dacian's head thrashed about as the outsized cockhead touched unexplored recesses of his rectal cavity, awakening fierce new sensations. Tantalised beyond resistance, Aspar felt the sting of the burning sap at the root of his manhood. His rod shook uncontrollably, like a poplar in a storm. Its colour deepened to a furious red, its surface coarsened by a web of jutting veins. Aspar's slit spewed out gobs of clotted seed onto the soft hair of his abdomen. The stranglehold of his orgasm around Surena's already compressed glans provided the final stimulus needed to suck out a second load from the Parthian's aching balls. His body arched and juddered as he shot spurt after spurt into the king's man-pussy.

Echoes of passion still rang through the hall as the two men clung together, drowsy with satiety.

'And now tell me one of your tales,' Surena murmured sleepily, cocooning his back and buttocks in the curve of Aspar's torso, and pulling his friend's arms about him.

A red streak of dawn over the distant mountains awakened Aspar. Surena was staring at him with a lazy smile, his chin resting on his hands. The other noblemen had drifted off to their quarters in the course of the night, leaving the two men alone in the vast hall. A breeze stirred the gauze curtain around the bed. For the first time since his departure from Rome, Aspar felt something close to peace.

The prince had invited Aspar to take part in manoeuvres he was supervising that day close to the city. Although Parthia was a cautious host to other peoples, such as Greeks and Jews, the army of the king was recruited exclusively from Parthians, both nobles and peasants; past experience had shown that the loyalty of troops recruited from amongst these foreign guests could not be relied on.

With threats both from within and without the empire, a constant programme of recruitment and training was necessary. Aspar would be able to drill alongside new recruits to the divisions of mounted archers.

After a light breakfast of fruit and camel's milk, the two men rode out together at the head of Surena's battalion. A straggling band of apprentice archers brought up the rear. Aspar was attired in the archer's uniform of leather leggings, silk tunic and domed helmet. A bow and full quiver bounced against his back. He was mounted on a stately Persian bay, a gift from Surena and a near-perfect match to Surena's own steed.

'I hear that the Romans indulge in mass orgies where many men make love in each other's company,' Surena blurted out with a scowl as they went. 'It is incredible that such a decadent people produces courageous warriors.' A sudden thought struck him. 'I hope you never took part in that kind of nonsense.' He frowned, turning to face Aspar.

Aspar suppressed a smile. 'But what exactly did we get up to last night?'

'That was not the same thing at all,' protested Surena indignantly. 'It's true that my men were present. But they are always with me. I don't even think about them. And anyway, no one would have dreamed of looking at us, so it was just the same as being alone.'

'You're right,' nodded Aspar, the corners of his mouth twitching, 'Terribly decadent, those Romans.'

Surena gave him a sheepish sideways smile. 'I don't really care what you did. As long as I don't have to hear about it. I only want to think about now. I know this won't last.'

Aspar made no reply.

Before starting the day's exercises, Aspar exchanged a few words with Hermes. He, too, was to be trained as a horseman in Surena's cavalry. As Aspar's henchman, he had been accorded the status of a nobleman and had been paired with a young Parthian aristocrat whose broad grin and ebullient manner suggested that he was delighted with the arrangement: his generous physical endowments meant that Hermes had much to offer both on the battlefield and in the gentler tussles of the bedchamber.

Surena explained that, naturally, Aspar would become his companion in warfare and that he would therefore personally undertake his friend's training. Over the next weeks and months, the Dacian king began to acquire the skills that made the Parthian archer such a deadly foe. At first, it was a question of developing the muscles needed to use the double-curved bow, whose compact construction and lightness belied the immense power with which it launched its missiles. This, combined with the lethal sharpness and strength of the arrows, made it a uniquely fearsome weapon that could pierce Roman mail, shields, helmets even, and tore through flesh as if it were rotten fruit.

But accuracy and speed in the use of the bow was only the start. Although he was a proficient rider, Aspar took many falls as he began to match his skill as an archer with the necessary prowess as a horseman: shooting forwards; backwards when feinting retreat; firing a volley as you charged within feet of the enemy's front-line and continuing to shoot while wheeling round in a U-turn back to a safe distance. But, though he found much amusement in Aspar's tumbles, Surena quietly glowed with pride at his companion's rapid progress.

Judging that the time was ripe for Aspar to meet Osroes, the King of Kings, the prince arranged a hunting party to which he invited the leading members of the Imperial Court. A devotee of the hunt, Osroes graciously agreed to attend.

Before they left for the mountains where the hunt was to take place, Surena led Aspar to his treasury. He showed the young king chests crammed full of jewelled gold and silver ornaments. 'These have been accumulated by my family for generations,' he said carelessly. 'Think how many armies we could pay for with all this, Aspar.' He took the king's arm and led him to a cupboard set in the wall. 'Here we keep the symbols of royalty,' he explained, throwing open the great oak doors to reveal a collection of diadems, armbands and torques. 'Some of these have been in the family since before the empire's foundation. Others are more recent gifts.' He reached to one of the higher shelves and lifted down a torque of twisted gold. Aspar felt the blood rush to his head in recognition.

'Yes, Aspar. Of course you know this. It was a gift from your father to mine when he came here with a delegation from Decebalus. It is your own symbol of royalty. Today, you will appear before Osroes as the king you were born to be.'

When Surena presented his companion to Osroes that afternoon, the Parthian King's manner was gracious but remote, and Aspar noticed that the nobles kept a respectful distance from the monarch, though they appeared relaxed enough with one another. The goal of the hunt seemed to be to seek and outflank the prey – mostly mountain lions – in such a way that the King was able to shoot and kill the creatures with relative ease.

Towards sunset, the party returned to the pavilion where a banquet was to be held in Osroes' honour. Aspar could see the King approaching the tent from the opposite direction in the shadow of a low cliff. Suddenly the Dacian froze. He was aware of many eyes turning towards him as he plucked an arrow from his quiver and let it fly in the King's direction with the swiftness he had learned in the months of drill with Surena.

As the King fell forward from his horse, Aspar was pulled from his own mount. He could see Surena's panicked face above him as he pushed his way through the circle of angry noblemen. Then the crowd parted and there stood the King. Behind him, a servant held in his arms the limp body of the lion that Aspar had spotted on the cliff above the sovereign's head: his arrow had struck the beast an instant before it had landed on the King's back.

'I owe you my life, Dacian,' said Osroes. He extended his hand to Aspar and raised him to his feet. Unexpectedly he smiled and turned to Surena: 'Truly, you have made a Parthian of him.'

That night at the banquet, Aspar told stories of the Dacian gods and found the Parthians an attentive audience. On his golden couch, Osroes lay unmoving, his intelligent gaze fixed on the young fair king from the north. After this, Aspar was a firm favourite at court, and was treated by the other nobles with something like awe. Whether this was due to his skill with the bow or with words, he was not sure.

When spring arrived, and with it the battle season, Surena returned from an audience with the King brimming with news. Incursions were to be made into Armenia; the king of that territory was on the brink of capitulating to Rome's demands and Orsoes was anxious to forestall any treaties that would imperil the empire. The best news, however, was that the King had decreed that the two friends should jointly command the expedition as generals of the Parthian army. Surena embraced Aspar enthusiastically. The Dacian could only stammer his gratitude for his friend's faith and generosity.

Amidst the practical preparations for the operation, Surena was concerned that the necessary prayers should be offered to the gods. With Aspar, he made sacrifice to Verethranga, god of victory, who boasted one of Ctesiphon's finest temples. The bronze statue of a muscular bearded man was familiar to the Dacian king.

'This is the hero the Greeks call Herakles, is it not?' he asked.

'Yes – to Parthians, Verethranga and Herakles are one and the same,' explained Surena.

Having made sacrifice, taken the auspices (favourable as ever, Aspar noted) and offered incense before the god, Surena and Aspar spoke the words of mutual dedication used by warrior–companions since the time of the Greeks. At the conclusion of the ceremony,

Surena called for a servant bearing a golden casket. He reached inside and lifted out two golden belts. The buckles were studded with large emeralds in a characteristic twisted knot.

'You know this sign?' Surena inquired eagerly, seeing a flicker of understanding in Aspar's expression.

'It's the Herakles knot, isn't it?'

'Yes, the ancient expression of a love that binds. On the battle-field, of course,' he added hastily. 'That is what two warrior–companions should mean to one another.'

As they rode out from the city, the men wore their belts. At Surena's insistence, Aspar also wore the torque and the Parthian his diadem, the symbols of kingship.

They had crossed the border and were some days into Armenian desert territory before scouts brought news of enemy troops – not a local force, but a cohort of Roman legionaries.

'Just as I thought,' murmured Surena, when he heard the news. 'The Romans are already here.' He gave a low whistle. 'Not quite the border patrol we had in mind. There must be nearly a thousand of them and three hundred of us. Imagine, though, if we could capture them with such a small band of men.' He thought for a moment and then turned to Aspar. 'We can do it, you know.' He looked up at the skies. 'The hundred and twenty days' wind has begun. We must follow stealthily and attack them on the march when the sand-storm is at its height and visibility is down to a few paces – enough for us to fire at point-blank range and then disappear from their sight.'

After two days of clear weather, the hot wind from the east, the scourge of soldiers and merchants alike, began to blow. The Parthian scouts having ascertained the exact Roman position, Surena and Aspar worked out the battle-plan and explained it to their commanders. The attack would be launched while the cohort was in marching formation, spread out and at its most vulnerable.

The Parthian forces, carefully avoiding Roman scouts or killing them silently with knives, would position themselves on either side of the column, far enough away to be concealed by the storm. The plan was to send in the heavy cavalry first in order to split the Roman force, separating the tribunes from the legionaries, the fighting men from those whose task it was to set up camp. Then, before the Romans could assume battle formations, the mounted archers would attack in waves, picking the enemy troops off like flies, retreating into the safety of the sandstorm.

As Surena launched the signal for the battle to begin, Aspar suddenly realised why the Parthians had always proved such fearsome enemies. From all sides came the chilling sound of their war drums. Rising and falling on the wind, they were like thunder mixed with the howls of beasts in the arena. Through this din cut the screams of the Parthian battle-paean. Aspar could only imagine the impact this made on the Roman troops, coming as it did from the blinding curtain of dust thrown up by the storm.

He and Surena fought side by side and, when it was their turn to attack, they were faced with a scene of utter disarray. As planned, the archers rode until they were but ten paces away from the enemy and able to launch their arrows with the certainty of a hit. The Roman legionaries ran this way and that in complete confusion, uncertain even from which direction the enemy was approaching and too disoriented to take up defensive positions. Aspar swerved back into the storm at the last minute, conscious of his companion at his side, and prepared to make another run.

This time, the scene was one of complete devastation. Bodies of Romans lay in heaps while many were still alive but mortally wounded, their limbs and torsos pinioned to their shields, shrieking in pain as they tried to pull the barbed arrow-heads from their flesh. Aspar launched his weapon and pulled the horse round with a sharp movement of his knees. At that moment, a Roman soldier on horseback passed in front of him, close enough for Aspar to recognise him instantly. He wore the uniform of a tribune, but the golden helmet that concealed most of his face was one that the Dacian king would have recognised anywhere – the mask of Vulcan that he had seen on Valerius that night in the Baths. The strange design was engraved in his mind's eye with absolute clarity. The man's gaze lingered on him for a second; Aspar could see the dark eyes staring from the holes in the golden face. He wondered if the tribune had recognised him, but then he was gone.

The battle was over in under an hour. The Parthians' lightning methods had decimated the Roman troops. By then, the wind had dropped slightly, but it was still not possible to see more than a hundred paces. Doubtless some Romans had escaped under cover of the storm, but Surena and Aspar supervised the counting of the many dead and the taking of hundreds of bewildered prisoners. These survivors were led off to their camp in the nearby hills.

The two leaders remained behind with just a few of their guards, and were checking among the wounded to see if any of those with less serious injuries could be taken prisoner, when Aspar looked up at the pounding of approaching hooves. He whirled round in the direction of the sound, instinctively seizing an arrow from his quiver and preparing to shoot. The horseman was heading directly for him, lance aimed at his chest and already just a few paces away. Aspar let the arrow fly and saw it hit its mark, just under the lower edge of the strange golden helmet where Valerius' neck joined his body. But in the instant before the arrow struck, Surena, having left his own bow on his horse, had stopped Valerius' lance the only way he had been able to – by throwing his own body in the path of the weapon.

As Valerius' body toppled from the horse, Surena sank back on to the sand, his body sliding down the lance that skewered his chest.

Aspar flung himself to the ground, cradling his friend's head with infinite gentleness, terrified to touch the lance and aggravate his agony.

'Now I have shown you what I vowed never to speak,' the prince managed to gasp, as blood from his punctured lung frothed up onto dark lips. He groped with his hand as though in darkness till his fingers found Aspar's belt. 'But the Herakles knot, Aspar: I did not mean it just for the battlefield. I did do my best to keep silent, though, didn't I? I did not want to stand in the way of your destiny.'

'You mustn't talk now. Our surgeons will tend to your wounds.'

Surena gave his head a slight shake. 'There's no hope for me in this life.' His dark eyes brightened as he looked up into Aspar's face. 'But Verethranga, god of heroes, will reward me, don't you think, my friend? I will ask him only for one thing. That one day we shall be reunited. It doesn't matter how long I have to wait. I'm used to that. However dark it is down there in the underworld, it will be full of light if you are there.' The warrior began to choke as the blood flowed more strongly from his lips. Then his breathing stopped and Aspar felt the body go limp in his arms like a discarded doll. He felt his throat tighten and the tears well up in his eyes. He had never stopped to examine his feelings for the young Parthian; both as a boy and as a man, he had simply thought of Surena as a part of himself. Now these feelings struck him with full force.

He was not sure how long he remained there.

A sound brought him back to himself, a voice calling out of the storm. 'Valerius?' He could see the outline of three Romans riding towards him. As they drew near, he recognised two tribunes and a centurion. Seeing Aspar, they rode towards him. Spotting the motionless body of Valerius, the centurion drew his sword and galloped towards the Dacian, who stared at him blankly.

'No!' called one of the tribunes sharply, cantering to the centurion's side in order to get a better look at Aspar's face. His gaze dropped to the torque at his neck. 'I know who you are,' he said slowly, 'I've seen you in Rome, haven't I? No,' he repeated to the centurion. 'This one we will have alive.'

Ten

It was with some trepidation that the straggling remnant of the cohort so decisively crushed by the Parthian expedition made its way back to headquarters in Antioch. Its mission had been to scare the Armenian king into submission and to strike fear into the rulers of Parthia. Roman intelligence had suggested that, with internal relations between the various kingdoms of Parthia at a low ebb, the troublesome (and rich) empire was ripe for the plucking. Yet here was the advance guard returning in abject defeat, with the bulk of its forces either dead on the field of battle or prisoners of Parthia. Even the standard of their legion had been captured, and all this had been accomplished by a mere handful of enemy soldiers.

Facing serious disciplinary charges, possibly even a death sentence for their part in the disaster, the two surviving tribunes decided to gamble everything on two incredible pieces of luck: that one of the enemy generals had been killed (though unintentionally) and, more significantly, that the other had been taken prisoner. Moreover, this was no ordinary general but the Dacian Slave King, celebrated in Rome and throughout the cultural centres of the Empire. So they took their time on the return journey, sending scouts on ahead to announce the news.

The tribunes' ploy worked. By the time the small party arrived in the City of Lights, Aspar's capture was the talk of Syria and the news had even spread to the outlying provinces. In the city's bathhouses and latrines, men lingered for hours discussing nothing else. The many social gatherings of bored, respectable matrons were abuzz with it. Even in the Grove of Daphne, which gave Antioch its reputation as the greatest of eastern flesh-pots, customers and temple attendants paused in their debaucheries to speculate on the legendary charms of the Slave King.

Aspar's arrival caused a near-riot which distracted the Roman high command from the glaring fact that their cohort had been routed by the enemy. He rode into Antioch on his Parthian steed, robed in the brilliant silks of a general, his blond hair and beard still dressed in the Parthian style, with Surena's jewelled belt around his waist and his father's torque at his throat. His reputation as warrior, king, prostitute and author had preceded him, and his appearance more than fulfilled the expectations of the sensual citizens of Antioch. Instead of mockery, he was met with cheers, and women threw flowers in his path from their balconies. His welcome was that of a military hero or a champion gladiator and, though he was a prisoner, it was common knowledge that he was also the victor.

Aspar had expected to be despatched immediately for Rome, probably to face execution as his father had. Instead, he was taken to the city's main fortress where he was placed under guard in a suite of rooms usually reserved for visiting dignitaries. Trajan, he learned, was about to personally lead a massive campaign against Parthia, hoping to deal the empire the same crippling blow he done had to Dacia seven years earlier. In view of the Emperor's imminent arrival, the generals decided that the wisest course of action was to play down the defeat in Armenia and focus on Aspar's capture.

A stream of distinguished visitors came to visit him in his well-appointed prison. From them, he learned that news of his defection to Parthia had reached Rome itself. He was taken aback to discover that, in order to cash in on his notoriety, his publisher had issued the unfinished second volume of his *Shield of Gold*.

One visitor, a rich merchant, kindly agreed to send a copy to Aspar in the fortress. As he perused it, he noted that even his final jottings before leaving the city had been gleaned from his desk at the House of Glaucus and incorporated into the text. He wondered vaguely who would be pocketing his royalties now, and wished he had made provision for this before leaving the capital.

Those requesting an audience with him ranged from wealthy predators hoping for his favours to prim matrons interested in discussing the finer points of his poetics. The latter returned to their literary circles with enthusiastic reports, while the former left disappointed and puzzled by Aspar's brusque rejection. Though the Dacian king had little interest in satisfying the curiosity of the citizens of Antioch or fanning the flames of his fame in the city, he welcomed the visits as a distraction from the thoughts that weighed on his mind. He was bitterly disappointed that his hopes had been dashed so close to fulfilment, but even this blow was eclipsed by the loss of Surena, which he felt more keenly than he could ever have imagined.

After several weeks of captivity, he bored of the visits and requested ink and parchment: writing would provide a more satisfactory distraction from his plight. It was with some annoyance, therefore, that he glanced up from his work one evening after supper, the silence disturbed by the sound of the metal-shod footsteps of guards in his ante-chamber. As they marched through the arch that led into his study, he opened his mouth in protest. But his words were cut short as the visitor they were escorting lowered the hood of his white robe: it was Zosimus.

The guards retired and the two men clasped each other in a long silent embrace. Aspar realised that in the months since their separation, the bitterness had faded and only his deep feelings of affection for the other man remained. There was no need for words, however. Their delight at being in one another's presence again was plain.

'I would have come earlier, but I was in Alexandria receiving a delivery from the east. The news of your capture reached me there and I sailed as soon as I could,' Zosimus explained, trying the fine wine with which the Roman authorities had supplied the Dacian. 'When I arrived at my villa, I found Hermes waiting for me: he told me about your victory.'

'Loyal, as ever,' murmured Aspar.

'Yes. He returned to Ctesiphon with the victorious troops, but as soon as he was sure that you had fallen into the hands of the Romans, he came here as fast as he could. Which apparently drew bitter tears from his companion, a young Parthian prince, I believe.'

'So I would imagine,' said Aspar with a smile. He looked up at Zosimus. 'Did he tell you about Surena?'

Zosimus shook his head. Aspar recounted in dead tones how Surena had taken the death-blow that had been meant for him.

'He must have cared for you a great deal. You should feel proud to have inspired such devotion.'

'It is a heavy burden to know that I live because he died.'

'But you can honour his memory by making sure that his sacrifice had a purpose. Did he know about your hopes of returning to Dacia?

'Of course.'

'So he has made that dream possible. That is the significance of his death.'

'Except that now it's no longer possible, so his sacrifice was sheer waste.'

Zosimus drew close to the Dacian and dropped his voice to a whisper. 'You are wrong, Aspar. Many legions are presently travelling east for the planned war against Parthia. Some of the generals have already arrived. And one of them is an old friend of yours – Proculus.'

'Proculus is here in Antioch?' exclaimed Aspar.

'Yes, I have met and spoken with him and he is willing to help you regain your freedom.'

'But surely that is too great a risk for him.'

'It's a risk he is prepared to take. The plan is this. He is to protest to the other generals against the favourable treatment you are receiving. You will be transferred to a fortress outside the city walls under light guard. He will insist that the move takes place by night so that you will not be recognised by the Antiochians. On the way, the guard will be ambushed and overcome. I will provide all that is necessary for you to travel through Cappadocia to Pontus from where you can cross to Dacia by sea. Unless, of course, you would rather return to Parthia.'

'I fear that Trajan's campaign there will be long and hard-fought. If I am ever to fulfil my father's wishes, I must take this chance to return to Dacia now.'

'Good,' said Zosimus, relieved. 'I am sure that is the right decision. Though of course, the road to Dacia will not be an easy one.'

'And Proculus? I would welcome the chance to thank him.'

'No,' Zosimus shot back, with a shake of his head. 'Antioch is crawling with informers – a meeting between you, however secret, could only compromise him.'

'Listen, Zosimus,' said Aspar thoughtfully, 'I'm going to need money for this journey – and everything I owned I left behind me in Parthia. But I do have these – my torque and this belt. Could you sell them for me?'

Zosimus eyes lingered on the typically Parthian belt, Surena's gift, with its Herakles knot of rubies. 'No, you must not sell those. They mean too much. I will ensure that you have enough money for the journey.'

'You are so good, Zosimus,' said Aspar affectionately, taking his hand. 'No one could have a better friend.'

Zosimus glanced away. 'I am only too keenly aware that I have fallen short of the pledge we made in Hispania. I fear that in the years ahead I may regret it bitterly.'

*

Proculus' advice was heeded and, a few nights later, Aspar was escorted outside the city walls by a small detachment of mounted guards. There was no moon that night (Proculus had borne this in mind, Aspar was certain) and his escort was too surprised to put up much of a fight when a band of warriors swept out of the darkness in the mountains outside Antioch. Aspar was taken aback to find that his rescuers wore Parthian uniforms. The struggle was over in minutes. The Dacian king was snatched from his horse and he rode off into the night, seated on the horse of one of his rescuers. Soon they were threading their way through a maze of narrow gorges. Aspar shared the mount of the tallest of the Parthians, a giant of a man.

'So, Aspar, once again we are on the run,' rumbled a voice from behind him. He recognised the booming tones of Hermes, who explained that the warriors were mercenaries hired by Zosimus. His hope was that, fooled by the uniforms, the Romans would pursue Aspar to the east , giving him a head start on his journey north.

As planned, Zosimus met the party just off the road to Commagene. He provided both Aspar and Hermes with the swift strong Parthian horses they were used to riding. 'The beginnings of your cavalry,' he smiled. He also furnished both men with false documents and carefully unfolded a map on soft parchment. 'See Aspar, I have drawn in the route I think you should follow: north through Commagene, crossing into Cappadocia, close to the border with Armenia. Then heading northwest through the mountains. If you hit the sea somewhere around Amastris in Pontus, the voyage to Dacia will not be too great. The problem will be finding a sea-worthy vessel. I know those waters and I don't think a fishing boat would be up to such a long journey. On the other hand, buying passage on a merchant ship would be too much of a risk. The journey by land should take about six weeks. The sea voyage – who can say?'

As he had promised, Zosimus provided them with money, but Aspar was astonished by the weight of the leather saddle-bags, full of gold talents. 'This is a fortune, Zosimus. Too much.'

'Hardly too much. You will certainly need it, if you are to raise any kind of fighting force,' Zosimus replied.

'But a gift this lavish would impoverish even the richest merchants of Rome.'

Zosimus laughed. 'Maybe I am richer than they. And anyway, I can always earn more. Perhaps it will make up for what I am unable to do.'

Aspar took hold of the Ethiopian's hand. 'Remember how in Hispania, when I gave you my mother's talisman, I said that from that day on you would be my lucky charm? Well, I was right. Charms of wood and metal are of little help. It is in ourselves and in our friends that we find real strength. I owe a great debt to all my friends – Surena, Proculus, Hermes. But if it were not for you I would have not have travelled this far on the road to my destiny. You saved me in Hispania, in Rome and now yet again. So you need never rebuke yourself. Without you, I would not be here.

'Once, you told me that my gods were with me. It is true that we can do nothing without the strength of the gods within us. But it is also true that without us the gods can do nothing.' Aspar chuckled. 'Now you have me talking in paradoxes, too.'

The first grey light was breaking over the desert and the dawn breeze blew steadily. It was time to leave. The two friends embraced in silence. Aspar looked back many times as he and Hermes started out on the long journey north. Even when he had shrunk to a dot on the horizon, the lone figure of Zosimus did not budge. Though the bitterness in his heart towards his friend had faded, Aspar found that the ache of parting had not diminished.

*

The two men resolved to travel under cover of darkness; for speed, they would keep to the arrow-straight roads built by the armies of Rome. They met few others in the desert wastes of Commagene and Cappadocia; merchants and private travellers preferred to seek the refuge of an inn at dusk, not wanting to risk an encounter with bandits. Aspar and Hermes had no such concerns, and were therefore taken completely off guard when, some miles north of the Syrian border, they found their way blocked by a band of men, some mounted, others on foot. Before they had time to react, they were surrounded.

As their captors raised their torches, Aspar saw that this was no small company: there were perhaps a hundred of them and not all were men – there were women and even children, and they carried shabby bundles of belongings as though they were prepared for a journey. Aspar started with astonishment as one of the men dismounted and addressed him.

'So it is true,' breathed the man in perfect Dacian. 'News of your coming has spread among the Dacian slaves of the region, but we did not dare to believe it until now. We have awaited this moment for years. King Aspar,' he said, bending one knee, 'we wish to return with you to Dacia – we want to fight with you for the freedom of our people.'

One by one, the rest of the crowd sank to its knees, even the tiniest child, who looked up at up Aspar with great blue eyes. There was a long moment of rapt stillness and silence as, enclosed in a tiny oasis of light in the vastness of the desert night, the Slave King and his people stared at one another in wonder.

Suddenly the expedition became fraught with hazard. It was easy for two people to travel without being noticed – impossible for a hundred. And they did not remain a hundred for long. As they travelled by night, always heading northwest towards the sea and avoiding well-used routes, groups of Dacian slaves would melt out of the darkness to swell their numbers. Often as dawn broke, Aspar would look back to find that the crowd had multiplied overnight. Soon they were several hundred strong. He was touched by their enthusiasm and optimism, but was also fearful for them, realising what a vulnerable target this undisciplined rabble presented to their Roman masters.

Pitching camp in a remote mountain region of Cappadocia, he and Hermes summoned a council of the men recognised as leaders by the Dacians.

'Clearly we have to continue on our way with all haste,' Aspar explained, 'but the longer we take, the more chance there is of attracting Roman attention. Antioch is crawling with legionaries – they could send a party north from there or else cut off our path to the sea with troops from one of the legions stationed in Cappadocia or Pontus.'

'They are looking for you, anyway, Aspar,' added Hermes, 'and they must have realised that the Parthian uniforms of your rescuers were just a ruse. Even now, they may have a search party on your tail.'

'And our masters will be hunting for us, too,' put in one of the Dacians. 'We are all wanted men and women in one way or another.'

'Exactly,' agreed Aspar. 'That is why we must be prepared to stand and fight if we have to. We must remain here in the mountains, and form ourselves into a force ready to take on Rome's professional fighters. But we cannot afford more than a few weeks' delay. It is now June. We must reach the sea before September, when the sailing season ends. It would be fatal if we were stranded in Asia Minor for the winter – the legions would certainly find us and wipe us out.'

'Some of us are warriors – we fought with your father and the other leaders in the wars with Trajan,' one of the Dacians volunteered with enthusiasm. 'But what do we do for weapons?'

'We will begin selecting men and training immediately,' returned Aspar. 'But, of course, proper equipment will be necessary. And we will not just be fighting in the Dacian style. Hermes and I will train a force in the Parthian arts of war. I have seen with my own eyes how effective these can be against the Roman army. Hermes, you must lead a party over the Euphrates into Armenia. I will give you all the money you need to buy horses – preferably Parthian horses – bows, arrows, spears, armour for the light and heavy cavalry. Our survival depends on this mission, my friend. I know, as you have proved so often in the past, that you will not fail me.'

In a few days, Hermes was back at the camp with the horses and much of the equipment they needed, purchased from Armenian rebel factions who opposed appeasement with Rome. In addition, he had obtained supplies of food and warm clothing, which would be required once they set sail for Dacia, as well as carts for transporting the women, children and baggage.

During his absence, Aspar had formed the men into infantry divisions, and was already drilling them hard. Those with some riding skills, who would form the heavy and light cavalry, had started practising with makeshift bows and arrows. They fell upon the fine Armenian weapons and armour like children opening Saturnalia gifts. The men now set to work in earnest. Even some of the younger women joined the infantry. The latter numbered around a hundred, strengthened by close to two hundred cavalry. Many of the slaves had lost husbands, wives and children; all had lost homes and freedom. They threw themselves into the tough training regimen with the wholeheartedness of those who have nothing more to lose.

Aspar organised the older women into groups charged with sewing uniforms and banners from fabrics brought by Hermes. He

worked with them to reconstruct the Dacian patterns of ornate tendrils so that they could be copied on to shields. One of the men, a
metal-worker, cast several dragon-headed standards. Once these
had been decked out with long colourful trains of silk, they were
set up alongside the training areas to inspire and encourage. Both
women and men would stand and stare at them, spellbound: they
had never thought to see such sights again. Aspar ordered an altar
to be built to the Dacian healing god Zalmoxis and frequent sacrifice was offered with prayers for a safe passage home. 'Not that
Zalmoxis will get us home – that's up to us,' Aspar muttered to
Hermes, 'but anything that puts heart into these people is helpful.'

At night, around a communal campfire, Aspar would recount
the sagas of the Dacian gods and heroes. Tears rolled down the
cheeks of the men and women as they listened, enchanted, to
each word of the tales. Even the eyes of the children sparkled, and
they looked up at their mothers as they recognised names from
half-remembered bedtime stories. These evenings around the
campfire, more than anything else, evoked their homeland for the
exiled Dacians; made it seem real and close, and strengthened
their resolve to see it once more.

By the time the Dacians broke camp, they had been transformed from an undisciplined mob into a miniature army. Scouts,
both cavalry and footsoldiers, kept a careful watch for enemy
troops in all directions. A contingent of light cavalry led the way,
followed by the infantry, flanked by the heavily armoured cataphracts. Then came Aspar and the other leaders, protected by
mounted bodyguards. Women, children and baggage in horse-
drawn carts were next, with a final group of mounted archers
bringing up the rear. The contrast with the amorphous group that
had arrived six weeks earlier was stark, but Aspar knew that the
greatest change had taken place in the hearts of these men and
women. A desperate hope had become a clear-sighted and practical determination to cut through the substantial obstacles that

stood in their way.

The first of these was several hundred miles of rugged mountain terrain as they crossed Asia Minor. This was especially hard for the children and the elderly and progress was slow. Skirting cities and avoiding busy routes added many miles to their travels. Carts carrying those unable to walk and vital baggage would often topple into ditches or lose their wheels on the boulder-strewn mountain paths, which caused further delays. Frequent stops were necessary to forage for the supplies required to feed the hungry travellers. The company of trained fighters was small; if they were half-starved, they would stand no chance against fit, well-fed legionaries.

By the end of August, according to the map Zosimus had given Aspar, they had reached the Pontine mountains. One morning, while he was riding towards the rear of the column, giving encouragement to a group of women and children, Aspar saw a scout riding towards him at top speed. He was shouting and appeared to be in a state of great agitation. 'King Aspar,' he gasped, as he drew near, 'the sea, the sea!' He gesticulated wildly behind him.

The mood of the crowd was transformed. A moment earlier, they had been tottering with exhaustion. Now, women snatched up their small children in their arms and began to run. Old folk hobbled forward as fast as they could. The warriors, used to marching or riding in tight formation, broke ranks and joined the general stampede towards the summit.

As he rode onto the ridge, Aspar gazed out over the silvery expanse of the Pontus Euxinus which stretched to the horizon. Across that land-locked sea, far to the northwest, lay Dacia, their home. A few miles along the coast, he spotted a city. If he had followed Zosimus' map correctly, that would be Amastris, which meant that the sea voyage would not be too gruelling – if only they could find suitable boats, and enough of them. Yet he felt no exhaltation, simply relief that they had made it this far and that the weather was still holding. The youthful king smiled indulgently at the scenes of jubilation around him. The adults laughed and hugged one another. The children jumped and danced, infected by the high spirits of their elders. Aspar let them have their moment of triumph; he knew that the hard times still lay ahead.

But he did not realise how soon they would arrive. When they were halfway down the mountain, scouts brought news of an approaching Roman force. It had set out from Satala, far to the east, and was on course to block their route to the coast. Aspar ascertained from the reports that the expedition consisted of two cohorts, around a thousand men. That was over three times his own fighting force and he determined that, rather than meet them on the coastal plains, the confrontation should take place in the foothills of the mountain range they were descending.

The Dacians attacked first. A small party of mounted archers ambushed the Roman troops while they were still on the march. They charged several times in waves and their arrows hit home. The Roman casualties were negligible, however, in terms of their total numbers and, when the cavalry withdrew into the foothills, the legionaries gave chase. They had assumed, as Aspar hoped, that the archers were the sum total of the Dacian forces and that they were therefore retreating in the face of overwhelming Roman superiority.

The party of archers rode between two hills into a large flat area ringed by scrubby dunes, continuing their retreat until the last of the Romans had passed through the gap. The consternation of the enemy was palpable when invisible Parthian drums began their thunderous howling and, with piercing war cries, the cataphracts came thundering down the dunes from every direction, ploughing into the Roman cavalry with their spears. Legionaries scrambled in panic to gather in defensive formations, but before they could, a continuous lethal hail of arrows was unleashed by the light cavalry. Between sorties, mounted archers on the edge of the battle stirred up clouds of sand so that each new wave seemed to emerge from nowhere, and always from a different direction, making it impossible for the foot soldiers to orientate themselves. At last, the archers withdrew, and Aspar sent in the Dacian infantry to finish off their work. Those Romans left alive were either too badly wounded or too demoralised to continue, and gave themselves up.

When the leaders were brought before Aspar, their manner was arrogant, despite their humiliating defeat. 'A full legion is less than three days behind us,' a centurion sneered. 'They will crush this rabble with ease.'

'Like my rabble crushed you?' volunteered Aspar with a smile. Yet he knew that what the soldier said was true. It was vital that they reach the sea and embark for Dacia before the legion caught up with them. His followers were keen to celebrate their first victory, but he cut their revels short and, after seeing to their few light casualties, ordered his small band to re-form, leaving the prisoners behind them, bound hand and foot, stripped of clothes and weapons.

They marched for two days without stopping before they found a natural harbour on a deserted strip of coastline. It was almost completely encircled by cliffs with an opening wide enough for one or two small craft to enter or exit at a time. Aspar knew that the legion, which was no doubt covering twenty to thirty miles a day on forced march, could not be more than twenty-four hours away. He despatched a company, led by Hermes, along the coast with instructions to hire or buy every seaworthy craft they could find. He would lead a similar quest in the opposite direction. They must be prepared to pay whatever necessary, he instructed Hermes, even if they used up the rest of the vast sum with which Zosimus had provided them. Poor fishermen would surely be persuaded by the offer of more money than they could hope to earn in a lifetime. But, Aspar pointed out, the boats must be ready to leave that night.

The sun was setting over the Pontus Euxinus, as Aspar nervously surveyed the fleet of small fishing boats crowding into the harbour. He knew that the legion was drawing closer by the minute. Hermes stood some yards off at the water's edge, engrossed in discussion with a crowd of fishermen.

'Let us begin to embark,' Aspar called out to him.

The Armenian strode rapidly up the beach. 'I think you should talk to these men,' he said in a lowered voice. 'They say the omens are bad for tonight. Birds have been seen flying inland. A storm is approaching. These boats are not built for heavy seas.'

'But we cannot delay,' Aspar insisted. 'Do we have any money left?'

'Some. Not much.'

'Offer them whatever we have. We must set sail immediately.'

Hermes returned to the fishermen. Aspar watched anxiously as they talked in raised voices. He swung round as someone called his name. One of the scouts had ridden down from the top of the cliffs where they were keeping a lookout for their pursuers. 'My king, the legion is in sight. I'd guess they are two, at most three hours away. They don't appear to be stopping for the night.'

Aspar turned back to the beach. The fishermen were shouting now, and gesturing at the sky. It was almost dark and women and children were seated in circles. A constellation of lamps lit up one by one around the curve of the bay. As though in reflection, stars sprinkled the clear ultramarine overhead. Approaching the fishermen, the young king passed a group eating supper. A small boy looked up from his food. 'Are we going in those boats?' he asked his mother.

'Yes, we're going with King Aspar,' she assured him softly. 'He's taking us home.'

Aspar quickened his pace. 'We must begin the embarkation now,' he commanded brusquely.

'But these men say they will not sail tonight.'

'We'll man the boats ourselves, then. We've navigated across deserts and mountains by the stars. We can do it at sea.'

Hermes drew close to him and lowered his voice. 'Aspar, none of us knows how to sail. And certainly not how to handle a boat in a storm. These men are well acquainted with the sea and its moods, and they are sincerely afraid of what might happen if we leave now.'

'We have no choice. I don't care about myself, but these people have put their lives in my hands, and the lives of their children. I have to get them out. Do you think the Romans will spare any of us if we remain here?' He was shouting now and the fishermen were staring.

'But Aspar, you have done everything possible. Even you cannot work miracles.'

'If that's what it takes to save my people, then I must.'

The fishermen had closed into a circle. After a pause, one of them came forward. He bowed slightly to Aspar. 'Your lordship, we've been talking,' he mumbled. 'We're family men ourselves and don't want to see anything happen to the women and children. We'll go with you, but on the condition that we stay close to the shore, just in case a storm blows up.'

'In that case, we must extinguish all lights,' Aspar shot back. 'No lamps on the boats. 'Nothing that will show the Romans where we are. And we must leave no trace behind us. They must think we have vanished into thin air.'

The young king hurried back up the beach and took the steep path up the cliffs. He looked at the sky. It was cloudless and the air was quite still. The moon had not risen. The stars were a belt of jewels stretched across the blue-blackness. Surely there would be no storm tonight. Seafaring men were notoriously superstitious.

He reached the rim of the cliffs. A group of mounted scouts peered anxiously into the darkness. Following their gaze, he felt a chill course through him as he spied an endless line of torches snaking through the darkness beneath the rearing bulk of a mountain range. It was hard to gauge their distance, but they must be some miles off, judging by the dim thunder of their marching.

An hour later, Aspar descended to the beach with the scouts. The embarkation had been quiet and orderly, despite the fact that the Dacians had anticipated this moment with such excitement. Even the horses were being transported in barges they had managed to secure. Now all but a handful of boats had left the harbour one by one through the narrow gap before turning west, dark and silent as a parade of mourners. The legion was perhaps an hour's march away, but by the time they reached the coast, there would be no sign of the slaves.

They had been at sea some hours when the moon broke the horizon behind them, red and swollen, veined with shreds of cloud. By its dim light, Aspar could see the fleet, a flock of dark birds strung out ahead, parallel to the coast. Far behind, it was just possible to make out a cluster of lights on the shore: was it a fishing village or had the legion reached the coast? One by one, the men and women in the boat noticed the ominous moon and nudged one another, shuddering.

A low bank of cloud grew, swallowing the large red disc and giving chase to the boats. Soon it had overtaken them, blotting out the stars above, and racing ahead to the distant horizon. A darkness descended over the sea, so dense that Aspar could not even make out his companions in the small craft. The fisherman steering in the stern called out occasionally to be answered by his colleagues in the vessels before and behind.

The air was so still that the sail sagged, and the boat hardly seemed to budge. Out of the solid blackness before them came the distant noise of a baby crying and, from behind, the nervous neighing of horses. Aspar could sense the fear of his fellow passengers and, to break the spell, struck up a conversation about hopes for their future in Dacia, but this was soon cut short. A blast of wind struck the sail and the boat leaped forward. Speeding through the choppy water, it pitched with increasing violence. Children began to whimper. Then, as suddenly as if they had passed under a waterfall, rain lashed down from the void overhead. The waves grew so high that the boat tilted steeply downwards into the trough, nosing up the other side.

'Secure the baggage and the children,' Aspar called above the roar of the waves. Water was sliding around their ankles and he gave orders to start bailing with cooking pots, helmets, anything to hand. He stumbled towards the stern of the boat, clutching at its sides and his companions for support. As it lurched downwards he fell back, striking his head against the mast and, when they rode up the other side of the wave, he was flung headlong and found himself sprawled next to the boatman, clutching grimly at the two oars he used to hold them on course. 'Should we make for the shore?' Aspar whispered, his mouth close to the man's ear.

'Too late,' came the reply. 'We'd be dashed to pieces.'

'Do you have any idea where we're going?'

'That's the only consolation,' the fisherman replied, 'we're moving in the right direction – due east. But a bit faster than I'd like. If this wind gets much higher, I'll have to lower the sail.'

Above the noise of the waves, thunder rumbled round them, slowly circling back and forth. A flash of lightning revealed the spectral sails of the other boats scattered across the wide expanse of boiling sea under a weight of churning clouds, a procession of ghostly shades. The women in Aspar's craft clutched their children to them, their keening merging with the shriek of the wind, while the men bailed in grim silence. Darkness walled them in again.

Screams cut through the noise of the waves as the prow tilted upwards until the boat was almost vertical and it seemed that they would all be tossed overboard. It hurtled on as though scaling the side of a mountain. Aspar felt a lurching in his stomach as when he had ridden a chariot fast uphill. For an instant they were returned to the horizontal plane and then plunged downwards at such speed that they were flung back against the wooden hull, their breath snatched away. Thunder cracked violently directly overhead and a fork of lightning just feet from the vessel showed them descending into a valley of white foam, an almost sheer cliff of water barring their progress. The fisherman fought to lower the sail, which lashed and struggled like a white demon. Some of the men tried to help him, swaying violently with the unpredictable movement of the boat.

The prow catapulted upwards. They were climbing the cliff again. The men working at the sail cried out as they tumbled back into the stern. Aspar heard a shout skim close to his ear and a body fall past him, over the side of the boat. He lunged to grab the man, but he was gone. The boat hurled on through the night, like a trident unleashed by the god, leaving the unfortunate to the sea's fury.

His hand still extended over the side, clutching at nothing, Aspar was overwhelmed with his own powerlessness. The waters yawned darkly beneath them, who knows how profound, while the wind-gods tossed them at will as they might a pebble on the beach. These men and women had trusted him and he had brought them to this. What pride had made him think that he could return them to their native land? He would have done better to send them back to the safety of their lives as slaves.

The boat had now let in so much water, despite the frantic bailing of all the adult passengers, that Aspar could not understand how it could still be afloat. A deafening clap of thunder sounded and forks of lightning hemmed them round, imprisoning them in a giant cage. They were alone on an incline of water so vast, so steep, that it seemed that the world had been tilted on its foundations. Up and up they soared, hardly touching the surface. Far above them, Aspar could see the foam-fringed line stretching in either direction, where the glassy water met the black sky. They shot towards it, piercing through the curtain of spray. For a sickening moment they hovered above black nothingness. Then they tipped over the edge of the world.

The boat somersaulted as it fell. Aspar's body struck the water with a sharp crack. The vessel landed on top of him, its side striking the back of his head and he sank into the cold darkness. His body felt heavy, dragging him down. He could not summon up the strength to fight it; he had fought all he could. Had he not taken on the might of Rome – and even the gods themselves? Now the moment had come to admit that he was beaten. It was time to give in. Down he went into blankness and, as he surrendered to the chill embrace of the depths, he felt a certain peace.

Faces rose up to meet him, familiar faces: Surena, Zosimus, Hermes, Proculus, Livius, followed by a mass of men, women and children. He stiffened. No. He couldn't give up. How many had believed in him, trusted him, taken terrible risks, even sacrificed their lives for him? He struggled against the downward pull of the waters. He must go back up to the world, back to the people who had relied on him, were even now relying on him. He was still alive. Some of them, at least, were alive, and he must do what he could to save them.

He fought with all the strength that was in him against the powerful swirling currents that seemed determined to keep him from finding his way back to life. With a desperate lunge, he broke the surface. A feeble, soundless flash of lightning showed an upturned boat, a few arm-lengths away. Men and women clung to it; children were draped over the hull. Aspar struck out towards them and hands reached out eagerly, hauling him to the frail refuge of the wreckage.

The storm had begun to subside and by its dying bursts of light, they could see isolated figures floundering on the surface, clinging to broken spars of wood. Recovering his wits, Aspar managed to find ropes fixed to the sails which billowed under the boat like a sea-monster. Using these as safety lines for himself and other volunteers, they made sorties from their own boat to haul in as many scattered individuals as they could find.

The night seemed to be without end and the chill of the water pierced to the bone. Yet they clung on, murmuring encouragement to one another. Then came a moment when the blackness did not seem quite so dense. Dark forms could be dimly discerned on the water which had now stilled to glassy smoothness. Feeble cries linked one group of survivors with another.

The first light of morning filtered through a white mist that swirled slowly over the sea. A dawn wind sliced a path through the haze and Aspar could see clearly the shapes of capsized vessels and broken fragments of others, all with shivering men and women clinging to them while children crouched together on the up-turned hulls. Though badly damaged, with masts broken and sails in shreds, a few craft were still afloat.

Above this scene of desolation, a dark shape began to condense out of the mist. The breeze blew once more and a white curtain wafted across the scene, obliterating whatever it was that Aspar had espied – or thought he had. Perhaps it had merely been a thickening in the swirling mist? Suddenly it was there again, now looming high – absurdly high, it seemed, from above the water-level. Aspar wondered if the intense cold was causing him to hallucinate. Then, he was gripped with fear as a square Roman sail slowly took shape out of the foggy gloom.

The ship drew closer. Behind it was another, and a third. The first ship approached in ghostly silence. A hooded man stood on the prow, robed in white. For a second Aspar wondered if they were already dead and that this was Charon come to transport them across the Styx to Hades. Then suddenly he knew beyond all doubt who it was, this charmed figure who had come, once more, to snatch him from the mouth of death.

It was some time before Aspar climbed the ladder on to the ship's deck. He had remained in the water to help as many as he could to safety. But long before he stepped aboard, his eyes had locked with those of Zosimus.

All over the deck, and on the four other ships in Zosimus' fleet, the rescued Dacians and the fishermen of Pontus were warming themselves at braziers and sipping hot broth. Zosimus and Aspar retired to the Ethiopian's comfortably furnished cabin on deck. Aspar huddled close to a bronze stove, a thick woollen cloak about his shoulders and, as he gulped down the hot soup, he stared at his friend.

'The moment we said goodbye outside Antioch I was finally convinced I must follow you.' Zosimus smiled, reading Aspar's thoughts. 'Ever since we parted in Rome, the life I had come to love so much had lost its attraction for me. In my heart I knew that, though it would be a hard choice, I would only be truly content when I fulfilled the pledge we made in Hispania.'

'Ever since I have known you, you have always been able to come up with just what was needed at the right moment,' said Aspar, 'but a fleet of ships? And how did you find us?'

'Rumours had reached Antioch of your Dacian army. From my own experience sailing these waters, I was sure that you would never make the journey in without sturdy, seaworthy vessels. I could offer you vital help and I could not shrink from the challenge. As soon as I heard you had formed an army, I set sail with my fleet, manned by Phoenician sailors – no friends to the Romans. I calculated that I would arrive in time to meet you on the coast. It was when we docked in Amastris that we heard that a band of Dacians was looking for boats. We sailed all night through the storm, hoping we would reach you in time.'

'Well you did – but only just.' Aspar reached over and touched the wooden amulet that hung at Zosimus' neck. 'I was right all those years ago not to rely on a piece of wood, but on a man who deserved my trust.' As he released the charm, his fingertips brushed accidentally against the skin of the other man's neck, and the Ethiopian let out an involuntary gasp. Aspar snatched his hand away, as though from a burning pot. For an instant, the two men froze, staring at one another, uncertain what their next move should be, conscious of the fragility of the moment.

But their hesitation did not last long. Their instincts overwhelmed them, just as the followers of Dionysus are driven to frenzy by an excess of wine. They collided, clasping one another convulsively, their famished mouths feeding hungrily from each other, tongues sparring fiercely. Bodies locked, they toppled onto Zosimus' straw mattress. The involuntary erections that, hidden beneath their robes, had raged fiercely throughout the preceding conversation, now discovered one another and chafed together with aching acuteness.

They wrestled on the bed, pressing the hardness of body to body – chest on chest, hip against hip, limb along limb, with brutal urgency, as though the long absence could only be assuaged by the intensity of contact in the present. Without pausing from their writhings, somehow they managed to shed their clothes, sighing and shuddering as flesh met flesh, groping and hooking with arms and legs as if every part of one man's body should contact every part of the other's.

Aspar wrenched himself from the vice of Zosimus' embrace, inhaling the sweetness of his lover's body as his head sank to the crotch. The Dacian's mouth hungrily devoured the pulsing purple cock, drawing deep groans from the chests of both men. Zosimus rapidly swivelled his body around his imprisoned dick until the hardness of Aspar's engorgement beat against his lips. He opened them, allowing the proud curve of the rosy prick to glide down the satin smoothness of his throat until he could clamp his lips firmly around the thick hairy base. Aspar let out a long moan as Zosimus constricted his throat against the glossy dickhead and began to massage it with unrelenting pressure.

The thirst of the two men for one another's juices was so intense that they milked each other's prick mercilessly with greedy gullets until rhythmic moans mirrored the copious jets that shot into their guts. Slowly releasing the still-tumescent weapons, they darted ravenous tongues over the hot red heads, savouring each other's semen, of which they had been starved for so long.

His hunger pricked by the creamy nectar, Aspar thrust his head between Zosimus' thighs and parted the meaty buttocks to reveal the circular frill of flesh. He caressed it with the flat of his tongue, saliva glands shooting painful streams as the musky hole stimulated his taste-buds. Prising the fleshy arselips apart with his thumbs, he delved deeply into the moist recesses with his tongue. At the same time, he growled with pleasure as he felt Zosimus' tongue probing his own hole, firing sparks of pleasure up his spine and to the tip of his cock.

After a few moments of this intense stimulation and intimacy, their semi-flaccid appendages reared up with renewed anticipation. Aspar spat hard into his lover's hole. As his tongue swirled around the ring of flesh, making it slick for penetration, he could feel it relaxing, ready to accommodate him. Pulling himself up between Zosimus' muscle-etched thighs, the young king mounted him from behind. He rammed his up-curved horn-of-plenty into the expectant love-canal with an impatient thrust that caused the other man to roar out his pleasure and pain. Aspar sighed deeply as he felt once again his own flesh sheathed in that of Zosimus, the bend of the other man's rectum seeming to match perfectly the angle of the king's own rampant manhood.

He felt the Ethiopian's sphincter clench convulsively around his rigid column as though determined to wring out every drop of salty love juice. Suddenly Aspar plunged frenziedly in and out of the lust-swollen anus, possessed by a burning desire to implant his seed deep inside his lover once again. His features were distorted in furious concentration as he noisily splattered the clear juices of natural lubrication which poured from the other man's arse. Sharp cries signalled Aspar's orgasm as a series of violent jolts racked his body.

Then he was on his back, knees pressed hard against his shoulders and Zosimus, enraged with desire, was plugging him with his rigid pole, knotted with veins like tendrils of a vine wound tightly about a stout pillar. Aspar felt himself drowning in an agonised sweetness as Zosimus rode him remorselessly to climax, his cock searing Aspar's intestines like a sword-blade hot from the forge.

Suddenly the room was still, as the two men lay entwined, drenched with sweat, panting and trembling from their exertions.

There was a gentle rapping at the door.

Zosimus slipped on his robe and Aspar pulled the covers around him.

The door opened in response to Zosimus' summons and Hermes entered. Aspar thought he saw a look of sadness pass across the man's features. But then they returned to the impassive expression he remembered from the time he had first seen the Armenian giant in Glaucus' house so many years earlier.

'We have thoroughly searched the area and taken all survivors on board,' Hermes reported briskly.

'And the losses?' demanded Aspar.

'Thirty, forty, maybe.'

Aspar looked stricken.

'But you still have your army,' insisted Zosimus.

'The horses are lost,' put in Hermes grimly, 'and most of the weapons.'

'I have brought Parthian horses – there are more than a hundred in the holds,' said Zosimus. 'And weapons – bows and arrows, and armour from Parthia. Roman spears and swords. Catapults and ballistas. Slings from Arabia and men who can train others in their use.'

Aspar could not hold back a smile: 'You've thought of everything.'

'The captain awaits your orders, my lord Zosimus,' put in Hermes.

Zosimus threw open the cabin door. Aspar followed, pulling a blanket around him toga-fashion, blinking in the brilliant sunshine of the fine September day. The captain turned expectantly to the Ethiopian.

'Northwest,' commanded Zosimus.

'Northwest, my lord,' repeated the captain, bowing in agreement and turning to give orders to his crew, before signalling the instructions to the other ships. The deck teemed with naked sailors hauling up the anchor, securing the freight, hoisting the sails.

Aspar and Zosimus moved towards the prow while the ship pulled round into the wind, leaping forward as the great white sail bellied, and set its course for Dacia.

*Men of violence, men of lust – the gladiators were legendary
as the sexual athletes of their age!*

Gladiator School
by Ben Elliott

78 AD.

Paris, a seventeen-year-old runaway, is loved for his beauty by the wealthy young Egyptian Lucius and by Publius, a member of the Praetorian Guard. But then, despite the fact that he is the son of a free man, Paris is sold to the gladiator school of Pompeii by Lucius' merchant father. As a sex slave to the hulking warriors of the arena – more beasts than men – Paris submits to their sadistic lusts. Only by satisfying these men can Paris gain the chance to train as a gladiator himself and win his freedom.

Having matured into a skilful fighter, Paris is then transferred to the Ludus Magnus, the great gladiator school of Rome, where he becomes one of the mightiest champions of the amphitheatre. But here, in an age of sexual excess unequalled in the history of the world, Paris is drawn into the wild and violent lifestyle of a leading gladiator and risks losing everything he has fought for, including the man he really loves.

UK £7.95 US $11.95 (when ordering direct, quote ZPR6)

Zipper Books are available from bookshops including Borders, Waterstone's, Gay's the Word and Prowler Stores.

Or order direct from:

MaleXpress, 3 Broadbent Close, London N6 5JG

FREEFONE 0800 45 45 66 (Int tel +44 20 8340 8644)

FREEFAX 0800 917 2551 (Int fax +44 20 8340 8885)

Please add p&p – single item £1.75, 2 items or more £3.45, all overseas £5